TWICE UPON A CRIME

A NOVEL

TWICE UPON A CRIME

A NOVEL

WHEN HOLLYWOOD BURNS YOU,
IT'S TIME FOR A REWRITE.

MARK S. WAXMAN

An Imprint of Roan & Weatherford Publishing Associates, LLC
Bentonville, Arkansas
www.roanweatherford.com

Copyright © 2024 by Mark S. Waxman

We are a strong supporter of copyright. Copyright represents creativity, diversity, and free speech, and provides the very foundation from which culture is built. We appreciate you buying the authorized edition of this book and for complying with applicable copyright laws by not reproducing, scanning, or distributing any part of it in any form without permission. Thank you for supporting our writers and allowing us to continue publishing their books.

Library of Congress Cataloging-in-Publication Data
Names: Waxman, Mark S., author
Title: Twice Upon a Crime
Description: First Edition. | Bentonville: Rogue River, 2025.
Identifiers: LCCN: 2024947781 | ISBN: 979-8-89299-003-5 (hardcover) |
ISBN: 979-8-89299-004-2 (trade paperback) | ISBN: 979-8-89299-005-9 (eBook)
Subjects: | BISAC: FICTION/Crime | FICTION/Romance/Romantic Comedy |
FICTION/Thrillers/ Crime
LC record available at: https://lccn.loc.gov/2024947781

Rogue River hardcover edition November, 2024

Jacket Design by Casey W. Cowan
Interior Design by Staci Troilo
Editing by George "Clay" Mitchell

This book is a work of fiction. Apart from the well-known actual people, events, and locales that figure in the narrative, all names, characters, places, and incidents are the product of the author's imagination or are used fictitiously. Any resemblance to current events or locales, or to living persons, is entirely coincidental.

DEDICATION

To living happily ever laughter.

Chapter 1
THE END

DAMN. I BROKE a nail.
   Forgive me. It's impossible to think straight at this moment, when I'm facing what could be the end of my life.

As a writer, I have a wild imagination. But never could I have envisioned myself being in this much danger. It was *so* not me. I mean, really, what the hell was a somewhat sophisticated, somewhat respected, somewhat cultured film professor doing in the middle of the night, inelegantly creeping on her hands and knees in the muddy crawlspace below a well-guarded California estate, about to break through the floorboards into a movie producer's mansion to exact revenge? I was placed in this extraordinary peril by an immature infatuation with the sexy, young man crawling beside me. It was as if we were starring in a bad romantic comedy.

Were we killed that night?

Well, as a professional storyteller, before you know the ending, let me share what happened in the beginning and the middle. I'll use the cinematic "flashback" technique that I teach my Screenwriting 101 students. And so, six weeks earlier....

Chapter 2
FIONA

TWO DOZEN MORTALS of various ages, colors, and backgrounds were scattered throughout the auditorium, staring at the thirty-foot tall silver screen, studying every second of a second-rate movie. Each of my self-deluded screenwriting students had high hopes of triumphing in the entertainment industry. They signed up for this adult night course at Santa Monica Community College thinking that in twelve weeks, and for a hundred and eighteen dollars, they would learn the tricks of the trade and the secrets to showbiz success. They wished someday their name would be up on that screen after the words "written by." The truth was, every student sitting wide-eyed in that room would be lucky to get a job selling popcorn in the lobby of a cineplex.

The film wouldn't be over for another twenty minutes, so I quietly sneaked out of the auditorium and sat alone in the courtyard, under a quarter moon, on the Abner C. Rosenthal bench donated in the name of his wife Naomi. A few coeds somnambulated around campus, exhausted from balancing two jobs, three kids, and four junior college classes. A student munching on a soggy tuna sandwich while gyrating to the music playing through her earbuds pranced over to me.

"Hey, Professor Logan," she said at high volume. "I got a writing gig."

"That's great, Miss...."

"Tamicka. Tamicka White."

"I'm happy for you."

She plucked her earbuds out. "Well, it's not exactly for a movie."

"For TV?"

"It's more like for a menu," she boasted.

"You're writing menus?"

"At that new fish restaurant on the pier, *For Cod's Sake*."
"Well, it's a start. Congratulations. Or should I say con-*cod*-ulations?"
"They pay me in food." She proudly held up her bartered tuna on rye.
"Would you like to finish my *Huckleberry Yellow Finn*?"
"Good writing. But no thanks."
"You sure? It's our top seller."
"Nah. I'm fine. Just dandy."
"What does 'dandy' mean?" she asked.
"Tip-top."
"What does tip—"
"It's late. I really gotta get back to class."
"Okay. Well, good seeing ya."

With that, Tamicka popped the music back in her head and sashayed into the night, leaving me to contemplate my so-called state of "dandy." I wasn't anywhere near fine or dandy or tip-top. Sure, at closer to fifty than forty, I was still able to contribute to society by exhaling carbon dioxide, which is good for the plants. But otherwise, I was at a point in my life where I realized getting my annual mammogram was the only time someone asked me to appear topless in a film. I was at a point where my memory was starting to go, that all I could retain was water. I was at a point where I could see the dark at the end of the tunnel, and the only light ahead was a freight train speeding toward me. Fine and dandy my ass, which—courtesy of daily yoga—had remained relatively firm and in place. Older people would say, "tip-top."

As I watched Cesar-the-custodian bag up the evening's trash, I found myself imagining the day they pack *me* up. The day they lower me under the grass. The day my daughter would place a sprig of lilacs on my casket. What would be said at the funeral? What would I wear? Who would deliver the eulogy?

I pictured the President of the United States leaning on the podium, squinting through tears at a teleprompter. "We've lost a national treasure. Fiona Logan was a strong, independent woman. A great patriot. A great teacher. For a junior college, that is. She was talented, generous, and brilliant." Madam President would blow her nose. "And Fiona was very, very beautiful. Spectacularly beautiful. In fact, I'm recommending that Congress vote to place Miss Logan's gorgeous face not on the one-hundred-dollar bill, but on Mount Rushmore."

One can fantasize. It's what this one used to do for a living. Now, I get paid very little to teach others how to do it.

Or perhaps our commander-in-chief would spare the platitudes and someone—maybe Cesar—would step forward at the gravesite to tell the *real* truth. "At holiday time, Miss Fiona was always good for a gift card to Starbucks or Target. That's one nice lady there. But life dealt her a bad hand. And she folded early by performing a perfectly executed swan dive off the campus belltower, landing spread eagle onto the cobblestone quad. Broke her glasses and everything. Took me a week to power wash the blood off."

As always, I made quite a splash, a rather dramatic exit. Like the time I stormed out of—

A backfire in the student parking lot snapped me back to my senses. I'd never kill myself. The belltower? With my acrophobia? No way. Besides, I had too much to live for. Like my daughter. My dog. Chocolate. I just needed some good luck. Just one speck of positive news. One out-of-the-blue, life-changing knock on the door. "You, Fiona Logan, are today's Publishers Clearing House winner." A half-eaten tuna sandwich wasn't going to cut it. I needed something cosmic to upgrade my state of fine and dandy.

Nor would my big break come from the scrawny man with thinning hair now approaching, another former student of mine no doubt, who sat uninvited next to me on Abner's bench. No rest, on that night, for the weary teacher praying to be a Powerball winner.

"Hi, Professor Logan."

"Barry?"

"Larry," he said. "I had you last winter."

"No one's 'had' me in years."

He dismissed my pathetic but factual quip. "Tuesday nights at seven. I never skipped your class."

"Thanks. Attendance is underrated." I squeezed my eyes close, wishing he would pick up on my go-away-this-instant-or-I'll-scream-rape vibe.

"I also took your advice," he said.

"To call your mother more often?"

"To write what you know."

"Oh, that old cliché. I hope it helped, Jerry."

"Larry. Mine was the script about a screenwriting student who couldn't think of a good story to write."

"I think I remember it. Ended with eighty blank pages?"

He grinned. "I'm no writer. I'm a welder for Delta Airlines. I just thought I could meet some cool chicks in the class," he said as he rose.

I looked up at him. "Sorry it didn't work out."

"Actually, it almost did. Remember that hot Indian babe, dot not feather, who sat on the aisle? Killer body?"

"Who could forget Fatima?"

"Roshni."

"Forgive me. I'm terrible with names, Gary."

"Larry. Anyway, her father will only approve a man with—how did he put it?—'a hint of potential.'" He held up a sketch pad. "So, I'm going to try art. I just registered for a figure drawing class."

"Nude models?"

He nodded. "I like checking 'em out before asking 'em out."

"This college is like your personal dating app."

"Yeah, life is good." He hiked up his sagging pants. "Well, I have a bus to catch. Bye." Mercifully, the welder wandered off.

"Bye, Terry," I said into the air.

What had happened to *my* life? To *my* art? I once was on top of the world. I blinked. Then, the world was on top of me. No, I was nowhere near fine. And miles from dandy.

I was tired of my whining. I refused to have a midlife crisis. I promised myself beginning that very night I would start making better choices. I would adopt a take it day by day philosophy. I would stay present, live in the moment, relinquish expectations.

Knowing me, however, I would follow my mother's dying words, "Stop testing how deep the water is with both feet."

At my *real* memorial, I hoped they would praise Fiona Logan as a loving, pretty-enough woman who gave her all. And enjoyed fantasizing. But not teaching it. Did I already mention that?

I drew a deep, life-affirming breath, exhaled it toward the trees, walked back to the auditorium toward my miserable job, toward the lie that my naïve students would write and sell a movie script, toward my new and improved attitude. And my soon to be dandier life.

I leaned against the wall near the stage, scrutinizing the reactions of my students as they watched the end of the film. I suppose my eyes lingered too long on one particular face belonging to the fetching young man in the front row. He was completely enthralled, absorbing every scene in the movie while several others around him answered texts or snored. At one point, he caught me staring. I quickly looked away, embarrassed by the impropriety.

Chapter 3

JACK

Through the light of the projector beam, through flecks of dust particles, I locked eyes with Professor Logan. I stupidly smiled, perhaps sending the wrong message. I wasn't flirting or anything, even though she was quite a looker. But I was there to learn. I was on a mission to become a serious screenwriter. Besides, I was in love with Beth.

Love? I didn't know what real love was. And without that knowledge, that understanding, that experience, how could I write a romantic movie? Or move to the next level with my girlfriend? Or stop looking at my teacher long after she stopped looking at me?

The reason I had always rushed to class early and sat in the first row was because, at six foot three, I needed the legroom, and I didn't want to miss one word of the lecture, one frame of the film. The instructor was a certified, bona fide, motion picture writer. And that's exactly what I wanted to be, though, as I was packing to leave Chicago for Los Angeles, my father called to say, "Listen to me, Kiddo. I know what I'm talking about. They're all commies, queers, and junkies out there in Hollyweird. Move back here to Dayton, where you can get a normal job, surrounded by normal people, look after your mother and me, and make something of yourself."

I had been at a crossroads in my life, stuck in the Windy City, trapped in an advertising agency, imprisoned in a suit, slowly climbing the corporate ladder, each rung distancing me further from my childhood goal of writing movies. That's what I really wanted to do. This was a now or never moment. I convinced my best friend, Kevin, to drive west with me, to room with me, to give the Golden State an eighteen-month shot. We were both single, adventurous, and at the last reasonable age when taking a chance and failing was still recoverable.

Other than sporting a good tan and having Beth in my life, I didn't have much to show for the last sixteen months. My California Dream was turning into a pipe dream. My big break was overdue. Was it time to move home, find a normal job, and make something of myself? If so, what would I do with Beth? She seemed to be the perfect one for me. But her life was in L.A.

Professor Logan was showing an obscure, low-budget action film titled *With Guns Blazing*. She had downloaded the screenplay so we could follow along on our digital devices. My eyes bounced between the script and the movie screen. It was fascinating and exciting to watch printed words written in private become moving pictures exhibited in public.

Before the end credits rolled, the overhead lights flickered on, and the film sputtered to a halt. A few students clapped, which woke the others. Professor Logan made her way toward the podium. She wore skinny jeans, a baggy sweater, and vintage Converse high tops. She had style. And grace. And, for whatever age she was, leading lady beauty.

As she glided across the stage, she spoke. "I wrote that piece of... let's say 'entertainment'... a few years ago, when I had to do what I had to do. I wanted to write something that I would willingly watch. But instead, the studio wanted blood and guts. So, we compromised. I gave them blood and guts." She paused, then added, "Mostly mine."

Professor Logan had arrived at the lectern. "Anyway, I put the whole paycheck on a sure-bet racehorse named Can't Lose," she said. "Well, guess what? It did."

Some in the class laughed. Most squirmed in their seats. I merely wondered who my tall, redheaded, bespectacled, blue-eyed professor was in real life. And why she wouldn't make blue-eyed contact with me again. I figured she was setting boundaries. Didn't trust men. Been hit on by too many who had taken her Introduction to Screenwriting, and who had stared, like I was, at the sexy instructor on stage. I was just riffing. Something writers do in their heads. All the time.

"If you learn nothing else in here," Professor Logan said, "remember this. Action sells. Also remember, writers sell out." She took a breath. "So, tonight's message is lights, camera, *action*." She closed her notebook, completing her lecture. "It ain't called emotion pictures. It's *motion* pictures."

I raised my hand.

"Question?" Professor Logan asked, looking annoyed, searching for the voice.

"Last week you said we should write about things we know. I don't know anything about gunfights and car chases."

"The reason you're lucky you got me for this course is that I'm a pragmatist, not a dramatist. I don't teach theory. I teach reality." She looked me straight in the eye. "Any monkey can write a script. I'm teaching you to write one that might actually get bought. Or what's the point?"

"Won't a good love story sell?"

"If you have a need to write from your heart, write lullabies and marry rich. In here, we write from our stomachs, from a need to eat, to eat somewhere you don't have to order through a clown's nose." The class tittered. Some applauded. I did neither. "I'm not good with names," she said, scanning her attendance chart. "Is it 'Larry' by any chance?"

"Jack. Jack Reynolds."

"Look it up, Mister Reynolds. The highest grossing films are action movies. These days it's not about the writer. It's about digital effects. *Superman*, *Spider-Man*, *Ironman*, *Aquaman*. All the 'man' franchises. Create a superhero, and you'll make super buttloads of money. And, admit it or not, that's why you're all here."

I heard a grumble from the back of the auditorium and watched Dean Bailey, a school administrator, march out in disgust.

"Next week, we'll discuss *The Avengers*, the most successful action franchise of all time."

I mumbled to myself, "*The Avengers* is a love story."

"Until then, see ya at the movies," Professor Logan said, switching off the podium light.

Chapter 4
FIONA

As I hurried down the school hallway carrying my heavy satchel, I heard, "Fiona. Fiona." Randall Bailey, our out-of-shape dean, had to run to catch up with me.

"What seems to be the problem, officer?" I said without breaking stride.

"You're taking it out on the students again," he said.

"I know. My shrink thinks it's really helping."

"If it weren't for the high marks you receive on the student evaluations—"

"I can't figure that out either."

"Bottom line, they look to you for guidance, Fiona. What they get is bitterness and disdain."

"I realize it's against school policy, but they also get something called—what's that word again? Oh, yeah. The *truth*."

I had managed to trigger Dean Bailey's eye twitch. "Listen," he said. "All these students need to know is how to write a script. Pure and simple."

I stopped walking, luckily for Dean Bailey, who was near cardiac arrest. "One writer out of ten thousand sells a screenplay each year," I stated. "And that one writer isn't in my classroom, including me. That, Dean Bailey, is what they need to know. Pure and simple."

"Teach them the basics, Fiona. That's your job."

"What I *should* teach them is to ask for a refund so they can study something, something like welding, something they can make a living at. As a writer, I'm not proud of ending my previous sentence with a preposition."

"Why do we have this same goddamn conversation every goddamn quarter?" he blasted.

"Because it makes you think you're goddamn God."

He swallowed hard, straining to be civil. "Teach them your craft. That's what they pay us for, and that's what we pay you for. Stop the editorials." His right eyelid was flittering like a hummingbird's wing. "And dress like a teacher, not a student."

For some unknown reason, I said, "Do you know who my husband was?"

The dean was a bit thrown. "I heard illustrator. Children's books?"

"That's *what* he did, and nobody did it better, but that's not *who* he was." I took a breath to compose myself. "When we walked down the street, if he saw a parking meter that was expired, he'd put money into it." I looked away. "It's been four years, and there hasn't been a day...." I turned back to Dean Bailey. "I'm teaching them that storytellers have a duty. We are the conscience of society. Haven't we had enough gunfights and car chases? Don't we have a responsibility not just to sell Milk Duds and Raisinets, but also to do good in the world? We should all do good, don't you agree?"

He was unmoved and colder than ever. "Teach them how to write, Fiona. Or I'll find another washed-up, burned-out hack who will."

I hated him. I hated that job. I hated my life.

The dean stormed off, past a few stunned students who had overheard us. They were gathered at the vending machines, including that good-looking guy from the front row.

Chapter 5
JACK

CO-EDS WERE FANNING out to their cars in the parking garage. Professor Logan threw her stuff angrily into the trunk of a haggard 1983 Mercedes coupe convertible. Her license plate read RIGHTER.

I walked up to her. "Professor Logan?"

"Speaking," she said.

"Cool car."

"Thanks. How can I help you?"

"I don't want to learn the craft. I want to learn the art. *Forest Gump, It's a Wonderful Life, Midnight Cowboy.* That kind of art."

Professor Logan slammed the trunk, turned, and narrowed her eyes. "Nobody wants those movies anymore. Certainly not your generation."

"I do."

"Watch 'em. Don't write 'em." She leaned against her car, trying to calm herself. "How old would a man like you be?"

"He'd be like thirty-one, like in November."

"Then you're old enough to understand that movies are for the masses. And smart enough to know what word is in *masses*."

"You're calling your audience 'asses?'"

"Too kind?"

"Movies are people's dreams."

"Movies are just light beams and sound waves dancin' in a room with strangers. Horny kids on dates, seniors on discounts, lonely widows on Prozac. Movies are a place to hide in the dark, to escape reality, to enjoy air conditioning, if only for a couple hours."

"Did you write that?"

Professor Logan got into her car. "Next week's lecture."
"Do you believe it?"
"Yup."
"Do you really think none of us will ever sell a screenplay?"
"I'm positive."
That pissed me off. Students need encouragement, not doom and gloom. "Are you on Prozac, Professor?"
I had googled Fiona Logan before I signed up for her course. I knew that her husband was her inspiration, her muse. That he had died, that she hadn't sold a screenplay since.
"It's Renford, right?" she asked curtly.
"Reynolds. Jack Reynolds the First."
"Your dialogue needs work, Mister Reynolds."
"Quentin Tarantino said, 'Having an ear for dialogue is—'"
"I'd love to stand here all night and debate the merits of the visual arts, but I have a dinner date."
"At this hour?"
"And he's waiting."
"On a school night?"
"I'm a grownup. I get to stay up as late as I want."
Professor Logan slammed her squeaky door and turned the ignition. The old engine tried to kick over. Eventually, it did. She sped away from campus, leaving me in a cloud of brown exhaust and with the fear that she was right. That I would never sell a movie script.

Chapter 6
FIONA

THE ARTHRITIC PIANIST wore a tobacco-stained tuxedo shirt and a pencil mustache as crooked as his fingers. He mindlessly played a maudlin medley of movie scores. The writer in me wondered what he was thinking when he played "My Heart Will Go On" for the one-zillionth time. Was he struggling to understand why his fellow Juilliard graduates had, decades ago, secured glamorous positions in symphony orchestras around the world, while he performed in the lobby of an upscale department store by day and played here at Rive Gauche Café by night? At least, I suppose, he could tell his relatives back in Des Moines that he was "in the industry."

With the somber theme from *Schindler's List* wafting in the background of Larchmont Village's trendiest late night in spot, the overly cheerful waiter cleared our dinner plates. In an hour, I would be home reading *Sense and Sensibility* for the one-zillionth time. I'd also be regretting and rejoicing, having jettisoned the overly eager man sitting across from me. My anticipation of a night blissfully alone grew until Eddie Harper, the aforementioned pursuer, extended the evening by asking to see the dessert menu.

"I couldn't, I really couldn't," I said, patting my stomach. When it came to sweets, I could, I really could. But I just wanted to go home. I did, I really did.

"C'mon. We'll split a *crème de la* something," he said, finishing his third scotch. "You need something sinful."

It was our fifth date. And, though he didn't know it yet, our last. It wasn't because he was boring or unattractive. On the contrary, Eddie was astonishingly good-looking, generous, and funny. And, as he endlessly reminded me, "a Hah-vard man."

But he had three fatal flaws, as if one weren't enough. First, Eddie was an alcoholic. And devoid of all self-awareness. For example, he thought he could hide his addiction from me, from the writer who majored in Perceptivity. Second, Eddie was a textbook narcissist. It was as though he received a royalty every time he said the word, "I." Third, and possibly the worst, he didn't like dogs. Deal breaker.

It was okay. My heart would go on.

WE HAD MET the month before in Gelson's sprawling supermarket. I was bent over the watermelon stand, uncovering a small price sign buried among the fruit.

"Six dollars?" I mumbled aloud. "How can a grocer sleep at night?"

A baritone voice behind me responded, "Are you asking *me*?"

Startled, I twirled around. And faced a breathtakingly gorgeous man in a breathtaking three-piece Armani suit. In my mind, at that angel-choir-singing moment, I named the attractive stranger Bond. James Bond.

"Sorry," I said. "I was just venting."

"I do that, too. Usually after eating a burrito."

I recoiled. "Really? A fart joke? At your age?"

"I get nervous around women with melons," he stammered. "That didn't come out right."

"Boobs. Burritos. Away, you mouldy rogue, away."

James Bond cocked his head like an inquisitive puppy.

"Shakespeare," I explained. "He wrote plays. Before you were born."

"Like *Henry IV*?" he asked. "Act two, scene four?" He flashed a double-dimple grin.

Oh my, he was good. But I wasn't in the market, so to speak, for a man. I stood there balancing on the teeter-totter of emotions. At my age, when a woman's hair starts turning from gray to black, was I to disregard Bond's pickup artistry or, for a change, be flattered and take a chance? Stay present? Live in the moment?

"I read that watermelons are ninety-two percent water," I said.

"I prefer to read fiction. Like Shakespeare."

"Shelling out six bucks on a teacher's salary for mostly water is outrageous."

"I'd be happy to buy you one," James Bond offered, nobly stepping forward.

Another decision, be thrilled or repelled? Or do as I normally did. Self-destruct. I chose emotional suicide. "Thank you. But that won't be necessary."

"Teacher. Wow." He saluted me. "On behalf of the nation, thank you for your service."

A subtle and unavoidable glint of desire passed between us, there in Fresh Produce with a slew of other shoppers strolling by, drawn in by our middle age flirtation. But playtime was over. I reminded myself I was retired from the Department of Romance, that I had made peace with dying as a single woman. I turned to leave.

"Maybe we could hang out some time," he quickly dared to suggest.

"We just did," I said. "And I can barely remember it."

I wheeled away, navigating my wobbly, creaky cart farther down the corridor, pausing to smell fruit and to examine vegetables. I wasn't surprise to hear Bond's voice behind me again. After all, he was a hunter and not nearly ready to give up the gathering.

"Me, again," he said.

"I saw a pretty lady in the meat section," I remarked, adjusting my beret. "If you run fast, you may be able to pick *her* up."

"Is that it? You've pegged me as a supermarket stalker?"

"My gender has been blessed with acute olfactory glands," I said. "We can sniff a predator six aisles away."

"For the record," he said. "I completely support Time's Up, Me Too, Stand Up, Sit Down, Head, Shoulders, Knees, and Toes."

"Do you have a job?" I asked. "Or do you do this all day?"

"I'm an attorney. I just do this on the side. Pro bono."

"Well, try pro-boning someone else."

Rebuffing an Adonis attorney despite my neediness. I had come a long way, thanks to therapy. I sighed and checked my shopping list on my phone.

"Let's start over," he requested.

"By now, most women would be sitting in your shopping cart. There. A crumb for your ego. Let's leave it on that high note." I reached into the wall cooler and pulled out a carton of organic eggs.

Undaunted, he sang along to "Moon River" being piped through the speakers above. "'Wherever you're going, I'm going your way.'"

"Is that the mating call of the double-breasted lawyer?" I asked dismissively.

"It's the desperate cry of a man who doesn't want to dine alone tonight."

I was tempted to acquiesce, but then came to my senses. "Well, it's been a thimble of fun. Now it's time to return to earth."

I started to go, but he blocked my cart with his. I noticed that the only item in his shopping basket was a supersize bottle of Chivas Regal. He was definitely a party boy. Definitely not my type. I swerved around his cart and made a sharp turn down aisle nine. Bond was on my tail. I accelerated. Bond caught up. We were rolling side by side, touring the market in silence.

"One can learn a lot about a person by what they eat," he announced.

I looked off. "I could call security, you know."

He bent over and poked his perfect nose inside my shopping cart. "Dog," he said, examining the contents of my basket. "Yoga three times a week. And—"

"Five cans of dog food and you guess dog? Brilliant. Who are you? James Bond?"

He grinned, confident that he had caught his prey. "How did I do on the yoga thing?"

"Four times a week. Not three."

"Shoot. Missed it by one Namaste."

"You'll recover." I had become me again, the law firm of Judgmental, Snide & Abrupt. "We're done here. My mother said not to talk to strangers." I turned my back to him. Was I just teasing? Was I just living in the moment? Was I discarding all the therapy?

"How did I guess yoga, you wonder?" He pointed to a big candle in my cart. "This is L.A. I figured the candle meant you were into all that hippie-dippy California stuff."

"The candle goes in my emergency kit," I said. "In case you hadn't heard, all of us hippie-dippy Californians are going to die in the next earthquake."

I didn't know why I had engaged in this vacuous back-and-forth in the first place. Well, yes, I did. Although I didn't want to be that gullible woman who falls victim to trite advances in the grocery store, I didn't want to be that woman who falls asleep, night after night, accompanied only by *Sense and Sensibility* rising and falling on her chest.

He studied my basket some more. "Vanilla ice cream, half gallon size. Means you're lonely."

"It's melting. Unlike my heart. It means I gotta go." I turned to leave. "Almost nice talking to you." I guided my cart around his and headed toward the checkout counter.

JAMES BOND PUSHED his cart behind me into the parking lot. "I think I could fall madly in bed with you," he said.

I glanced over my shoulder. "Are you really following me?"

"No. You're leading me. Leading me on."

"I'm not available."

"My gender has acute olfactory glands, too. We can sniff out lies."

"I'm married," I disclosed.

"With one potato in your basket and no wedding ring? Sniff, sniff."

"I have a boyfriend."

Bond pulled alongside me, sniffing the air. "The nose knows."

"Okay, I don't have a boyfriend."

"Busted."

"I'm a lesbian."

We had arrived at my car. "It's none of my business," he said. "But I think you need a heterosexual man with whom to eat ice cream."

"You're right."

"I knew it."

"It's none of your business." I opened my trunk. "I'm not lonely," I said. "I'm a loner."

"I give up."

"Look, I don't mean to be rude."
"No, really. You win."
"I just like my privacy."
"Then how about a private dinner with me?" he asked.
"That's one too many people."
"Tonight. I'll even shower first."
I began loading my trunk with groceries. "I'm about to scream."
"Wonderful. I'm thinking eight o'clock. Your place or your place?"
"What's wrong with your place?" I snapped. "Is your wife there?"
"No. She's, uh…."
"Oh, this should be good."
"She dines in heaven."
I froze.
"And her husband is completely lost," he added. "And doesn't know how to do this."
"I'm so sorry. Really."
"It's been three years. I try to be charming. But I come across creepy."
"'Creepy' would be generous."
We just looked at each other.
"I'm Eddie." He smiled and offered his hand. "Creepy Eddie Harper."
I lowered my glasses and shook his hand. "I'm Fiona. Fiona 'attracted-but-not-interested' Logan."
"Hello, Fiona," he said.
"Hello, Eddie," I said. "I'm sorry you're alone. But I'm afraid I'm not looking for a relationship."
"Last thing on my mind. We can just be drinking buddies."
"You're a guy. I know *exactly* what's on your mind. Besides, my last fling went down in flames. My heart suffered third degree burns. So…."
"So, we'll fire up that candle of yours. Share the potato. Eat your ice cream for dessert. And read Shakespeare to each other. The perfect remedy for heartburn."
"Gosh. Just when I thought you might be sincere."
"I am what I am, and that's all what I am," he said.
"Shakespeare?"
"Popeye the Sailor Man." He pressed on. "Look, neither the history

nor future of civilization will suffer from your having dinner with a Harvard man tonight. I think it would do a world of good for your scorched heart and my empty heart."

"If you haven't noticed, I haven't finished my hate-all-men phase."

"One date. A chance to hate one more man. Anyway, none of this will matter after the big quake kills us."

I was falling for this guy. I really didn't want to start something I couldn't finish. My heart couldn't take another hit. I had to resist, in the name of self-preservation. "Shoo. Scram. Skedaddle," I said with absolutely no authority.

"Abandon you, just like that? After all we've been through?"

A good-looking, unrelenting lawyer, who made me laugh inside. What was a girl who had sworn off dating to do? Put her cans of dog food in the trunk, drive off, and wonder if this adorable admirer could have been different from the rest, could have been my soulmate, the next love of my life? Or jump in now with both feet?

I slammed the trunk close, opened the driver's side door, and turned to Eddie. "No dinner. No dessert. No sonnets."

"Three strikes. Is that it? I'm out?"

"We can have coffee. Tomorrow. In a public place."

TWENTY-SEVEN DAYS LATER, Eddie Harper scrutinized the dessert menu as if it were the Dead Sea Scrolls. And then, the effects of all the liquor, from a day of drinking, from generations of Harper drinkers, staggered in. I had tried to look past Eddie's troublesome dependency on our previous dates, but when I realized I had rarely seen him without a drink in his hand, it was time to take my leave.

"Will you marry me?" he said, slumping forward, slurring his words.

"I thought you'd never ask."

"I'm not kidding. I'm really asking."

Our waiter swooped in. "Have you chosen a dessert?"

"This lovely woman just accepted my proposal of marriage," Eddie announced.

"Congratulations," the waiter said matter-of-factly. He worked in L.A. He'd heard it all.

"We'll celebrate with one *crème brûlée* and two spoons," Eddie said. "And bring me a bottle of your best champagne so that my fiancé and I can toast to our future together."

The out-of-work actor zipped off with the order.

"*Crème brûlée.* That thing's full of sugar. You'll be up all night," I said.

"As they say in France, zat's zee plan, *ma chérie*," he affirmed. "We'll be up all night."

I had faced that moment so many times before in my history with men. The same old sadness surged through me as I took a deep breath and tried to steady myself for the standard "I'm sorry, this isn't working out" speech.

"This is our night," Eddie said. "We can stay up as long as we want. Do whatever we want. Do it over and over again as many times as we want. *Carpe diem.* Is that French?"

"Eddie—"

"Let's get Eddie a little sweaty tonight. What do you say?"

Drawing on a professional writer's command of language, I said nothing.

"I promise you'll be begging for more," he said. "They all do."

He was experienced enough to know that he was very drunk, talking too loudly, and generally being a Hall of Fame prick. He had been spurned enough to know he had blown it once again. Just as I was about to speak, he spoke. "Don't screw this up, Fiona. I love your name. Is it French?"

"We're not having sex tonight."

"My god. You *are* a lesbian."

"I wish I were. It would make this so much easier."

"I think 'lesbian' is French."

"I want to say this in the most sensitive way," I began. "I like you. I think this could have developed into something nice, maybe even long term. But your drinking is a problem for me. And for you. Certainly, for a 'future together.'"

He became petulant, like a scolded schoolboy. "With your beautiful red hair and gorgeous black blouse, I think I'm going to call you Ladybug, which in English means a lady who is starting to bug me."

I very sincerely said, "I'm sorry. We're over."

"We've had a ton of dates," he huffed. "All we've done is talk and eat. How long did you expect me to go without getting some poontang?"

I slowly folded my napkin. "Here's some free advice. Referring to love-making as 'getting some poontang' isn't an aphrodisiac."

"You're *meshugganah*. Is that French?"

There was no reason to make this any harder or last any longer. "Damn you, Eddie. Why do you have to be a selfish, drunk, dog-hater? Otherwise, we might have had a shot."

He literally rested his face on the tablecloth. "Marry me, Ladybug."

I looked away. "Either I *am* a lesbian, or I'm destined to be a spinster. Either way, I'll be better off than being with you."

He cast his eyes up from the table. "I own a fifty-four-foot sailboat with a king-size bed. I usually reserve that juicy piece of intel for when getting laid needs a little nudge." He reached for my hand. "Come sail away with me, Ladybug, Ladybug."

"I'm sorry, Eddie. Really."

"I don't understand you."

"Neither do I."

Eddie sat there, pouting. "So, we're not sleeping together tonight?"

"Right."

"Darn. How about tomorrow night?"

"Picture the word 'never.' Now sailor, picture the ocean."

He sat up and smacked the tabletop. "I want sex."

"I'm afraid you hit on the wrong shopping cart."

Eddie took out his gold money clip, peeled off a crisp one-hundred-dollar bill, and forced it into my palm. "Fuck me, whore. Take me home and fuck me."

Patrons ceased their conversations. Busboys stopped in their tracks. The peppy piano rendition of *Raindrops Keep Falling on My Head* came to a halt.

"Thanks for dinner," I said evenly as I stood up.

"You're an ugly old witch." he bellowed, just as the champagne arrived.

"And thanks for showing your true colors before wasting any more of my time," I said. With all eyes on me, I strode out of the restaurant, but not before stuffing Eddie's hundred-dollar bill, which I could really have used, in the pianist's tips goblet.

Outside, on the sidewalk, I heard a thunderous applause for my dramatic exit coming from the restaurant.

Chapter 7
JACK

LABORING ALL DAY at a boring job and attending Professor Logan's night class wore me out more than when I worked in the steel mill during my college summers.

My hands were filled with my gym bag and a pizza, an ironic pairing, as I made my way down the fifth-floor, outside corridor. I hated my tacky, Polynesian-themed, Culver City apartment complex, Palm Gardens. On the other hand, this Dayton native loved the fact that I wouldn't see a single snowflake all year.

I unlocked the front door and pushed it open with my foot. I entered my small, two-bedroom apartment, decorated with half flea market furniture, half IKEA. I crossed to the kitchen and plopped my stuff down, then checked my pinging phone. It was a text from my roommate Kevin saying, *Staying at Shanelle's tonite.*

I moseyed into my bedroom, opened the sliding glass doors, and walked out onto a small balcony. I had an unobstructed view of the lit-up water tower on the back lot of Sony Pictures Studios, formerly MGM, where *The Wizard of Oz* was filmed. I watch that movie every year.

I rested against the railing and let the night air cool my face. Would the Great and Powerful Oz, I wondered, allow me someday to be part of motion picture history?

PROFESSOR LOGAN HAD told me to work on my dialogue. So, I lay in bed with my laptop, scrolling through the many scripts I had downloaded over time. I examined the speeches, reciting them out loud to experience the full effect of every line, the power of every word. My teacher stressed that how a character talks is just as important as what a character says. In addition to moving the story forward, the dialogue should indicate to the audience where the character is from, how educated he is, what her personality is like.

"Frankly, my dear, I don't give a damn."

"Love means never having to say you're sorry."

"I'm going to make him an offer he can't refuse."

"Life is a box of chocolates, Forrest. You never know what you're gonna get."

"Are you on Prozac, Professor?"

About that last one, I agreed. Not exactly a classic line.

THE STARLET IN her near-topless Versace gown stood on stage, fumbling to open the envelope. "I'm just so nervous. They told me a billion people are watching," she squealed.

My heart pounded in my ears. My mouth was dry. My skin was wet. This would be my night. The culmination and celebration of a lifetime quest.

"The Oscar for Best Original Dialogue goes to...." the starlet teased.

Those around me in the theater held their breath. I scooted to the edge of my seat, ready to spring forward, ready to retrieve my award. Ready to deliver my acceptance speech, written with unforgettably original dialogue. Ready to thank the Academy for its dedication to excellence. To thank my mother and father for their unwavering support. To thank Beth, who was home sick with the flu, for her abiding belief in my talent. And to thank my plus-one for the evening, Professor Logan, for motivating me by guaranteeing I'd never sell a script.

The starlet continued, "A.I."

The ovation was deafening. A life-size robot in a Giorgio's tuxedo goose stepped down the aisle toward the stage to claim its gold statuette.

As the camera closed in on my reaction, Professor Logan leaned over and enveloped me in a comforting embrace, followed by a long, steamy smooch on the lips that rivaled the movie kiss on the bow of the *Titanic*.

I was stunned, shocked. And surprisingly thrilled.

Until I awoke from that silly dream. Everything about it was artificial, and nothing about it was intelligent. It was all the figment of a hopeful writer's vivid imagination.

Chapter 8
FIONA

O<small>N A DISTANT</small> hillside, the lit-up Hollywood sign loomed like a sentinel in the night as a stark symbol of dreams still to be realized, and those yet to be dashed. I pulled my fading red Mercedes into the garage of my old but full-of-character Spanish-style, twelve-unit building, Casa del Sol, which housed a mixture of lower-income families and struggling singles. Not so long ago, I lived in a five-thousand square-foot home where Mulholland Drive meets Beverly Glen Boulevard, where tour buses clogged the star-studded mountain neighborhoods, where autograph seekers camped outside celebrity gates.

Lugging my things, I walked through a well-tended garden, pausing to pluck a dead petal off a Double Delight rose. It had been a long night after a long day. I was beat, and I was still single. I also still had a stack of unreadable scripts to read, note, and grade.

I continued wearily down the dingy hallway to my ground floor apartment, Unit #6. Displayed on the door was a polished brass plate, MANAGER.

As soon as I opened the door, my beloved basset hound, Rathbone, jaunted over to greet me. He wore his signature red bandana around his neck.

I stooped down to kiss him. "Hello, baby. How was your day?"

My small, well-organized dwelling was filled with junk mail, newspapers, magazines, books, videos, DVDs, scripts, and photographs of my family. Original illustrations and oil paintings by my late husband adorned the walls. I turned on Spotify and let Bruce Springsteen's *Dancing in the Dark* light up my living room and lift up my spirits.

The buzzing rivers of traffic welcomed Rathbone and me as we stepped onto the rooftop deck of our apartment house. Armed with my nightly glass of Chardonnay, I eased my tired body into a cushy lounge chair. The marquees of movie theaters sparkled before me, and sirens sliced the night. Eddie who? No loss. Lesson learned. Moving on.

Looking out over the City of Angels, and in anticipation of my big meeting the following morning, I raised my glass. "Hello, Hollywood. You haven't seen the last of Fiona Logan," I said. Then, I quoted *Gone with the Wind*, "'After all, tomorrow is another day.'"

It seemed like a dream. The way he carried me to the bed. The way he expertly unclasped my bra. The way he breathed warmly in my ear.

So many questions rushed in. Clearly my conscience was working overtime to protect me from this moment. How, at my age, did I end up in something as sordid as a one-nighter? Why was I breaking my own moral code? Where was my usual restraint? What happened to lessons learned? Why was I about to violate my personal principles? Why now become a traitor to my values? Hadn't the Eddie Harper fiasco taught me anything? Eddie-thing at all?

Enraptured in a steamy indulgence, I arched my back, moaning in expectation. The embers crackled in the fireplace, our only source of light. He lifted my skirt, and his fingers walked up my inner thigh, inch by arousing inch. I felt like the heroine in some cheap romance novel. This couldn't be happening. Not to Fiona Logan, mother of one, wife to none. Retired lover to all.

The entire scene was absolutely out of character for me. Nevertheless, a growing passion wrest control of all reason, all senses. I had never envisioned experiencing anything this spontaneous, this exciting, this scandalous. I couldn't stop. Didn't want to. And feeling, not guilty, but for the first time in years, liberated and sexy. After a lifetime of abiding by society's rules, didn't I deserve a few rapturous hours of unrepressed, irresponsible ecstasy? Hadn't I earned the right to take a chance, to let go?

Yesterday, I would have politely said, "I'm flattered. But I'm sorry. I can't do this." Tonight, however, I tore his shirt off in a frenzy like it was on fire.

It didn't matter that we didn't know each other. What mattered was that we had followed an impulsive primal instinct. The nameless, chiseled Viking had dared to take the willing hand of this nameless, demure Gypsy, and we had left the masquerade party in the lobby of the ski lodge. He carried me slowly up the spiral staircase to his suite as we acted upon our urge to be in the moment, and for one erotic night, two strangers would stay present and unite in pure hedonism. For this New Year's Eve, December would end with a bang, as it were, and January would begin with a wild, irresistible, simultaneous, orgasmic scream.

At the stroke of midnight, as church bells echoed throughout the Alpine valley, he lowered me to the bed. I threw my head onto the satin pillow, my hands squeezed the bedposts of the brass bed frame, and just as the mysterious buccaneer was about to ravish my craving body, my hound dog gave a frightful bark.

I abruptly opened my eyes to his slobbering, hungry face. It was breakfast hour. Rathbone's front paw was petting my lap. And no sexual fantasy of his master would forestall the sunrise feeding.

I pushed myself out of the lounge chair, grabbed my empty wine glass and Converse high tops, and headed down off the roof to serve my precious companion, who licked me awake every morning.

It was a dream. A corny, unromantic, lowbrow, barbaric dream. Fortunately, my hairiest best friend rescued me from such a perverse apparition. Unfortunately, I was beginning another day without sex, without love. Without any relief in sight.

The curse and blessing of being a writer is that I can't ever turn my imagination off. Especially when I'm sleeping. That's when my mind creates characters and plots and images, amplifying, so says my therapist, my own suppressed fears, aspirations, and desires.

I'm sometimes shocked by the show my subconscious stages in my slumber. The racy images, the embarrassing, cheesy "writing," the representation of Fiona Logan as a person completely opposite of who I am in my waking hours, confound and intrigue me. I simply don't harbor those kinds of fantasies. I'm educated. I'm refined. I'm mature. A booty call with a pirate? Arggggh.

My dreams, on a good night, provide useful material for my work. Of late, however, they have been taken over by my declining hormones, which would have been great if I wanted to write porn. Which I didn't. So, come dawn, I open my eyes and know it's time to face a blank computer screen and its insatiable blinking cursor, all in effort to restart a career by making stuff up.

Chapter 9

JACK

Daybreak. The coastline was deserted. Low-flying pelicans dove for breakfast. I jogged along the beach, splashing through the surf of the Pacific Ocean. My sunrise routine of driving to land's end, indulging in an invigorating run and ocean dip before going to work, was a form of meditation. It was how I worked out problems in my movie scripts. The ones I had hoped to write. The ones that, according to Professor Logan, would never be read, much less produced.

"Wait up," a high-pitched voice shouted.

Behind me, charging across the hard sand, came Violette, who claimed she changed her first name each year on her birthday. This year, she also had a head of bright purple hair. Perpetually between jobs, this frisky transplant from Louisiana was one of the regular runners who busted butt every morning on the two-mile stretch between the piers of Santa Monica and Venice. Violette was a poster girl for California, bronzed and Botoxed. She resided in my apartment building and was my chief consultant for living the California lifestyle. Violette was the one who suggested, "If you're going to wake up in L.A., begin every day by making love to the beach."

"Hey, Buck." She called me "Buck," short for Buckeye, Ohio being the Buckeye State.

"Good morning, Sunshine."

We ran side by side along the water's edge, listening to each other pant. It was kind of a turn on.

"A bunch of us are going to the pier tonight to get stoned and ride the Ferris wheel. Don't you dare tell me you can't make it," she said, batting her purple eyelashes.

"Sorry. Promised my girlfriend a movie."

"This phantom girlfriend of yours is getting in the way of some good times."

"Don't date a doctor. They're never around."

"Lucky you."

"What do you mean?"

"If she's never around, she'll never find out," Violette said in a tempting tone.

"Find out what?"

"About us."

"What about us?"

"About us doing it, dummy." She whipped her head, tossing sand out of her hair. "Do I have to spell everything out for you?" she giggled.

"Yeah, I get it now."

"You're so Oh-hi-oh, Bucky," Violette said, licking a bead of sweat off her top lip.

"It's just that—"

Too late. She had rocketed ahead of me, calling over her shoulder in her seductive southern drawl, "Don't worry. I'm not giving up on you."

I studied her long, violet hair and spectacular rear end as she sprinted down the strand.

MY FIFTEEN-YEAR-OLD, SKY-BLUE Prius hybrid weaved through lanes on Fairfax Avenue, battling morning traffic. I parked behind Bliffer's Bakery in time to see, on the loading dock, full-bodied Shanelle Grant, age twenty-nine, with my big, black roommate, Kevin Adams, thirty-three. They were in the throes of playful kissing and serious groping. I watched and listened. That's what writers do. Study human behavior, noting every detail. You never know when you'll need to recreate the scene for a script. I had introduced Kevin to Shanelle, my workmate. And they hit it off from the beginning.

As the fondling festival turned wild, Shanelle groaned, "Ohhh, Kev." She wrapped her leg around Kevin's hip. He, in turn, took a wide grip of her ample butt. They needed to be hosed down.

Breathless, Kevin separated himself. "We're gonna get arrested."

They laughed and exchanged one last kiss before Shanelle dismounted Kevin and Kevin mounted his pearl-white Harley motorcycle. I was envious of how comfortable they were expressing uninhibited affection in public.

As Shanelle entered the bakery's backdoor, I got out of my car. Kevin motored over to me. We bumped fists.

"Have you been here the whole time?" he asked.

"I didn't sleep here, if that's what you mean."

"You were spying."

"Couldn't take my eyes off you two."

"You're sick," he said.

"It was like watching good porn."

"Is there such a thing?"

"Yeah. When your girlfriend is the star."

We laughed. If I never made another friend, I'd be quite satisfied. Kevin, a social worker, was solid gold.

"Did I get any mail?" he asked.

"Nothing important. I left it on the counter."

"Miss me?"

"You ever coming back?"

"Ask Connie Lingus," he said, strapping on his helmet.

"Who's that?"

He indicated the bakery. "My porn star."

We laughed and high-fived each other.

"I'm late. Gotta fly," Kevin said. He took off, but circled back to say, "I miss you, Dawg."

I'd do anything for that guy, including, if I had to, live alone in the name of his blooming romance.

I entered my place of business. The sign above the bakery's front door said, *Meeting Your Kneads*. You could smell the freshly baked bread a mile away. A Fairfax district institution, Bliffer's Bakery was known for its pastries, cakes, and fresh Friday morning challahs. Bliffer's was also known for its five-foot tall, eighty-six-year-old owner, Benny Bliffer who, as I put on my apron, was berating wiry Ricardo Sanchez, the morning-shift baker.

Shanelle, a talented and aspiring R&B singer, was removing trays of hot bagels from the oven. Duncan, a recovering everything, was the dishwasher who, with headsets clamped to his Mohawked head, had effectively tuned out the here and now. This eclectic back-of-house staff engaged in a routine but skillful dance, an accomplished daily ritual of the opening hour in very tight quarters.

Ricardo took me aside. "Warning. The troll's out for blood," he said, just as Benny ambled up to me.

"I guess you were in the neighborhood," Benny said.

"Benny."

"Nice of you to stop by."

"I'm only two minutes late."

"Late is late."

"I fell asleep in the shower. Won't happen again."

"Better not," Benny groused as he moved away to target his next victim.

"I'll come in two minutes early tomorrow," I called after him. "I love you, Benny."

Shanelle passed through, carrying a hot tray. "Behind you," she cautioned. "We had 'the talk' last night."

"How did it go?" I asked.

"He said yes."

"Touchdown."

"He really wants to move in," she said, her eyes glistening. "It's a slippery slope from there."

"It's what you want."

"I ain't lettin' this one get away. And I hate being indebted to you."

Benny cornered Duncan, who strummed his air guitar. "And I pay you for this?" Benny said to Duncan's vacant face.

"I hope it works out," I said to Shanelle.

"Sure changes things," she said.

"Sure does."

Eleanor, a.k.a. Mrs. Bliffer, entered through double doors, which connected to the storefront area. She was constantly trying to set me up with Jocelin, one of her eight granddaughters. "The bright, not pretty one." Eleanor was convinced that Jocelin needed, in her words, "a goy to deflower her."

"Good morning, Eleanor," I said, wrapping her miniature body in my arms.

"Good morning, Jackie, my sweet."

Benny pursued Ricardo, waving a work order in the air. He yelled, "We're the bakery to the stars. George Clooney wants a Bundt cake in the shape of a penis? You don't ask, 'with or without circumcision.'"

"*El me esta volviendo loco,*" Ricardo said to no one in particular.

"Oh, yeah? You're driving *me* loco," Benny screeched.

Before I left for California, I had read an ad on the L.A. Craigslist, *Bakery Salesperson/Cake Decorator wanted. No experience needed. Flexible hours. Good penmanship wouldn't hurt.* Before applying, I watched a ton of YouTube videos to learn how to decorate baked goods.

The work was steady, the pay sucked, but it gave me plenty of time to think on the job about the scripts I tried writing at night. Besides, Eleanor found my copywriting skills to be "icing on the cake."

Benny handed me a clipboard. "Missus Goldblatt changed her mind again," he said. "Now she wants a pair of doves for each year her parents have been married. Sixty years."

"A hundred and twenty doves?" I exclaimed.

"By four o'clock."

"That's twenty doves per hour."

"What? You got something better to do?"

"I could use a nap."

Benny rolled his eyes.

"I love you, Benny."

He turned to leave, then stopped. "Also, something schmaltzy written on top."

"Piece of cake."

He shook his head and rallied the troops. "C'mon, people. Shake it and bake it."

I pushed through the double doors and walked into the store area. The powder blue walls of the bakery featured dozens of autographed photographs of Hollywood celebrities with their arm around Benny. My favorite was Muhammad Ali. Benny's head came up to the champ's belt buckle.

I greeted the staff and moved to my cake decorating station situated in front of the street window, where passersby would pause to watch the artist at work. I settled on my stool and almost disappeared behind the Goldblatt's four-foot-tall, six-tier anniversary cake. I sized it up like Rodin studying a block of Carrara marble.

"Sixty years. That's a lot of flockin' birds," I murmured.

Chapter 10
FIONA

BEGINNING MY MORNINGS in the flower garden and inhaling its earthy aroma allowed me to connect mind to body. I was alarmed by a plaintive whimper, looked around, and realized that the high-pitched squeals had come from an exhausted me. I couldn't hold my plank pose any longer and collapsed face first onto my yoga pad.

I rolled up my mat and headed into the house. This was not going to be just another pointless day. This day, I was going to Paramount Studios to try to sell my latest idea for a movie. I had to look good. I had to look *now*. I had to fulfill my high school yearbook's prediction for me, Most Likely to Look the Youngest the Longest.

Standing in front of my full-length bathroom mirror in bra and panties, applying lipstick, with Rathbone at my side, I took a moment to examine my once striking face. Some had compared it to Lucille Ball's. The early years. I puckered my lips. "If you weren't such a boozer, Eddie Harper, you could have awakened to this today."

I pulled the skin near my cheekbones and watched wrinkles and sags disappear. Turning sideways, I looked at myself in profile, keeping the tightness with one hand and sweeping my red hair up with the other. Then, I let it all fall back. "What do you think, baby?" I asked Rathbone. "Who's winning? Gravity or me?"

According to Rathbone's blasé expression, I looked good enough. To be accepted just for who you are is the sole reason to own a dog.

"Today's your day, Lucy," I promised my mirror. "You're going to crush it."

Although they didn't have any idea who I was, the out-of-towners gathered on Melrose Avenue outside Paramount Pictures Studios didn't take any chances when I drove my Mercedes convertible, top down, through the iconic front gates. They aimed phone cameras at my face, which was hidden by a huge sunhat and oversize sunglasses. The ghost of Lucille Ball was returning to her original lot.

Nabbing the first open spot, I parked, got out of my car, and charged toward my appointment. I caught a glimpse of myself in the reflection of the commissary window. "You've still got it, kid," I said, trying to pump myself up.

I had dressed in my power outfit, Navy gabardine DKNY pantsuit, white T-shirt, and my good luck shoes, red Armani sneakers. Red, white, and blue. I made a statement. "She may not be the youngest, but she's America's most patriotic screenwriter."

I found the historic DeMille building and hurried into the lobby. A lanky receptionist sat behind a half-moon glass desk, unconsciously scrolling through her Instagram. The waiting area was empty except for fifty-six-year-old Kim Fleishman, the sixth child of a Japanese mother and Jewish father. He identified as a Jupe.

Kim had sunk deep into a giant leather couch. His fat knees were higher than his little head. Despite having gone nearly bald, he flaunted a petite ponytail, dyed jet black. He wore designer jeans, a western vest and boots, an open silk shirt, orange kerchief, and an earring. Kim was my agent. He was also gay. My gay-gent. And, for some unthinkable reason, on this day, he was dressed as a dapper cowboy.

"You call this eleven thirty." He struggled to swim out of the divan.

"You call this proper meeting attire? What's the trick 'r treat costume for?" I said, eyeing Kim's get-up.

"Took me six weeks to set up this fuckin' meeting," he fumed, trying to keep his voice down.

I took in his whole ensemble. "You need a lasso to tie the look together."

"And you waltz in here like—"

"Missed a belt loop there, Curly," I pointed out as I waltzed toward the reception desk. I had known Kim forever. He was so much fun to tease.

Kim madly fumbled to re-thread his belt, but he wasn't through reprimanding me. "One does not keep the studio waiting." He hustled to my side.

"Ah, the eleventh Commandment," I said, removing my sunhat and sunglasses. I checked in with the receptionist. "Fiona Logan here to see—" I turned to Kim. "Hey, Tex. Who is Fiona Logan here to see?"

"Zane Prescott," Kim said, still smoldering.

"Is Mister Prescott expecting you?" the receptionist asked.

"No," I said. "He's probably expecting a man half my age."

Undaunted, the frizzy-haired receptionist picked up the phone and dialed. Something about me caused her to look more closely at my face. "Are you somebody?" she inquired.

"No. I'm a writer."

"Christ, Fiona," Kim flared.

"Because you look like that chick from that movie," she said. Then, she spoke into the phone, "A Miss—" She went blank.

"Logan," I whispered.

Kim edged me aside and called out, "And her agent, Kim Fleishman."

"…are here for Mister Prescott," the receptionist said. She listened for a moment, then hung up. "They'll be right with you." She stared at me again. "You know, the one having the affair and kills that guy, but it turns out she really didn't? That chick."

"Not me," I said.

"She played the sister in that other movie," the girl said. "About an asteroid or something."

Kim steered me back to the waiting area. "Twenty goddamn minutes late," he hissed through his capped teeth.

"My dog didn't go off," I said.

"What?"

"I know. Can you believe it? He overslept."

"Is this a hormonal thing? Really, Fiona, you're getting goofier by the day."

He deserved an explanation, an excuse, but I didn't have a good one, so I told him the truth. "It's atychiphobia."

"And what is that, Professor?"

"Fear of failure." I wasn't kidding. My face may have said, "Bring it on," but my stomach was screaming, "Bring on the Pepto-Bismol." I was scared to death. I couldn't fail. I wasn't going to get too many more chances to present my wares, my words. As I grew older and older, the stakes of these pitch meetings became higher and higher, while my confidence was plunging lower and lower. I'd still be in bed were it not for some nagging inner drive to find a way to pay my bills. Writing assignments always had.

There were a shrinking number of films being produced, and there were too many qualified writers desperate to make theirs one of the few. I was no longer on the coveted list of *B* writers. Trying to get a studio executive excited over my story—trying to convince him or her or they that it would be a box office bonanza—was nearly impossible. I used to be good at it. I had to prove to myself that I still was. But I could already feel the sweat pooling under my arms.

Kim placed his hands on my shoulders. "You'll do great, sweetie. Just stay calm. Stay centered. Use your meditation methods. And don't forget to begin the meeting with some light banter. Get them to like you right off the top."

"Light banter. Okay."

"Ease into the pitch, make Prescott see your story, don't be afraid to use your feminine wiles, then close with an up number and a ballad."

"Thanks. I'll do my best. But if I start to sabotage myself—"

A male assistant, dressed all in black, entered the foyer. "Miss Logan?"

"And Mister Fleishman," Kim said, shaking the assistant's hand with both of his.

"I'm Troy, Mister Prescott's assistant. This way, please."

"Git along, little doggie," I said to Kim.

He walked ahead of me as we followed young Troy down a long, narrow hallway bordered by movie posters and trophy cases. My performance anxiety was setting in, right on schedule. I tried pushing it away by focusing on Kim's puny ponytail. It was like a tiny pendulum swaying back and forth, hypnotizing me into a needed state of relaxation.

But I should have taken a Prozac.

Chapter 11
JACK

Elizabeth Watson, my smart, freckled, and pretty girlfriend, walked into the bakery. She waved at me, while making her way across the floor. Though she was always pale from her indoor captivity, Beth looked great in her hospital scrubs.

"Makin' house calls?" Shanelle said, hugging Beth.

"Treated that stud of yours yesterday. Cut his hand on the rim. A man his age has no business slam dunking," Beth said.

"Best slam dunk I've ever had, girl," Shanelle replied.

They cracked up. I watched as Beth exchanged friendly ad-libs with the staff. Everybody loved her. Except Eleanor. She was holding out for a Jack and Jocelin wedding announcement.

"Well, surprise," I said, exchanging a perfunctory peck on the lips.

Beth read the inscription on the cake. "'Sixty years—soaring on the wings of love.' Who came up with that tearjerker?"

"A former linebacker for the Ohio State Buckeyes."

"You were born in the wrong century."

"And Max and Miriam Goldblatt will be forever grateful that I was." I resumed my handiwork. "So, what's happening?"

"I got off early. Thought we could grab lunch together," she said.

"Grab a cookie. I gotta work."

"Well, that sucks."

"I know. I hate making money for a living."

"How about tonight?"

"Yeah. Let's have lunch tonight," I said.

"What's your problem?"

I stopped working. "Kevin and Shanelle are moving in together."

"Sweet. It's about time."

"I'm happy for them, but I can't afford that apartment on my own."

Beth took that in. "Everything happens for a reason. One apartment door closes, another opens."

I paused. "So, you think the Door Gods are telling us something?"

"Solves a lot of problems," she said.

I offered Beth some icing off my finger. She sensually licked it. If the AMA ever published a *Girls of the OR* magazine, Beth would be its centerfold.

"We're coming up on a year, Jack. Most of the time, I'm at your apartment anyway."

"I know. It really interferes with my dating."

Beth moved closer to me. "It's sorta the next step, after a year. Kinda what couples do, after a year." Her tongue circled my finger, licking more icing. This doctor knew just how to raise my blood pressure. "Why pay two rents? Doesn't make sense. Did I point out the fact that it's been a year?"

"Yeah. So does your mother every time we see her," I said, smiling.

Benny buzzed by. "Visiting hours are over, Doc. Your boyfriend is behind schedule."

"Looking good, Benny. Have you been exercising?" Beth asked.

"Yeah. Exercising my right to kick you out of here," Benny said and limped off.

Beth turned to me. "Let's get some take-out tonight, snuggle up, and talk more about the Door Gods." She beamed, embraced me, and left.

Chapter 12
FIONA

Zane Prescott's office was decorated in black. Walls, rug, couches, desk, artwork, lampshades, coffee mugs—all black. Even his windows were tinted. Zane, dressed in a black suit, black shirt buttoned to the top, black shoes, no socks, and was in his late twenties. He was *GQ* perfect, right down to his slicked-back black hair and five-day black whiskers. He sat back in his black chair, stealing looks at stock market updates on his computer screen. He never bothered to stand up nor offer a handshake.

Taking notes was Zane's adolescent development executive, Lucas, who was dressed identically to his boss. But Lucas out-blacked everything around, including his boss, as an African American.

Kim broke the ice. "So, uh, we really appreciate your taking the meeting."

"I've been looking forward to it," Zane said absent-mindedly, glancing up from his phone. "They tell me Fiona wrote some great shit back in the day." He lifted his coffee cup. "Is anybody else's latte cold?"

Lucas sprang up to freshen Zane's coffee.

I made a feeble attempt at light banter. "Sorry I was late. It's genetic. My ancestors arrived on the *June Flower*."

Zane forced a fake smile and a phony giggle.

Kim jumped in. "Actually, we were a bit tardy because some big rig jackknifed on the 405 and—"

"So, tell me your latest and greatest movie idea," Zane said, cutting to the chase and challenging me. So much for light banter.

"I don't have a movie idea," I said. The room fell silent. "It's *more* than a movie idea," I gloated.

Zane wasn't impressed by my opening salvo. Kim, however, loved my style, my sense of timing, my painstakingly well-rehearsed, seemingly-impromptu sales pitch. That's how movies were sold back in the day.

Kim leaned over to Lucas and tittered, "More than a movie idea."

"It's sequels," I said. "It's merchandising. It's a TV spin off. It's—"

"It's almost lunchtime," Zane said. "Am I ever gonna hear this thing?"

Kim looked at me, his most fed-up and un-sellable client, hoping I wouldn't suddenly stand up and storm out as I had done before.

Sure enough, I stood up and moved toward the doorway.

Kim dropped his head.

At the door, I executed a precise military about face. "We start in darkness," I said dramatically.

Kim looked up, relieved.

Zane checked his black Apple Watch, bored.

"There's a spark. A pair of hands have just lit a match," I said.

"*Mission Impossible*," Zane commented. "Classic. Go on."

"The match is dropped—"

"By the way, love the shoes," Zane said.

I pressed forward. "…igniting a floor drenched in gasoline. We—"

"Uh, huh. Got it."

"We cut outside. It's night. A building explodes. The building is—"

"Wait for it," Kim said, leaning over the edge of his seat.

"A fire station," I said.

"We're talking comedy?" Zane asked.

"We're not." I marshaled on. "We see fire engines trapped inside, engulfed in the irony. Firefighters jump from their second floor sleeping quarters. It's an inferno. All we hear is breathing, heavy breathing, like someone is—"

"Wait for it," Kim uttered, interrupting my flow again.

"Having sex," I said.

Zane threw a sideways glance at Lucas. "Psycho drama, Lukey-boy."

"It's an action picture," Kim claimed.

"Okay," Zane said. "Action. There's nothing wrong with action."

I started again. "The camera—"

"We like action," Zane said. "Right, Luke?"

Assistants, like Lucas, are instructed not to speak in meetings even if asked a direct question, so he just nodded and gave Zane a thumbs-up. Then, Zane's intercom sounded.

"Sorry," he said, picking up his desk phone. I waited. "What?" he said into the phone. After listening to the response, he put his hand in the air. "Two seconds." He punched a line and began talking. "We still on?"

My shoulders fell. I detested this guy. This business. This town. The whole kit and caboodle. I once wrote a children's book called *Kit 'n Kapoodle* about a lost kitten and the poodle that rescued her. Marvin, my late husband, did the illustrations. It didn't sell. God, I missed Marvin. Especially at moments like this, when *I* needed rescuing.

Zane spoke into the phone, "Yeah, we're running a bit late here, but—" Suddenly, he snickered and looked to Lucas. "Can you believe this mofo? Demands to talk, then puts me on hold."

Lucas just shook his head in disbelief, lips sealed.

After a long delay, Zane cupped his hand over the mouthpiece and said to me, "Firemen jumping. Heavy breathing. Having sex. What else?"

I tried to recapture the mood, my rhythm, my composure. "The camera slowly—"

Zane shot his palm toward me. "Wait." Then, into the phone, "Sure. I could leave now. Let's—" Again, he looked at Lucas. "I'm on hold again. Interrupts my meeting, now this. What a dick."

Lucas gave a thumbs-down.

Zane drummed his fingers on his desk. Everyone waited in silence. And waited. Finally, Zane nodded to me. "The camera slowly...." he said.

"Moves to reveal—"

Instantly, Zane held up his hand, listening into the phone. Then, cheerfully said, "Start warmin' up, Monty. Because today, bro, I spot you nothing." Zane hung up, smiled, and looked at me. "You know Lamont Williams, right?"

"I don't know anyone," I said.

"Black dude, but Jesus can he write."

Lucas looked away.

Zane prepared to leave. "So, look, I'm not gonna sit here and grinfuck you folks all day. I've already got a couple pyro movies in the works."

I moved to the window, seething, my back to the room.

"Pyro movies?" Kim said. "There's actually a category?"

"They're called genres. But look, if you have anything else, anything, just call Troy and he'll get you in to see Lucas. Kid went to NYU. Full scholarship. Knows everything."

In the reflection of the window, I saw Zane stand and grab his gym bag. Lucas took his cue and stood as well. As Zane put on his Canali suit coat, he said to my back, "Good pitch, man, really. I could see it all. The flames, some sicko setting fires, wackin' off."

Kim was there to sell this project. He wasn't going to leave the room until he closed the deal. He rose. "Here's the twist," Kim said, heroically. "Turns out the sicko is a woman."

I spun around. A woman? Oh, really?

"Ah, ha." Zane gasped. "Well, thanks for coming in."

"She's a shrink, specializing in pyromania," Kim said, not giving up.

"There ya go. All kinds of surprises," Zane said, backing toward the door.

"She set the whole thing up in order to seduce the arson investigator," Kim said. "Three magic words. 'Summer blockbuster.'"

"Those are two words, my friend. My two words? Goodbye," Zane said.

"That's one word," I mumbled.

Kim tried desperately to salvage the pitch. "And, wait for it. The arson investigator is a woman."

I did a double take. More women? I returned to staring out the window, trying to locate my car.

"Girl on girl shit," Zane said. "Very in. Let's hope one of them is Asian. No offense intended."

"None taken. I'm half flattered," half-joked my half-Asian agent. "Tell him the title, Fiona."

I had long ago lost interest but always enjoyed making up titles. "*Pyro Lesbo*," I said, turning toward the group.

Kim disregarded me and stepped daintily in front of Zane. "It's called *Burning Desire*, and you know Fiona Logan can write the hell out of it."

"We'll chew on it, okay?" Zane said. He stepped around Kim, stopping at the door. "Going back, think about taking Sepulveda instead of the 405."

"Yeah," Kim said, dejectedly. "Good luck with your tennis game."

"Racquetball," Zane said. "Tennis is for sissies. No offense meant."
"Fiona plays racquetball." Kim blurted out.
"And I'm black," I said perkily.
Lucas stifled a laugh.
"You really should think comedy," Zane said, exiting.
Kim, Lucas, and I were left standing there.
Then, Lucas broke into a wide grin and turned to me. "When you said '*Pyro Lesbo*,' I 'bout pissed my pants."

KIM AND I left the DeMille building without saying a word. We walked quickly through the studio lot sharing a frosty silence. I couldn't wait to get home and pour myself a drink. And read *Sense and Sensibility*.
Finally, Kim spoke. "You gotta play the game, Fiona."
"Racquetball? I don't look good in goggles."
"Because when you don't play the game, like showing up late, they walk out early." Kim stopped me, taking my hand in his. "Sweetie. Why are you self-destructing again?"
"Because I like borrowing money from you."
"Look, I love you more than both my fucked-up sisters."
"I'm so flattered."
"But, Fiona, the anger, the animosity just spews out every time you open your mouth."
"Maybe I should talk through my ass, like you."
"What?"
"Where do you come off making the arson investigator a lesbian."
"I was trying to save your movie."
"Well, next time, save your breath." I broke away and started walking aimlessly around the backlot.
Kim had to skip to keep up. "Wake up and smell the future, Fiona. What's it going to be? Cashing checks or clipping coupons?"
"Alliteration will get you nowhere."
"This is exactly what I'm talking about. You need an attitude-ectomy."

"He never even looked at me," I said. "And 'grin-fuck?' Who comes up with these expressions?"

"Don't blame the Zane Prescotts of the world. They don't give a damn that you took time off to care for a dying husband, and that your comeback tour hasn't exactly been a smash hit. You're the one who stopped thinking, stopped writing, stopped living."

"Stop talking. I have alethophobia."

"Fear of?"

"Hearing the truth."

Suddenly, I was overcome by sorrow. I looked skyward. "Marvin, you bastard." Kim gave me a moment to collect myself. It didn't work. "I forgot where I parked my damn car," I said. "I'm lost. I'm freaking lost." The irony was palpable. I was walking in little circles, searching for my car, my life.

Kim had been through this with me many times before. Like any good friend or dog, he just let me rant. Such is unconditional love.

"When you adore someone so much," I said. "Then watch him disappear day by day, you can't just bounce back from that. You can't just cozy up to your computer and think of clever ideas for something as trivial as a movie." I was crying. "I'll never find my car."

"Marvin wouldn't want you to mourn forever," Kim said.

"It's all his fault."

"It's time, honey, to do what he would want you to do. What I need you to do. It doesn't matter what you write, just that you write."

"Let's face it. I don't care anymore."

"That's why you went into therapy. Something should have changed by now."

"Yeah. Instead of writing movies, I'm writing game show questions and teaching a stupid night class, just enough to buy gas for my guzzler." I headed off in another direction. "Where the hell *is* my guzzler?"

Kim loped after me.

I turned and faced him, filling my lungs with air and blowing it out. "No. I really don't care anymore." I looked around. "Somebody stole my car."

"I won't let you destroy yourself. It's costing me ten percent and my best friend."

"Which bothers you more?"

"Oh, blow me."

"Sorry, wrong gender."

Kim rightfully became enraged. He took a note card from his pocket and flung it at me. It floated to the pavement. "There's your other appointment for the month. You don't need me there. You don't need me anywhere. You don't need me period." He stomped off.

I picked up the card and hollered at him. "What I don't need are any more of these waste-of-time meetings."

Kim stopped, spun around, stomped back, and unloaded. "You ungrateful C-word. Do you have any idea how impossible it is to find you *any* kind of meeting?"

"Just call Troy. He'll get me in to see Lukey-boy."

Kim threw his hands up in frustration. "You're hopeless."

"This from a man who shaves his arm hair."

"If you want to be taken seriously, set your dog an hour earlier, and show up on time."

"It wouldn't have made a bit of difference. That punk had no intention of offering me a deal."

We were toe to toe. Onlookers pretended not to be listening.

"Why not? Sexism, ageism, cronyism? All the above? How long are you going to play the victim?"

"As long as you keep deceiving yourself."

"What does that mean?"

"It means neither one of us is getting rich!" I yelled. "Or younger."

"What are you saying?"

"Maybe we're both hanging onto a loser."

We'd had fights over the years, but this one escalated way beyond what we would later deeply lament.

"I'm not the loser here, girlfriend," he shouted. "In fact, if they had a contest for the biggest loser in the world, you'd come in second. Do you know why, Fiona?"

"See ya at the movies." I turned and clomped away.

Kim shrieked after me. "Do you know why you'd come in second?"

I never looked back, but I, along with a number of stagehands on a smoke break, heard Kim scream at the top of his lungs, "BECAUSE

YOU'RE A LOSER." He wasn't finished. "Another observation. Your therapist has transformed you into something worse. You should fire her."

"Wrong, girlfriend," I screamed over my shoulder. "Wait for it. I should fire *you*."

"You don't have to," he cried out, head bobbling, ponytail swirling. "I QUIT."

Chapter 13
JACK

ONE OF THE things I loved most about Beth is that, in many ways, she was old school. She preferred white tennis balls, film to digital cameras, and to watch DVDs rather than stream the latest movies on Netflix. We stood back-to-back in an aisle at the Culver City Library, browsing movies on discs. Beth faced the Horror section. I faced Romance.

"See, if we were living together, you would be watching my flat screen," she said. "All fifty-two inches."

"I'd rather watch your flat chest, all thirty-two inches."

She punched my arm. "Asshole."

"I'm joking, just joking. I worship your itty bitties."

"My giant TV, my gourmet cooking, my soothing backrubs, plus all the free tongue depressors you want."

"It's sounding better all the time," I said. "Except my tongue isn't depressed."

With great enthusiasm, Beth grabbed a DVD of the movie *Saw*. "I'm getting this."

I glanced over at the title. "'You can watch that one alone."

"It's so bad. I've watched it twenty times."

"Don't you see enough blood at work?"

"No. That's why I'm also taking *Saw 2* and *Saw 3*."

I had focused on a particular DVD with a picture of two young lovers on the cover. I took it off the shelf and read the credits printed on the back. "'Written by Fiona Logan.' That's my writing teacher," I exclaimed.

"Cool. What's it about?"

I read the description out loud. "'Opposites attract when a shy classical violinist meets a gritty rock guitarist.' It's called *Heartstrings*."

"You can watch *that* one alone."

"I thought she was just a hard ass," I said. "But who knows? Maybe she's a romantic at heart."

"Yeah. Just like me." Beth laughed, waving her horror movies.

Professor Logan didn't look right. She was dressed in some kind of skirt and blouse number and standing on stage in businesswomen's shoes. She was finishing up her lecture with little gusto. But, as always, I was hanging on every word.

"I once had an important job working with the extraordinary director Wes Anderson," Professor Logan said. "A brilliant man. I'll never forget the words he spoke to me. 'Black. No sugar.'"

There was no reaction, except from me. I cracked up. She deserved a round of applause. So, I clapped. She scoured the audience searching for the lone student who got the joke. Her eyes met mine. She took a tiny curtsy.

"Until next week, see ya at the movies," she said, gathering her notes.

After class, I headed to my car in the parking garage. I smelled smoke and hurried over to the source. Professor Logan's red Mercedes. She had the hood up. Clouds of black billowed out. I hesitated to make my presence known. She wasn't the most approachable person.

"Professor Logan?" I said.

"Speaking," she said.

"Should I call the fire department?"

She turned toward me. "Ah, the night stalker," she said. "No. There's not much left to burn."

"Can I help?" I asked.

"Yeah, blow hard."

We just stood there watching the fire burn itself out.

"I can give you a lift," I offered.

"I could use a lift." She sighed. We let that linger in the smelly air.

Nobody looks good under the green glow of institutional garage lights. But that night, at that moment, Professor Logan looked radiant. I wanted to know more about her. Which parent hadn't she worked it out with? Why all the cynicism? What mistakes had she made? When was the last time she laughed? Or went skinny-dipping? Or made love? I kept staring. I really had to stop thinking about her that way.

She looked into the distance. "Ever have one of those lives?"

"I could call you an Uber."

"Thanks. But by the time it gets here, my meeting will be over."

"You have a meeting at this hour?"

"A pitch to some producer."

"At this hour?"

"Yes. At this hour."

"I didn't know producers were open this late."

"You have a lot to learn," Professor Logan said, slamming the hood. She looked at her reflection in the car window and mumbled, "All dressed up and nowhere to go."

"I rented *Heartstrings*."

"Must be the head gasket," Professor Logan said to herself. "That'll be a small fortune."

"Don't tell anyone, but I cried at the end."

She looked at me, reading my face. "It's Mister Reingold, right?"

"Reynolds. Jack Reynolds. My dad calls me J-Rey. But my mom prefers—"

"Tell you what, Mister Reynolds. You really want to learn the art? Well, the art of writing a script begins with the art of selling the story. Drive me to my meeting, and you can witness first-hand the artist at work."

"At this hour?"

"Forget it."

"I just meant—"

"You'll never learn it in my classroom. I promise you that."

In everyone's life, there comes a moment. A moment that changes their destiny. This would be my moment. I could watch a true professional screenwriter in action. There's no price on the value of an experience like that. It's why I came to L.A. So, there was no way I was going to pass up this opportunity. Although I would be late for our late dinner, I knew Beth would understand and be thrilled for me. God knows I had waited many nights for her. Don't ever date a doctor.

Chapter 14
FIONA

I couldn't be late again. Not for what may have been the last pitch of my career. I had no other choice than to convince the idealist from my front row that he would learn from this inside look at the industry. I was probably violating some sacred school policy by taking a student off campus, but Dean Bailey was ready to dump me anyway.

With one wrist draped over the steering wheel, Jack drove his Prius northbound on the San Diego Freeway like a maniac. He talked nonstop and as fast as he drove. I was his captive and terrified audience.

"Don't laugh. I work at a bakery, decorating cakes, selling cookies, delivering bread, whatever they need me to do. Really nice people, and the schedule allows me to write scripts at night. I gave myself a year and a half to make something happen. My time's almost up. Either I hit the jackpot soon, or I go back to Ohio and run my dad's hardware store. I don't know if I've got what it takes, but all I've ever wanted to be is a screenwriter, to write something that will affect people forever, like *African Queen* or *It Happened One Night* or—"

His phone went off. The ringtone played the first few bars of "As Time Goes By." He held up his phone, enjoying the timing. "Or *Casablanca*. Excuse me." He checked caller I.D., then stuck the phone to his ear. "Hey. I'm driving. I can't talk." He listened. "I'm going to a meeting." He listened. "Yeah, at this hour." He tossed me a look and listened some more. "I know, I know. I'm sorry. I'll explain everything later." He listened, then, "Thanks. Don't wait up. Good night." He ended the call. "That was my girlfriend. Beth. I should've called her, told her what's up. But I got so carried away here."

"You've got a girlfriend?"

"You're surprised?"

"Not that it matters, but cake decorator. Likes old movies. Drives a Prius. Do the math."

"Not that it matters, but I'm straight," he said. And without missing a beat, he continued telling me his life story. "Anyway, money's tight, and my roommate's moving out, and the rent's high, so either I get another roommate or sell a script or—"

I interrupted by saying, "In the meeting...."

"Yes?"

"Observe."

"Observe. Okay."

"Don't talk."

"No talk. Right."

"Eyes and ears only," I said.

"No mouth. Got it."

"'Hello.' 'Goodbye.' Seriously, that's it. Do you understand, Mister Reynolds?"

"Yes. But can I talk now?"

"Go ahead."

"Can I ask you a favor?"

"What?"

"Can you call me Jack? Mister Reynolds sounds like I'm ancient."

"I'll call you whatever you want. Now, get in the far right lane."

Jack smiled and pointed his Prius toward the offramp. "I read every book I could find about writing, and each one said to experience life," he rambled on. "So, after grad school, I bought a one-way ticket to Europe. For a year, I went from country to country, town to town, girl to girl—"

I pointed my finger out the windshield. "Get off here."

"Then, it was back to the States. Job after job, mostly copywriting gigs, crappy apartment after crappy apartment, failed romance after failed romance. I saved enough money to come out here, to the motion picture capital of the world, to give screenwriting a serious shot. I never imagined I would be sitting next to an honest-to-God movie writer on my way to an honest-to-God show business meeting."

Such exuberance. Such optimism. Such a dreamer.

So young. So clueless.

So honest-to-God cute.

We arrived at a two-story, stark building in a sketchy strip mall on White Oak Avenue, way north of Ventura Boulevard. The sputtering neon sign read House of Skin. We parked and walked past dozens of drunk and rowdy coeds to the main entrance.

"What kind of studio is this?" Jack asked.

"Welcome to Hollywood, the motion picture capital of the world. Anybody with cash can call themselves a producer."

He read the words blinking under the neon sign. "'Topless Entertainment.' Wow. This is shaping up to be the best field trip I've ever had."

I led the way. I had never been inside a strip club. Never had the inclination. I felt safe having a muscular man by my side. A Neanderthal bouncer with the name Steve sewed on his windbreaker opened the door for us. The place was packed. Music pounded. Lights strobed. Laser beams pulsated through artificial fog. Jack was fixated on an exotic dancer making whoopee with a metal pole. We had to shout to be heard over the noise.

"This is a business meeting," I yelled. "Keep your eyes in your head."

"I was looking at the pole. My dad sells that kind for tetherball at his hardware store," he said, flashing a million-dollar smile.

I stepped up to the scantily clad hostess. "I'm here to see Roger Bowman," I hollered.

"Take the stairs," she yelled back, indicating a glass-walled office on the second floor, which overlooked the club. Jack and I weaved our way through the steamy crowd to the staircase.

"What's the rule, again?" I asked Jack.

He replied mutely by zipping his lips.

As we reached the second floor, we saw three young writer types sitting on folding chairs in the hallway outside a door marked *Roger Bowman Enterprises*. We took seats at the end of the row and sat alongside each other in silence. Jack read a text on his phone.

"She made her special soup."

"Practice being quiet."

"Butternut squash."

"It freezes."

We heard an egg timer ring in the office. After a moment, the door swung open, and a bald Roger Bowman escorted out a slouching hipster writer. Bowman, in his mid-50s, wore a magenta velour tracksuit. I bet he weighed three hundred pounds, slightly less than the gaudy platinum bling around his neck, wrists, and fingers. He had his arm slung over the downtrodden writer's shoulder.

"Thank you, Arnold. We'll talk," Bowman said, chewing on an unlit cigar. Then, he turned to those waiting. "My ten-forty-five cancelled. Who's got eleven?"

"Here," I said, jutting my hand in the air like the overachieving student I once was.

"You're up," Bowman belted. "Let's go."

Jack and I followed him into his office. Bowman could barely squeeze through the doorframe. His office was adorned with erotic art and sports and movie memorabilia. A cooking timer sat on his disorganized desk. He consulted an appointment book.

"Which one of you is the writer?"

"I am," I said. "Fiona Logan. My agent Kim Fleishman set up this meeting with your secretary."

"An agent?" Bowman said. "You're a real pro. I'm impressed." We shook hands. He covered my hand with his other hand and held on too long. Sizing up Jack, he said to me, "Must be take-your-kid-to-work day."

"Mister Reynolds—uh, Jack—is my associate."

Bowman shook Jack's hand hard. "Hey, Mister Associate," Bowman said, followed by, "Wink, wink, wank, wank."

"Hello," Jack said. And that's all he said, as agreed.

Bowman pointed his stogy toward a small sofa. "Sit down." He perched on the front edge of his desk. Poor desk.

Jack and I huddled next to each other, thighs awkwardly touching.

"So, here's the spiel," Bowman began. "I've made fortunes, lost fortunes. This month, I'm ridin' a good wave. Lucky for me, sex-crazed college boys are in heat year-round. You gotta love those false ID's." He walked to his glass wall overlooking the action below. "Drink up, fellas. The tits are on me." That gave him a good laugh. He turned his attention back to us. "My accountant says it's time to take some spare change and make another picture. Low budget, tax shelter, write-off sort of thing. We've earmarked forty grand for the script."

I felt Jack shiver and heard him murmur, "Forty? *Thousand*?" I shot him a stern look.

"Here's the catch. I need the script in three weeks," Bowman said. "I'm listenin' to one idea every fifteen minutes. I'll stay here all night 'til I hear one I like." He wound the egg timer to fifteen minutes. "All right, young lady, your fifteen minutes of fame starts right now. Dazzle me."

I stood up. "Okay. Are you ready?"

"Ready?" Bowman smirked. "I'm not even wearin' underpants."

I audibly gagged. Had my livelihood really come to this? Pitching to some gross slob in a strip joint at this hour? I tried to gather my senses, set the mood, set the stage, be the artist at work. I felt Jack's eyes on me. It made me nervous. It also made me feel that I had something to prove. I wanted to show off for him. Why? Was I a pervert? A child molester?

"So," I said. "We see a hand in the dark."

"Gotta stop you right there," Bowman said.

"What's wrong?"

"I don't get it."

"There's nothing to get yet."

Bowman turned to Jack. "If it's dark, how do we see a hand?"

Jack squirmed, struggling to stay true to his vow of silence.

"There's just enough moonlight to see the hand," I said. "Does that help?"

Bowman scratched his skinhead, then looked at Jack. "If she says so." He walked around his desk and dropped into his chair. Poor chair. "Doesn't matter, I guess. She's such a sexy broad, I'm happy to just look at her for fifteen minutes."

I could tell Jack was impressed with my quick thinking, my fearlessness. I could also tell he despised this snake as much as I did. Out of professional pride and a dwindling bank account, I forced myself to continue.

"The hand lights a match and drops it, igniting a floor drenched in gasoline. Suddenly—"

"Whoa, sugar. I don't need to smell every little fart. Just tell me what the fuckin' movie's about."

My acid reflux kicked in. "It's an action movie," I said, soldiering on.

"Action's too expensive. I'm one man. Roger Bowman, not Roger Spielberg. What else you got?"

"It's actually more of a psychological thriller," I said.

He turned to Jack. "Well, which is it?"

I jumped in. "It's about a pyromaniac who—"

"Stop. Just stop." He turned to Jack again. "Look, I need somethin' spicy. You know, a date night flick for"—he pointed out the window—"horny toads like them."

Jack nodded, lips sealed tight.

"There's a spicy woman in the lead," I said.

"Nope. Not feelin' it." Bowman rose.

I tried to save the pitch and save face in front of my student. "Actually, two spicy women. Lesbians."

"Forget it," Bowman said.

"Asian lesbians."

Jack seemed rather stunned and spontaneously wailed, "Hell-oh." Technically, I suppose, the outburst wasn't an infraction of our contract. Nonetheless, an irritation.

Bowman stopped the egg timer. "I got out of pornos ten years ago. Look, here's what's goin' to happen. Go downstairs. Have a drink on the house. And think up a story." He addressed his next remarks to Jack. "Somethin' your age would like to see. Wouldn't hurt if I turned a profit on this fuckin' thing. I've got a batch of alimonies. I can never remember how many." He consulted his sixty-thousand-dollar Rolex. "Come back in an hour." He glanced at the timer. "You'll have a good twelve minutes left, if I haven't found anythin' else in the meantime."

I felt both humiliated and infuriated and headed to the door. That's when Jack dared to venture beyond "hello, goodbye," a transgression that would change both our lives forever.

"Tell him," Jack said to me.

I turned around.

"Tell him the *real* idea," he said.

"Tell him 'Goodbye,'" I said tersely.

Jack continued to defy my directives. "She was only joking about the lesbians on fire. She does that just to get people's attention. She kids a lot. She's such a hoot."

"I don't have time for kiddin'," Bowman said.

"Neither do I," I said. "Let's go."

"So, here's our real idea, Mister Bowman," Jack said.

"You write together?" Bowman asked.

Jack and I responded at the same time.

I said "No."

Jack said, "Yes," and quickly continued. "An attractive older woman and a romantic young man fall in love with each other."

"A May/December thing?" Bowman asked. "I knew you guys did more than write together."

I felt my face burning.

"We writers have a saying, 'write what you know,'" Jack said sheepishly, throwing his arm around me. Then added, "Not everyone approves."

Bowman winked at me. "I know the feelin'. I'm datin' a twelfth grader."

I grabbed Jack's arm to leave, but Bowman stepped in front of us. "So, it's a love story?"

"Love. Romance. Hanky-panky," Jack asserted. "Spicy panky."

"No Oriental muff divers?" Bowman asked.

"She was just joshing," Jack said. "Part of her charm. We're so proud of her."

I was fuming, ready to lash out. But it was a lost cause, and part of me was curious to see where this was going. For the first time, I saw Jack as someone other than the eager student. I was now in the front row of *his* show. And he was holding his own.

"Does it have laughs? I like a good laugh," Bowman said.

"Tons of laughs. It's a laugh riot," Jack said. "Comedy is our jam."

"Maybe a little flesh?" Bowman said. "A nipple here, a nipple there?"

"A nipple, nipple everywhere," Jack bragged. "As many as you want. Made to order."

"I love this kid," Bowman said.

"We could even name one of the characters Areola," Jack said.

"Areola." Bowman howled, turning to me. "Where did you find this guy? He's hilarious. And you have an agent. This is great." He relit his cigar. "So, how does it end?"

Jack looked at me. "Tell him, Fiona."

It was the first time Jack had said my first name. It sounded so natural, like we had known each other for decades, been writing partners for years.

"They live happily ever laughter," I said, still inside Jack's gaze.

Bowman doubled over in laughter.

I took Jack's arm again. "C'mon. It's past your bedtime."

"I'm fuckin' lovin' this," Bowman crowed. "We gotta make this movie." He wiped sweat and tobacco-tainted saliva from his ruddy face. "Is it expensive?"

"Expensive?" Jack repeated. "You could shoot the whole damn thing under your desk. No sets. No stunts. No special effects. Cheap, cheap, cheap. Right, Buttercup?" Jack said to me with a sly grin.

I was speechless. Observing. Not talking. Mad. A little giddy.

Bowman settled back into his ailing chair. "But tell me, what's the story?"

"The story?" Jack echoed, like he had never heard the word before.

"Yeah, that little detail." Bowman blew a smoke ring from his cigar. "Sorry to piss on your parade, people."

"Fiona?" Jack meekly squeaked. He seemed bewildered. Suddenly adrift. Panicked.

"I might not be the sharpest bulb in the drawer," Bowman said. "But I'm no movie moron. I know they usually tell a fuckin' story."

Jack was good on his feet, but he had just stepped in quicksand. I had a fast debate with myself. Dive in and pull my pupil out or stand back and watch him sink. Pity, and that paltry bank account of mine, ended the inner dispute.

"All joshing aside, we worked out every aspect of the story," I fibbed, having no idea what I was going to say next.

Jack smiled in relief.

"So, let's hear it," Bowman said.

Jack looked at me. I looked at him. He said, "Uh, it starts, well, in the beginning."

He was lost. He needed help. I threw him a rope. Just to get him going.

"Our two main characters," I said, taking off my Versace glasses.

"Plan the perfect crime," Jack said authoritatively, gesturing to me to continue.

"And they escape with a million dollars," I said. "Perfect crime. Million dollars. Maybe a cheap car chase. The whole ten yards." I was getting swept up. Loosening up. Living it up.

"Nine yards," Jack said, bringing me down to earth.

"The big question is, will young people go see it?" Bowman asked.

"We've designed it specifically for the youth market," Jack claimed.

"It's targeted exclusively to both genders," I tossed in. "And all genders in between."

"When it comes to the moviegoer demographic," Jack said, pointing out the window. "We guarantee those horny toads will hop to the box office in herds."

Bowman walked to the window, stopped, and became pensive.

Jack and I exchanged looks.

"That's the story?" Bowman asked, still facing the window.

"What more is there?" I said, preparing to lie again. "Orson Welles once jotted down an idea on a dinner napkin. All it said was *Rosebud*. The next thing the world saw was *Citizen Kane*."

"I always liked Orson Welles," Bowman said. "He makes me look thin."

"Did I mention spicy?" Jack piped up.

"So, it's a love story. Low-cost. Funny. Spicy." The disgusting pig mulled.

"Designed for the exact audience you want to reach," I added.

"And let's not forget those nipples," the endearing cake decorator said. Then, to place the cherry on top, in a deep announcer's voice, Jack said, "Areola, a gorgeous and experienced woman, falls in love with Johnson, a handsome young man in the romantic comedy *Happily Ever Laughter*, coming this summer to a movie theater near you."

Bowman spun around. He put his arms straight out, his fingers framing a camera shot, imagining the credits. "*Happily Ever Laughter*. A Roger Bowman Production." He punched the air. "Sold. That's how I do business." He grabbed his crotch. "If I feel it in my balls, BOOM! I buy it." He shook our hands. After. Touching. His. Balls.

"Forty thousand? Just like that?" I said.

"You hand me a script. I hand you a check. Just like that," Bowman answered.

Jack pumped Bowman's hand. "Thank you."

"No contract?" I asked.

"No," he said.

"We won't disappoint you, sir," Jack said. "I promise."

"No paperwork?" I asked.

"No," Bowman barked.

"You won't regret this," Jack said. "We'll work around the clock."

I didn't trust Bowman, and he knew it. He withdrew a wad of cash from his pocket and dealt an even bunch of bills to each of us.

"Here's the only paperwork that matters," he said.

Jack's eyes popped.

"A grand apiece. Call it a signin' bonus. My word is better than any fuckin' contract." He threw open his office door. "Now, get out there and write me a movie."

"We'll start tonight," Jack said. "Gotta buy some paper first."

"I want that script in my hands three weeks from today. One day later, and the deal's off," Bowman said, guiding us out the door. "Don't be late. And don't you lovebirds let me down."

"Make room on your mantle for the Oscar," Jack said as I towed him away.

"Keep your cougar in a cage," Bowman said. "I think she's got the hots for me."

Chapter 15
JACK

PROFESSOR LOGAN TOOK long, angry strides through the parking lot of the House of Skin.

I tried to stay even. "It was so interesting being in a movie pitch," I said. "Thank you very, very much for letting me come. I learned so much." It was clear she was enraged and wasn't going to talk. I filled the dead air. "I have less than eleven hundred dollars to my name. Plus, the thousand he just gave me."

No response.

"I could see what was happening in there."

No response.

"Forty thousand dollars for three week's work. That's a super buttload of money," I said.

No response.

"I knew if I could just—"

Fiona stopped walking. She jabbed her hands into her hips. Her eyes were fuming. "What? Come up with some nothing-of-a-story, your nice, ancient professor would write it?"

"No. *We* would write it. And who said anything about an 'ancient professor?'"

"Who said anything about *we*? I work alone. And I don't even do that anymore."

"I can't write this thing without you."

"You should've thought about that before you shot off your mouth up there."

"I was trying to help you."

"Help me? More like, help yourself to my meeting."

"I was only—"

"Breaking your 'hello, goodbye' promise. You still owe me one goodbye."

"I don't know about you, but twenty grand would make a huge difference in my life."

"I spent a solid year on that pyromaniac idea. Researched every minute facet. Wove the most intricate plot. Twists and turns every minute." The woman had become unhinged. She reached into her purse, withdrew her wad of Bowman's bills, and handed them to me. "It's your idea. You pitched it. You sold it. You write it."

"No," I said, backing away, refusing to take the money.

She threw the cash at my feet. "It's all you're ever going to see. Trust me, Bowman's a joke. A blowhard. The very definition of Hollywood scum." She turned and stormed off.

I yelled to her back. "Professor. I'm sorry if I offended you."

"Thanks for the ride. I'll find my own way home." She kept walking, shoulders back, red head held high.

I stood there alone in the strip mall parking lot. I bent down, scooped up the money, and sauntered toward my car. Feeling awful.

"Goodbye," I whispered, paying my night's debt to the nutty professor.

As soon as I got into my car, I called Beth. She answered with a slight edge to her voice.

"You won't believe what an incredible night I've had," I said.

"Is it over? Because it's midnight, and I'm starved."

"Huh? You waited dinner for me?"

"Go ahead. Make it quick."

"Hey, this is a big deal," I said.

"Don't be a baby. Just tell me."

"Okay. Long story short. I got a job."

"You already have a job."

"A *writing* job," I said. "A *script* writing job."

"And they're paying you?"

"A buttload."

"How much is a buttload?"

"Forty grand. Twenty per butt cheek."

"Forty thousand dollars just for writing?"

When someone says it that way, it *does* seem out of proportion to the rest of the working world.

"It was supposed to have been split between me and my writing partner, but—"

"What writing partner?"

"My teacher. Her car blew up. I drove her to the strip club. The owner didn't like the Asian lesbian idea, so I jumped in with the nipples—"

"You were at a strip club? With your teacher?"

"We were meeting a producer. He owns a strip club."

"You skipped dinner to go to a strip club?"

"I didn't choose the venue. You seem to have forgotten the part about forty-thousand dollars."

"How great for you."

"Great is an understatement. This is the moment I've been waiting for."

"Well, whatever word is greater than 'great,' count me in."

"I'm not quitting the bakery, of course. But I can now officially call myself a Hollywood screenwriter."

"And you can now officially afford your apartment without my financial aid."

"What?"

"Come over. I'll heat up the soup. We'll talk. The Door Gods are getting restless."

"I'm so on top of the world right now, I just had to tell someone. It's too late to call my parents."

"I'm not just 'someone,' Jack. I'm your girlfriend who sat home alone tonight."

"I'm sorry. I couldn't pass this up."

"I know. I'm just really tired. And hungry." She waited a beat before saying, somewhat disappointingly, *"And I have my period."*

There was silence. I could picture Beth in her fluffy white bathrobe, sitting on the love seat in her cozy window alcove. After her evening shower, she loved to nestle with the pillows and catch up on emails while letting her thick blond hair dry. I could picture her perfectly toned body and silky skin slathered in wild lavender moisturizer. I could picture her studio apartment filled with fresh flowers and votive candles, waiting for me to walk through the door. I could picture us living together. So, why was I feeling sad when I should have been feeling happy? What was wrong with this picture?

"Congratulations, Jack. Really. I'm just being a bitch. A famished, menstruating, selfish bitch. See you soon. Drive carefully."

"I'll pick up a bottle of champagne, and we can celebrate my script assignment and—" I stopped, realizing she had already disconnected.

I sat there in my car, in the parking lot, in the dark, holding my phone and two thousand dollars in cash. I saw my writing teacher waiting on the corner. She had perfect posture. Must have studied ballet at some point. I wasn't about to leave her alone, outside a strip club to fend for herself at that hour. I would stay put as long as it took before her ride arrived.

As I was about to call out to her, insisting that I drive her home, an Uber sedan pulled up. She got in and slammed the door. The car drove past me. I couldn't be sure, but it looked like Professor Logan's head was buried in her hands.

A FEW DAYS had gone by. I had emailed Professor Logan several times to apologize. She wouldn't reply. But I'm a man of my word, and I had promised Roger Bowman a finished script on time. And by God, I would spend every spare minute I had to create one. After all, it was the first time in a year and a half that anybody had paid me a cent for writing, other than *Happy Birthday, Bobby* on a coconut cake. Only one problem. I didn't know what the hell I was doing. Oh sure, I had written many practice scripts. But never a professional one. And certainly not one in three weeks.

The cleaning crew had long gone, leaving me alone in the bakery. I sat on my stool, staring at my laptop. I'd made a few measly notes about the story but hadn't written one word of the script. There was a polite knock on the front door. I looked through the storefront window. Beth stood in the darkness, dressed in her hospital scrubs. I unlocked the door. She puckered her lips for a kiss. I accommodated.

"It's kinda late," I said. "Sorry, ma'am, we're closed."
"Your phone's off," she said, entering.
"That's because I'm working my tail off."
"I only have an hour."
"I'm writing." I relocked the door. "When I'm not decorating, I'm writing."
"Kevin said you'd be here."
"He's moving his stuff out tonight. It's way too noisy over there. and—"
Beth stopped me with a kiss. A long kiss. She provocatively fingered my belt buckle. "I thought we could play doctor," she whispered in my ear.
"I really shouldn't—"
She kissed me again. Harder. Longer. Wetter.
"I'm writing," I said, breaking away.
"That was last night's excuse. I'm getting jealous of this script."
"It's only been five days."
"Nights. Five nights."
"This opportunity is my lucky break. I'm not gonna blow this job."
"Did somebody say blow job?" Beth slipped off her backpack. "Is the nightshift here?"
"No, not yet."
"Ever do it in front of a bunch of bagels?"
"Can't."
"Can't or don't want to?"
"Can't want to. I have a deadline."
She swept her hand gracefully along the countertop. "I bet there's lots of whipped cream in this place."
I was melting. "You're such a slut."
"And you so love it." She guided my hand under her scrubs top.
"Stop," I said, sounding like a teenager on prom night.
"I'll let you suck a cherry out of my bellybutton." She alluringly untied the sash of her scrub pants.
"Beth, please."
"C'mon. You've had a day of squeezing frosting bags. I've had a night of emptying colostomy bags. This physician thinks we both could benefit from a little consensual sex."

"I'm stressing out, Babe. I'm really stressing out."

She took a step back, examining my eyes. "It hasn't just been the last five nights, Jack." She used her doctor voice. "It's been the last couple of months. You've been distant. I feel you pulling away."

Beth had dead-on diagnostic insights. It was one of the qualities that first attracted me to her. I had been feeling conflicted about us since early summer. I had been dissecting our differences. I questioned whether we had enough in common for the long haul. I had been scrutinizing the adage, "opposites attract." Attract, maybe. But stick? All I could think to say was, "Soon, I'll have forty thousand dollars in my pocket and time to think. Until then, let me write. Let me finish this." I grinned. "And let me take a raincheck on that whipped cream."

She hugged me. In our embrace, she whispered, "I don't want to add to your pressure. We don't have to live together. I can wait," she said. "A day or two." She smiled.

I disengaged and brushed one of her blond bangs aside, then kissed her lightly on the forehead. "Go back to work. Heal people. Do no harm."

"Okay. But, seriously, Jack. We've been sharing the same toothbrush. Might as well share the same address. It's the next logical step. And it could be, *will* be, fun."

"Beth."

"Yes?"

"I get it."

She gave me one of her sad faces, touched my arm, and let herself out.

Chapter 16
FIONA

I WAS STRESSED out. I tried to distract myself by reading a two-year-old issue of *Vanity Fair*. I cleaned my purse. I did some deep yoga breathing. All this because I had been sitting alone in the waiting room of my dentist's office for over an hour. Dr. McGee, though never on time, was the best in Beverly Hills. Still, going to the dentist made me nervous. Because pain hurts.

The receptionist sat behind her desk, on the phone, arguing with Verizon over her latest bill. I forced myself to think happy thoughts. I practiced some visualization exercises. My default was to imagine Crystal Cove, my favorite fishing hole, in Lone River, Colorado. It calmed me for the time being, until my mind circled back to Dr. McGee and his instruments of McTorture.

The hunky doctor and I had exchanged very few words in our dental history together, mostly because his banana-bunch fingers were usually stuffed in my mouth. "Swish. Slosh. Spit," was the extent of his communication. Ours was an odd relationship, much like I shared with most of the other one-on-one "hands-on" mechanics who maintained my body. Chiropractors, gynecologists, dermatologists, masseuses, and hairdressers. Don't get me started on proctologists. As Dr. McGee worked on me, I would try to make eye contact through his protective face shield. He preferred to remain aloof, though our noses were only inches away. We were two humans in a small room together, dedicated to keeping my choppers chopping. Such a bizarre contract. In order to inspect the backside of my incisors, Dr. McGee would lean over and into me. Our foreheads would almost be touching, his long wavy bangs falling in front of my eyes. I would smell his aftershave, feel his breath cross my brow. His body heat through his lab coat. His broad shoulders straddling mine. His pelvis pressed against my elbow. Dr. McGee's highly-educated fingertips would soon be tickling my ivories, groping my gums, fondling my tongue, coated in my saliva. How is this intimate practice considered socially acceptable? Legal?

I wondered what he thought of me, if he thought of me at all. Or was I merely his next drooling face in a monotonous day filled with a succession of gaping, carp-like mouths, a chain of cavities, canker sores, and cleanings? Working inside the center cave, the largest hole in our body, the funnel of all our spoken words, with plaque buildup and stinky breath?

Writers think of such things when they're looking to distract themselves, when they're anxiety-ridden, like when they're sitting on the chair in the lotus position waiting for their dentist to inflict severe physical and financial pain.

I was filing my nails when the door to the hall swung open. A voice attempting to sound like Humphrey Bogart's exclaimed, "Of all the dental offices in all the towns in all the world, I walk into hers."

I looked up. Destiny and dentistry had collided. Together, they had delivered unto me one Eddie Harper.

"I was going to call you today," he said, standing over me. "Really, I was. I would swear on my child's life, if I had a child and hadn't given up swearing."

God, he was handsome. As if I weren't already nervous enough in that office, seeing him again only increased my uneasiness. "Do I know you?" I coyly asked.

"I think it means something. You, me, and Doctor McGee."

"Sounds like a 70s song," I scoffed.

"I choose to believe we were meant to run into each other. Again."

"Don't overthink it."

"I'm here for a loose tooth. What're you in for?"

I held up my nailfile. "Soon to be assault with a deadly weapon."

He placed his hand on the arm of my chair. "I'm sorry. I am truly sorry for what I said and how I acted. It was despicable, even by my low standards."

What could I say after that? He took responsibility and made a preemptive strike, a manly apology. It was genuine. At the core, Eddie was a good guy. And I would be foolish not to cut him some slack, if not marry him.

He stepped back so I could take in his whole figure. "Ask me how I am."

Nerves got the better of me. "How am you?"

"Thanks for asking. Fantastic. I'm three weeks sober, and look who I just ran into."

"I'm happy for you."

"You should be happy for *you*."

"I'm about to get a two-thousand-dollar crown. Why should I be happy?"

"Because I'll pay for it."

"You tried buying me once before, remember?"

"I was drunk." He eased into the chair next to me. "I want us to start over. I'm a new and improved Eddie."

"I'm an older and wiser Fiona." I filed my thumbnail, the one I had just bitten off.

"Milady," he said quietly.

"I have cholera. Stay away." I was slowly surrendering under his spell.

"Dinner tonight? Candlelight and soft foods?"

"Don't do this," I warned. "You'll embarrass yourself. Again."

"Give me a minute to plead my case."

"*Vanity Fair* says that groveling can be hazardous to your health."

"Sixty seconds of your life. If you still feel the same way when I finish, I'll wait in the hall for my appointment."

"I'm not going to discuss this in a dentist's office."

The nosy receptionist seemed disappointed.

"You're right," Eddie said. "We'll talk about it after dinner. After flossing."

"I'm sure this works wonders for you in a courtroom, or in a singles bar, but—"

"You were the straw...."

"Let me guess. You were the camel."

"...that broke my back, which was a good thing."

"Fifty-five seconds left, councilor."

"I needed something or somebody to jolt me, to make me look at myself. You really helped me to change. I joined AA the morning after our last date. I got into therapy that afternoon. And took my first yoga class that night." He touched my hand. "I'm trying, Fiona."

"You're not taking yoga."

"Sure am. We'll have something to do together."

I looked at him skeptically.

"Please give me a do-over," he said.

"Why?" The real question was why was I still engaging.

"Because I know something about us that you don't."

"What?"

"That we're right for each other, that we speak the same language, we know who we are, what we want. We don't have to continue the search, scour dating apps, suffer through blind dates, be set up by well-intentioned friends, roam supermarkets. We found each other. There's no reason to look any further."

"If you stop now, you'll walk away with a shred of dignity."

"One more dinner. I promise it will be the best decision of your life." He checked his watch. "There you have it, my closing argument for our future, in less than a minute."

"Does this work on other women?"

"It only needs to work on you."

"Keep working."

"I wouldn't put us both through this if I didn't think we could make it together, Ladybug."

"Did you know that ladybugs practice cannibalism? It's a fact."

By now, the receptionist had closed her little rippled glass window because she was berating AT&T about her slow internet service at home.

"One more chance. Please," he pleaded.

God, he was handsome. "The truth is, I'm not ready for a relationship," I said. "I just can't seem to shake this persistent case of philophobia."

"My name's not Phil."

"Philophobia. Fear of falling in love. Look it up."

"I have a cure for that. Eddie. Eddie Harper. Sailboat owner."

"For your ego's sake, it's me, not you."

"When will you be ready?"

"When I'm strong enough to deal with our inevitable break up. Because sooner or later, most affairs of the heart fall apart. I can't take that kind of hurt anymore. So, I'm not going to waste yours or anyone else's time, effort, or crown money."

He dropped his head. I had cannibalized him.

To make sure he was dead, I took one last bite. "And, let's not forget that you called me an 'ugly old bitch, a whore, and *meshugganah*.'"

"I know you won't forget, but I know you'll forgive."

The waiting room door opened. Dr. McGee's masked assistant called out, "Miss Logan?"

I stood and turned to Eddie. "I hope you continue with all your changes. And that they will lead you to liking yourself."

"This isn't over. Our mutual friend, Fate, won't allow that." Then, in a lousy impression of Arnold Schwarzenegger, Eddie said, "I'll be baaack."

I actually looked forward to his coming baaack. Maybe he and Fate were right. Maybe Eddie and I were, at this time in our lives, meant for each other. If nothing else, God, he was handsome. I was swooning. Maybe it was from the scent of disinfectant.

As THE NEEDLE injected Lidocaine into my gums, I realized it was far less painful than my having rejected Eddie for the second time. My chin began to tingle, and my gut told me that this wasn't the last I would see of Eddie Harper. He was love-struck and obsessed. I was accessible and susceptible. And more than slightly enamored.

I was numb in so many ways. It was time to drill. It was time to spend money I didn't have on a rear molar nobody would ever compliment. It was time for Dr. McGee's fat fingers to crawl inside my mouth, to crown me Queen Fiona. Maybe today was the day he would ask me out, we would fall in love, and have a big wedding. I could rid myself of Eddie and no longer struggle to pay my bills. Move into a real house with a picket fence and sleep next to a human being that didn't have fleas. And... and....

"You're all done," Dr. McGee said dispassionately on his way out.

"Ank yew," my dumb, numb mouth said.

The agreement with my only child, Charlotte, was that I wouldn't bother her unless an emergency arose. No calls, no letters, no emails, no texting. I was, however, allowed a once-a-week, Sunday FaceTime visit. Charlotte was a junior at USC, currently studying in Spain as part of the semester abroad program. This was to be her breaking away period. She was declaring her independence. Because of the time difference between L.A. and Madrid, I had to initiate the call on Saturday at midnight my time, which greeted Charlotte first thing Sunday morning. She called the internet connection "Charlotte's Web." I called those weekly conversations our "Screen Play" time. And they were very special. Kept me grounded.

I put on makeup, brushed my hair, lowered the lights, and clicked on her number. Rathbone and I sat in bed waiting for Charlotte to answer.

"Hello, Char," I said as her pretty face popped up on my iPad.

"Hi, Mumsie. Hey, Rathbone."

"What's that manhole cover doing on your head?" I asked.

"It's mi sombrero de torero."

"A matador's hat?"

"Don't you like it?"

"Kind of flattens your head."

"Paco gave it to me."

"This is the first I've heard of a Paco."

"He's a matador."

"Sweet Jesus."

"You told me not to come home unless I sampled everything in Spain," she said.

"I meant the tapas."

"You'd really like him."

"Hey, I never mat-a-dor I didn't like."

"Wanna say hi?" Before I could answer, Charlotte had carried her laptop into her bedroom. *"Paco. Say ola to mi madre."*

I saw what every fearful parent of a daughter away at college dreads. A bearded overnight guest in my little girl's bed, thrusting a sloshing pitcher of sangria toward the camera, and saying, *"Gracias, Meesas Logan, for mi Charla-bella."*

"*De nada*, Paco. Please don't plunge a sword through my child's head."

"Mom." Charlotte brought her laptop onto her terrace. I could still hear Paco laughing in the background.

"I don't really need to see this," I said.

"Thank you for not being judgmental."

"So, I won't ask how everything's going."

"It's awesome. I love this city."

"And its male population, so it seems."

"I'm not coming home," she kidded.

"Still need to sample a flamenco dancer?"

"Did that Tuesday."

"What?"

"Calm down. We just flamencoed." She laughed. *"But he can do the splits with a rose in his mouth."*

"Charming."

"And with me on his shoulders."

I groaned involuntarily. "Is my baby rebelling? And I mean that non-judgmentally."

"I'm just doing what your baby's mother always said. Rise up to the occasions of life. Speaking of which, how's your love life?"

"Do you really want to know?"

"No. Which means 'no' in Spanish. But I hope you're having fun."

"I'm fine. Or dandy, as ancient people like to say. I'm doing my gardening, doing my yoga, doing my teaching, doing my love life dodging—"

"Oh, yeah? Dodging who?"

"A determined lawyer."

"That's awesome. Rise up."

"Don't say 'awesome' in English anymore."

On his way to the bathroom, a nude Paco tiptoed behind Charlotte, waving a towel like a matador's cape in front of his private parts. "*Olé,*" he cried out.

"Mom, can we do this later?" Charlotte asked, grossed out by the antics behind her.

"I insist."

We said, "Love ya," at the same time and hung up. I couldn't fault her. She was me at twenty. *Olé.*

Chapter 17

JACK

I WAS ON the recumbent bike at the gym, hoping to purge myself of some pent-up tension. I tried writing while peddling, but beads of sweat dripped from my nose onto my legal pad, running the ink. There's nothing more boring than exercising on a stationary bike, so I thought I'd multitask by phoning my folks. Since they didn't hear from me on Sunday, I was afraid they would start frantically calling L.A. hospitals and mortuaries. Welcome to the life of an only child.

"*Hello,*" my dad said. My mom always let him be the one to answer the landline.

"Hey, Pops."

"*Who's this?*" he asked.

"I know, I'm sorry. I meant to call last week, but—"

"*Let me tell your mother.*" He shouted, "*Lorraine, pick up. It's J-Rey.*"

"*Jackie?*" my mom said, getting on the extension. "*My God, where've you been?*"

"I've been very busy."

"*Too busy to call?*" she said.

Somebody dropped a heavy barbell in the weightlifting area. I jumped in my seat.

"*Was that a gunshot?*" Pop asked.

"No."

"*I'm tellin' ya, it's always something in Los Angeles,*" Pop said.

My eyes followed a cute girl skipping rope across the gym floor.

"*We heard you're having a tidal wave,*" Mom said.

"Heat wave, Ma," I said. "How're you doing?"

"Heat waves, earthquakes, fires, floods, shootings," Mom said. "Every time we turn on the television, it's some catastrophe in California. Why you couldn't find a job in all of Ohio beats me."

"It's not the job. The boy had to get away," Pop explained.

"I'm not a boy."

"Get away?" Mom whined. "From what? Us?"

"Hold it. I've got some good news," I said.

"About you and Elizabeth?" Mom asked hopefully.

"Let the boy talk." Pop injected.

"I got hired to write a movie script."

"Terrific, Champ." Pop said. "Isn't that terrific, Mother?"

"I'm letting the boy talk," she sulked.

"I'm having a hard time getting it done, but I will."

"Of course, you will," Pop said. "You're a Reynolds."

"And Elizabeth?" Mom inquired weakly.

"She's busy, too. We hardly see each other. She works all the time."

"Well, that's what you have to do to make it in this world, son," Pop said.

"She's a wonderful girl," Mom added. "I hope you stay with this one. I mean, we're not getting any younger, and it wouldn't be bad having a doctor in the family, what with their prices these days."

The movie *When Harry Met Sally* was playing on the TV screen above the pack of exercise bikes. One of the staff members turned up the volume as Meg Ryan was about to fake an orgasm in the famous diner scene. Her escalating yelps of ecstasy echoed throughout the gym and unfortunately through my phone.

"Now what's happening?" Pop asked. "Someone being attacked?"

"The lady next door is having a baby."

"What?" Mom exclaimed.

"And how's everything with you guys?" I asked, eager to change the subject.

"We're fine here," Pop said. "Don't worry about us. We're looking forward to seeing you at Thanksgiving."

"Me, too. Welllll...."

We all knew what drawing out the word "well" meant. It was the universal code for "this call is over," a cue to wrap things up.

"You take care, Kiddo," Pop said. "And your script job. How terrific is that?"

"*Will Elizabeth be joining you, I hope?*" Mom asked, adding, "*For Thanksgiving?*"

"We'll see," I said.

"*Well....*" Pop said.

"*Well....*" Mom said.

"Well," I said. "You guys be good, and I'll call you on Sunday."

"*Don't forget,*" Pop said.

"*We love you, Jackie,*" Mom said.

"Back atcha. Bye," I said.

I hung up. I was drenched. That two-minute call was more exhausting than the twenty miles I had just peddled in place. Meg Ryan was a little breathless, too.

I WAITED UNTIL an amicable morning hour to launch my assault. It was only ten a.m., but already eighty-eight summer degrees. I hoped she would be in a congenial mood despite the heat. I walked into a charming courtyard with a colorful garden, through a mosaic-tiled archway, and down a hall, following the sounds of a familiar voice. I came upon an open door and peeked inside. I found my target in the center of an empty, freshly painted living room of a Spanish style "For Rent" unit. With her back to me, Professor Logan stood atop a step ladder, attending to a ceiling fan. She wore cargo shorts, a blue denim work shirt, and a worn out toolbelt. She had earbuds in and sang along quite loudly and quite off-key to the Bee Gees's classic, "How Can You Mend a Broken Heart." She couldn't hit the high notes, but she had soul.

A basset hound rested at the base of the ladder.

I poked my head farther into the room. I knew she'd still be angry with me, and that she'd be even angrier when she saw I'd tracked her down. I was taking a big chance. But isn't that how we get ahead in life?

I was there to make a peace offering. And nothing says peace better than what I was holding. A powder blue cardboard pastry box from Bliffer's Bakery.

"Excuse me," I said.

She didn't hear me. I raised my voice, "Uh, PARDON ME."

"I'll get to it when I get to it." She plucked out her earbuds and turned. Upon seeing me, her jaw dropped, and her face flushed.

"Hello, Professor Logan."

She stammered. "I'm really just the handyman, but my agent negotiated a 'managed by' credit. Now, I live rent-free."

"I'd take that deal any day."

She straightened her hair and resumed her work. "How did you get my address?"

I took a tentative step into the room. "Rosario. My friend in the admissions office."

"I could have her fired."

At least she was talking to me again. That was a positive sign. Firing Rosario, if she was serious, would be a major bummer.

"I saw your car in front. I'm glad it's working again."

"Head gasket. Wasn't cheap. But cheaper than the tow."

The big dog lumbered over to sniff me. I kneeled down to pet him. "Does he bite?"

"If I give the command."

"What's your story, big fella?" I said to the dog.

"He's a rescue. Turned out, he saved me," Fiona said.

"What's his name?"

"Rathbone. After Basil Rathbone, an actor."

"The actor who starred in fourteen Sherlock Holmes movies and lost the Oscar twice to Walter Brennan? That Basil Rathbone?" I rubbed Rathbone's neck. "Aren't you something?"

"Careful. He might lick your face off," she said. "Now, how can we help you?"

I straightened up and slowly stepped forward. "I need a favor."

"What sort of favor?"

"I have a problem."

"What type of problem?"

"A problem getting you to do me a favor." I took another step.

She stopped working and looked down at me from atop the ladder. "What page are you stuck on?"

I just stood there. "I've called your office. You haven't answered any of my messages."

"Page one?" she asked.

"Or emails."

"It's beyond inappropriate for a student to come uninvited to a teacher's home. I could have you expelled."

"How about a teacher taking her student to a strip club?"

That stopped her cold. Touché. "I noticed you weren't in class last night," she said.

"I had to write. Or try to write."

We waited for the roar of a low-flying helicopter to pass. "Hand me the slip joint pliers, please."

I found them in her toolkit.

Grabbing them, she asked, "How did you know which pair was the slip joint?"

"Growing up, I worked weekends in my family's hardware store."

She fiddled with the fan for a bit. "Turn that switch on, will ya?"

I flipped a switch on the wall, and the ceiling fan began to spin and blow her red hair, like in a fashion shoot. I bet she once was a model.

"Look at that," I said. "Not bad."

"I've got my dad to thank for this," she said. "Made sure his three girls would survive. Taught us to shoot a BB gun, chop wood, and rotate tires. I can even throw a spiral."

"Bet that comes in handy."

Professor Logan climbed down the ladder, unfastened her toolbelt, and stood looking at me, foot tapping, eyebrows raised.

"Yes," I said. "I'm stuck on page one."

Chapter 18
FIONA

I CONTINUED CARRYING out my daily, menial chores, though I was thoroughly humiliated having Jack Reynolds see me in that light. He tagged behind me as I straightened the lounge chairs and umbrella tables around Casa del Sol's small swimming pool. While I scooped leaves out of the water with a skimmer, Jack moved to my side, still holding his little blue pastry box. Rathbone settled at my other side. I was starting to sweat under the September sun. Not an attractive sight or odor.

"Do you have to do this every day?" Jack asked.

"Saves on a gym membership."

"Can I help, Professor Logan?" He bent over and removed a leaf out of the pool.

"Yes. You can go home and work on your script."

"But I'm stumped. I'm lost. What does it mean when you just sit and stare all day and night at a blank page?"

"It means you're a writer."

"I need help."

"Don't ask me to write with you."

"Write with me."

"Sorry, Jack. I'm tired, and I'm re-tired," I said. "And besides, you got yourself into this fix. Now, write yourself out of it."

"I'm trying." He extended his arms and presented the powder blue pastry box to me.

"Earrings from Tiffany's?"

"I'm sorry I jumped in at the meeting."

As much as I wanted that blue offering, I didn't take it. "You meant well. And I'm sorry ol' Mount Logan erupted all over you. You're a nice guy and didn't deserve that. But I'm still not writing with you."

"Then, I'm still stuck on page one."

I wiped the sweat from my brow. "Review your class notes. You begin with an outline."

"I don't have time."

"After the outline, you write a treatment."

"It's due in nine days."

"Look around my garden. I wouldn't have those sunflowers if I hadn't planted the seeds," I said in my best mentor's voice. "You can't just start writing without first creating a plot, inventing characters, establishing relationships, identifying locations."

"See? That's exactly why I'm here. I need a pro."

"Sorry. I've got to turn in three writing gigs I found online. A eulogy, a resume, and a marriage vow. But first, the pro has to sand a fence."

"I'll pay you twenty thousand dollars not to sand it."

"You're standing on my skimmer," I said.

He looked down and stepped off the net.

I walked away, leaving Jack by the pool, holding his blue pastry box. And, presumably, in his pocket, was my half of the two thousand dollar signing bonus.

Chapter 19

JACK

Professor Logan leaned over, using a bright yellow watering can to irrigate the property's vegetable garden. I had no idea how old she was, but she had the buns of a college track star. Like a duckling, I continued to follow her and Rathbone along a woodchip path as she moved to prop up a fallen tomato vine. She took great pride in her work.

"I hope you didn't quit your day job," she said.

"No. But I left early today. Coming here was more important."

"After writing all the dialogue," she said. "You rewrite the script about sixty-seven times. Then, if you simply can't live without rejection, you turn the damn thing in. Bowman will make you rewrite it a few more times for no extra money, then you'll never hear from him again. And the movie will never get made. And you'll hate yourself for being fooled by a fraudster. That being said, finish. Just finish it. You'll learn a lot." She stooped down to sniff the roses. "It's not the destination that counts. It's the journey. Along the way, always stop to smell the roses."

"Great advice. Show me," I said, stepping in front of her. "Teach me." I moved closer. "Help me." I moved even closer. "Join me in the journey."

"If you remember nothing else I've taught you, remember this. You'll put blood, sweat, and tears into your writing. Hollywood will drink all three and spit you out."

"So encouraging. You should be a life coach."

"Here's a small secret I never told the school. I can't teach creativity. I can show you where to set the margins and how to procrastinate. I can read your screenplay and pretend to like it. But I can't teach you how to be a born writer."

"I can write this thing," I said. "I know I can. But I'm overwhelmed. I've started and stopped the script a dozen times because it just wasn't good enough. I've got just over a week left. The pressure alone paralyzes me. I just need someone who's been through all this." I mustered up the nerve to take one last step closer to her. "Go through it with me, Professor Logan. Please."

She looked at the blue pastry box. "What flavor is the jewelry?"

"Banana strudel. It's our specialty." I gently placed the box into her hand.

"Will power. That's my specialty," she said, handing the box back to me and walking away with Rathbone faithfully trotting behind her.

"So?" I called after her. "Will you—"

"Thanks for the unwanted visit." She was behind a row of hedges when she poked her head over the top and said, "You have a good attendance record. You take good notes. Now, practice what I preached. And finish." She was out of sight when I heard her add, "Lose my address. Or I'll flunk your ass."

I NEEDED TO write in a place other than my apartment or Starbucks. Maybe new surroundings would foster fresh ideas. Somewhere quiet, without distractions. After work, I went to the dilapidated Fairfax Library on 3rd Street, a short walk from the bakery. Since the birth of the internet, libraries weren't so much about the books they contained as they were about providing safe havens for latchkey kids, hangouts for the homeless, and air-conditioned shelters for the elderly.

A stinky skeleton with a dirty tarp pulled over its head snored in the chair across from me. We were the last two visitors left in the incandescently lit room. I stared off through a barred window, hoping for some inspiration. Before I knew it, the sun had set.

The custodian gently shook the old man's boney shoulder. "Lucky," he said. "We're closing in five minutes."

Lucky's face peeped out of his vinyl fortress, opened his liquid eyes, and looked around, trying to remember where he was and, while he was at it, *who* he was. "Yeah. Thanks, Dennis," he muttered. He turned and looked at me. "What's your purpose here, my good man?" he asked in a surprisingly erudite voice.

"I'm writing a movie."

He craned his neck to glimpse at the blank page on my laptop screen. "Is it a silent movie?"

"It's a work in progress."

"Doesn't look like your work has progressed very far," he sprayed through chipped teeth.

"Believe it or not, I'm going as fast as I can."

"Better finish what you want to finish because we're all finished at the finish line." I detected a slight New England accent. "We're all running, but in the end, we're all running to the same spot, to the same eternal resting place. It's a damn rat race, my brother. But even if you win, you're still a rat."

"So true." What else was I going to say?

"We're all dying." He raked his fingers through his ratty beard. "We're all finished."

"Finished? I'm just trying to get started."

He pointed to the institutional clock on the wall. "Look at that clock. Look closely. Listen closely. See the second hand sweeping the face?"

"Yes, I do."

"Time," he said, nodding all-knowingly. "Watch it move forward. Listen to it tick off the seconds."

"I see. I hear."

"You're watching time go by as you grow older, second by second, minute by minute. You're listening to your life count down, tick by tick." He grinned, exposing blue gums. "Then, you see and hear nothing. That's when you know it's game over. Finished. You're dead."

"Thank you for—"

"For changing your life today? It's my duty, my calling. Save one Time-Killer at a time. It's how I spend the time I have left."

I packed up my things and stood. "Well, it's been so very enlightening talking to you."

"I am the Truth, my fellow traveler. We're dying from the moment we're born." He gestured toward the stacks. "We're surrounded by books of knowledge. Yet not one of them will deliver you the truth you seek. Why not? Because they are filled with lies. It's a lie-brary."

I backed away, moving cautiously toward the front doors. "I wish I could stay."

"I'm merely pointing out how fast life goes, how one has to maximize every fleeting moment. Because, well, tick, tick, tick."

"You tell 'em, Lucky," Dennis cried out, leaning on his push broom, a well-chewed toothpick hanging off his bottom lip.

Lucky climbed on top of our round table. He stood tall, stretched his arms to the heavens, and continued his sermon from on high. "Value every beat of your heart, every breath you take, every tick of the clock because every second that passes is one less moment that you will live."

Dennis applauded. Lucky took a deep theatrical bow. I slipped away and sprinted back to the bakery to get my car, having not written one word all day.

Time was running out. My script was dying. Minute by minute. Second by second.

Tick by tick by tick.

Chapter 20
FIONA

I WAS SORRY to see Jack wasn't in the audience. He would have benefited from that night's lecture, *The Laxative for Creative Constipation*. He was probably somewhere trying to unblock writer's block.

"If you're stuck, stymied, and stumped, try playing what I call the Opposites Game," I told my class. "Flip the script. Make your male character female, the adult a child, or vice versa. If he's black, make him white or brown. If she's yellow, make her red or green. If it's a contemporary story, set it in the future. If the scene takes place during the day, change it to night. If it's scorching hot, switch it to snow." I walked out from behind the lectern. "Wanna get unstuck? Shake things up. Turn things upside down. Take a chance. It works in life. It works in writing." To shake things up, I moved downstage and sat on the apron, letting my legs dangle below. "Frequently, this exercise will reboot your script, sometimes in the most unexpected and wonderful ways." I looked out at my zealous students. "If you learn nothing else, remember this. As a writer, you're God. You can do anything you want. Any questions?"

A girl wearing a hijab, sitting alone in the back of the auditorium, raised her hand.

"Yes?" I said.

"Is this going to be on the final?"

"Name?"

"Tamara Vaziri."

"Miss Vaziri, this course is full of useful information. It's not intended to be memorized for a test. I don't care about exams. I don't believe in grades. If you're here and have a pulse, you'll pass. Some of the writing lessons you learn from me may apply to other aspects of your time on earth. There are no finals in the real world. Or in my classroom. I'm just trying to help you do something we all masochistically want to do. Write a screenplay. And to live a good life." The bell rang. "See ya at the movies."

I heard a door slam at the back of the hall behind Ms. Vaziri. I figured Dean Bailey had been spying on me again. My suspicions were confirmed when his lifer assistant cornered me after class.

"The Dean would like to have a little chitty chat before you leave," she said smugly, with a look that suggested "chitty chat" meant "turn in your gun and badge."

———

I LIKED CLEANING the laundry room in the basement the first thing in the morning. I was on my hands and knees, unclogging a blocked vent under the dryer when Jack walked timidly down the steps into the small, stuffy, Clorox-smelling room. He had another blue box of pastries in his hand. Sugar, his negotiating chip.

Rathbone greeted him with his tail wagging. The traitor.

"It's six a.m. Do I have to get a restraining order?" I said.

"I'm sorry the school laid you off."

"Fired," I said. "And weren't you banned from this property?"

"You can't flunk me anymore for coming here."

It was too early in the morning to start arguing. "I heard the new teacher is good."

"I'll never know. I dropped out," he said.

"Why?"

"I liked the old teacher."

"The *old* teacher," I said to myself as I scrubbed out the drum of the washing machine.

Jack took another step into the room. "Why did they fire you?"

"They said I was a bad influence."

"That's not true."

"And that I'm sarcastic and jaded."

"That's true," he said, setting down the blue box. "I can't believe they wouldn't even let you finish the term."

"Thanks for the reminder." I started sweeping the floor and panning the dust balls.

"Can I help, Professor Logan?" he asked, taking off his backpack.

"Yes. Stop calling me professor. I'm no longer your teacher."

"I still need a teacher, Miss Logan." He grabbed a cloth and wiped down the countertops.

"Fiona. It's Fiona. The Logan is silent."

"Guess what," he said.

"You're still on page one."

"Wrong."

"Congratulations."

"Page two. I put my name and date on page one."

"It's never too late to quit."

"Nothing sarcastic or jaded about that." He waited for me to react. "What happened to, 'It's not always the destination that counts. It's the journey?'"

"Jack, cut bait now," I said. "If you can't start, there's no way you can finish. Certainly not by your deadline. And even if you do, there's no way that low-life Bowman is ever going to pay up."

"Let's imagine, just for giggles, that the glass is half full, that we finish the script on time, that it's not awful, and that the low-life's check clears. There's still one way we can find out."

"Too many we's," I said firmly.

"We both can use the money," he reasoned. "There's forty thousand dollars just waiting for us."

I stopped sweeping. "And what do you bring to the party? Pastries?"

"The same thing you bring. Age. Your experience and my youth. There, I've said it." It stung. But he didn't take it back. "What I meant," he said, "is that you know story structure, and I know what stories my peers like."

"I'm form? You're content?"

"The perfect partnership, right?"

"Look, Roger Bowman's a fake and a flake. We'll never see the money."

"We've seen two thousand dollars."

"Probably counterfeit."

"Come on, he trusted us. We should trust him. Besides, what do we have to lose?"

"Seven days."

"It'll be a great seven days, Fiona. I promise you."

It sounded strange though pleasant having him call me Fiona. "You're so naïve," I said.

"You're so negative."

I looked him square in the eyes. "If you learn nothing else, remember this. The writer always gets screwed." I didn't intend the double meaning. Nor did he pick up on it, I think.

"One week. That's all I'm asking," Jack said. "Look, I can write this damn script, but it won't be very good. I'm not very good. Yet. With you, I'll learn to be great, and we'll turn in something we can both be proud of. What do you say?"

Just then, Maurice, a British slacker who was six months late on his rent, appeared in the doorway of the laundry room. "Fiona, my love. Forgive the interruption."

"I'll get to it when I get to it," I growled.

"A couple things." Maurice started.

"Who wants what?" I asked.

"A pigeon flew into Juanita's kitchen," he said. "Did some damage. She's rather traumatized."

"I'll be up in a minute."

"Also, I've got toilet issues again. It's backed up, oozing brown chunky lava as we speak. Could've been the prune smoothie."

"Thanks for the details. My life is now complete."

"So, I can count on you?" he asked.

"I'll get my plunger. And I'll console Juanita."

"As managers go, you're aces. Cheers." He turned and pranced off.

It seemed symbolic that I was in the basement, at the bottom of my life, at the end of my rope, at the beginning of my day. I was disgusted. I was embarrassed. And once again disgraced in front of Jack. Why did I care what he thought of me? He was just some former student. No more than a stranger. Just another wannabe screenwriter. Another misguided dreamer in store for a rude awakening.

"Fiona," the wannabe, misguided stranger said. He reached into his pocket and pulled out a roll of cash, tied with a blue silk ribbon. "This belongs to you."

I stared at the money, my share of our signing bonus.

"Seriously," he said. "Now, without your teaching income, wouldn't twenty grand help pay some bills?"

It would be absolutely foolish to work together. A waste of time. Of energy. No question about it. I declined the money, but snatched the blue pastry box as I walked up the stairs out of the basement.

Chapter 21

JACK

I WASN'T A great salesman. But if nothing else, I was—as they say in Ohio—as persistent as a winter cough. I waited as Fiona did repairs on her car. I felt she was ripe for convincing, that she was cracking. The brown chunky lava business had put her over the top. I just needed the right dialogue to close the deal.

We were in the long driveway that ran alongside the Casa del Sol complex. Fiona was lying on her back, under her old car, reconnecting a faulty gas line. I lay down beside the Mercedes. Rathbone lay down beside me. Fiona had a gob of grease on the tip of her nose, which I felt awkward about pointing out. So, I didn't.

"Just imagine if you had twenty thousand extra dollars right now," I said. "You could have a mechanic fix this. Or better yet, you could buy a car that actually runs."

She turned and glared at me. "I'll never part with this old clunker. Brings back great memories."

Silence. Total silence. I held my breath. Then, a breakthrough.

"If I were batty enough to agree to this dimwitted idea of yours," she began.

My heart soared.

"There would be rules."

"Yes, sir," I said, snapping a salute.

"Dos and don'ts. If I say 'do the research—'"

"I do the research."

Fiona wiggled out from under the car. She was filthy. Her glasses were perched on the end of her nose, just above the grease spot. "If I say 'don't talk—'"

"I learned that lesson."

Fiona stood. I stood. We faced each other.

"Furthermore," she said, pushing her glasses onto the bridge of her nose.

"You sound like a lawyer."

"If we disagree on something, *anything*, it's my word—"

"Over mine."

"You're the apprentice."

"You're the boss."

Fiona clapped her hands free of dirt. "And never, not for a moment, think that we're—"

"Writing partners."

"We're just—"

"Helping each other out," I said.

"One script. That's it. After that, I go my way—"

"And I go my way. And never the twain shall meet."

She took my hand and shook it. We never blinked. Her fingers were long, her pastel skin soft. For a brief instant, before we let go, we were holding hands.

"And stop—" she said.

"Finishing your sentences."

Fiona got into her car and sat behind the wheel. "More rules. I do the driving and talking. You do the sitting and listening. Got it?"

"You lead. I follow. Understood."

"Then, give me my cash and climb in."

I quickly took the roll of money out of my pocket and handed it to her. "Where are we going?" I asked.

"To get our story."

I triumphantly jumped into the two-seater convertible.

Fiona cranked her engine, to no avail. She tried again. Nothing. I was about to get out and look under the hood, when it coughed a couple of times, then caught. And away we went, two people just helping each other out. One with grease on her nose.

I felt proud of my accomplishment of changing her mind. Miss Logan, I mean Fiona, could be so stubborn. So funny. So frustrating. So... I was about to say "sexy." Good Lord, where did that come from? I had no business continuing to think like that.

Chapter 22

FIONA

Reality check. I needed the money. I needed to write again. I needed someone to motivate me. To show me some attention, some respect, maybe even some adulation. And so, I needed to agree to Jack's absurd proposal.

We drove downtown to the headquarters of the Los Angeles Police Department. During a drought in my movie writing profession, I wrote episodes of almost every cop show on TV. I did a lot of research, took many ride-alongs in squad cars, and even contemplated a career in law enforcement. Who was I kidding? I can't stand guns, violence, car chases, or wearing my hair short.

Jack sat quietly beside me, but because he kept jiggling his knees and cracking his knuckles, I could tell he was brimming with excitement. He was like a little kid. His smile widened when we approached the security gate of the underground parking structure. And he was very impressed that the guard remembered my name and admitted my Mercedes to guest parking.

Our footsteps echoed, as we walked through the basement to the bank of elevators.

"In the meeting—" I said.

"Hello. Goodbye," Jack promised.

"No more." For a woman who had earlier fetched three-day-old feces out of a toilet, I was enjoying this power. "Starting right now. No more talking."

"Can I just say one more thing?" he asked cautiously.

"What is it?"

"You have a small dab of grease on your nose. Hardly noticeable."

I began wiping my nose fiercely, probably spreading it. "Why didn't you tell me?"

"I thought it was cute," he mumbled through pursed lips.

"I don't know about you, Jack Reynolds," I said, shaking my head. He thought it was cute? Or he thought I was cute? Either way, someone was noticing me.

Lieutenant Manuel Lopez was a forty-year veteran of the LAPD and my contact for all things police related. He had the lumpy face of a bullfrog and the heart of a saint. Manny would do anything for me. He closed the door to his small Media Relations office and gestured for us to sit.

"I didn't exactly dress for the occasion." I chuckled.

"You always look good," Manny said. "Even that smear on your nose is charming."

I could feel my face redden. "And thanks for seeing me on such short notice." I madly rubbed my nose with my sleeve. "Next time I'll shower."

"You always have top priority, Fiona," he said. "It's been a long time."

"I hope you got my Christmas cards."

"Every year," Manny said. "Charlotte has certainly grown."

"Hello," Jack volunteered without warning.

"Well, hello to you, young fella," Manny said.

"That was Jack," I said. "Jack Reynolds. He's my, I guess you would say, 'writing colleague.'"

"It's a pleasure meeting you, Jack."

"Hello," Jack uttered again.

"I've known this little lady since the dinosaurs," Manny said. "She could have been a detective. Smart as a fox and, in case you haven't noticed, quite foxy."

"Manny, if you were only single. And rich."

He laughed. "So, what brings you?"

"We sold an idea for a script," I said.

"Back in the game. Good for you, doll."

"We have to create a great story. We have to invent interesting characters. And we have to come up with the perfect crime."

"You do, or I do?" Manny said.

"Just one example," I said. "Then, we'll be on our way."

"You're asking me to tell you how to carry out a crime and get away with it?"

We all laughed. "It's a movie, Manny."

"I'm a sworn officer of the law. I don't plan crimes. I get there in time to cover the body."

"We don't want any killing," Jack blurted out. "Whoops. My bad. Sorry. Hello."

I stepped in. "It's a romantic comedy. A caper. A romp. We need a soft crime. Nothing too messy."

"Putting a lot of restrictions on me," Manny said, rising and pacing. "Okay. The perfect crime. Have you ever heard of The Double Steal? And I ain't talkin' baseball."

Jack shook his head.

Manny returned to his desk. "It's the preferred choice of the mob and crooked cops. And it goes a little somethin' like this." He arranged objects on his desk to help illustrate his explanation. "This stapler represents Bad Guy number one." He balanced a small bottle of Maalox on the stapler. "The Maalox represents a ton of cocaine."

"No drugs. Nothing dark," I interjected. "It's a light comedy."

"Understood," Manny said. "Let's just say the Maalox is something of value, which Bad Guy number one has acquired illegally. How's that working for you?"

"Much better. Thank you," I said.

Then, Manny slid his calculator toward the stapler. "Bad Guy number two, the calculator, comes along and steals the Maalox." He picked up the Maalox, put it on the calculator, and inched it away from the stapler. He held up his scissors. "Uh, oh. Bad Guy number three, the scissors, is up to no good." Manny snatched the Maalox between the scissor's blades. "He steals the Maalox from Bad Guy number two." With the Maalox pill bottle clenched in the scissors' mouth, Manny carried the booty across his desk to safety.

Jack furiously took notes on his laptop.

"Now," Manny said. "Bad Guy number three sells the Maalox on the black market, pockets the money, and makes a clean getaway."

"Wow. So foolproof and so easy," I said.

"Bad guy number two can't call the authorities and say he's been robbed," Manny said. "Because what bad guy reports a theft of something he stole to the police?"

"And Bad Guy number one can't report the theft for the same reason. They're all guilty," I added.

"Ba-da-bing." Manny said. "The perfect crime? Rob a thief. And that's the story of, that's the glory of The Double Steal." He turned to Jack. "There's your crime, your story, and your movie."

"Fantastic," I said.

"Goodbye, goodbye," Jack stammered like he had Tourette's.

I quickly jumped in. "Thanks, Manny. I owe you. Again."

"Anytime, doll," he said. "And you, Jack—"

Jack burst in with a terse, "Goodbye."

Manny continued. "Take care of my gal here. I hope you write a masterpiece together." He swung open his office door. "I'll text you a list of contacts you might want to talk to. If you need anything else"—he handed Jack his business card—"just give me a call."

"You're the best, Manny," I said as I hugged him. "See ya at the movies."

"Hope it's this one," Manny said.

JACK SKITTERED DOWN the hall, all abuzz. "We got our story," he gushed.

"No," I said. "We've got the bones of our story. Now we need the flesh and blood."

"Where do we get those?"

"From the flesh and blood of others."

Chapter 23

JACK

WE WENT DIRECTLY to a famous writers' hangout for breakfast, *Du-Pars* at the Farmer's Market in the Grove Shopping Center in West Hollywood. As I waited for Fiona to return from the restroom, I looked around at all the other struggling screenwriters hectically pounding away on their keyboards. And there I was, finally among them. I had arrived. I was a working writer.

"Did you order?" Fiona asked, returning to our table.

"Eggs Benedict for me with pancakes and bacon on the side. A half-grapefruit for you, just as you asked." I noticed she had put makeup on and her hair up. And the tip of her nose was perfectly clean. I made an attempt to stand as she slithered into our booth. I banged my knee on the underside of the table. What a dork. It was like I was a middle grader on his first date. Why should I have felt nervous in front of her? Why should I have felt anything in front of her?

"Let's get started." Fiona took out a stack of colored index cards from her handbag and fanned them across the table like a croupier in Atlantic City.

I fired up my computer.

"We begin at the beginning. The research phase," she said. "You can't write without knowing what you're writing about."

"I like your hair that way," I said. "You know, on top."

"You need to concentrate."

"I am. It's just that some girls have squirrelly heads. Up goes the hair, out pop the ears. Boing. Doesn't work. But your ears are the right size and shape. Like two exotic half-shells."

"We have one week. Do you want to talk about my ears and miss our deadline?"

I rubbed my sore knee as I prepared a response.

"Listen, Jack. We're not dorm buddies out for a snack and chat. We're business partners racing the clock. We don't have time for anything but the task at hand. You need to stay focused. Think of the next seven days as a crash course in screenwriting, your free graduate school. At the end of this, if we work like ditch diggers, you'll have your name on a movie script and, doubtfully but maybe, some folding money in your pocket, both of which will be worth far greater than some night school certificate. So, sit up, pay attention, and no more talk about ears."

"A final comment, if I may."

She dropped her head, exasperated. "What?"

"With a long and graceful neck like yours, the hair up style really rocks."

"Now, can we do what we're here to do?"

I put on my game face. "Writers, start your pencils."

"Here's the plan," she said. "We'll split up and get twice as much done in half the time."

"Right. Send me in, Coach."

Fiona failed to hide a smile. "Before we can consult the experts, we have to figure out what the crime is."

My phone rang. It was Beth.

Fiona emitted a heavy sigh.

"My girlfriend," I said.

"Keep it brief."

I nodded and took the call. "Can't talk."

Beth asked whether she should start booking our flights for Thanksgiving.

"Beth, not now. Please. I'll call you later." I hung up.

Fiona took an exasperated breath. "We have to figure out what exactly our characters steal."

"Okay. What exactly do they steal?"

"We sold Roger Bowman on a million-dollar theft. So, they have to steal a million dollars or something worth a million dollars."

"This is great. I like writing."

She rubbed her temples. "They steal a diamond ring. Write it down."

"Small problem."

"What? You can't spell 'diamond?'"
"I mean—"
"*D... I... A....*"
"Jewelry? Is that the most creative thing we can think of?"
"We?"
"Diamonds are so yesterday," I muttered.
"There's no time for originality. And diamonds are forever."
"That was a good Double-O-Seven movie, but—"
"The first idea that comes up goes down. Put it down."
"But maybe—" My phone rang again. What was left of Fiona's patience was waning. So was Beth's, apparently. I answered the call. "Still can't talk. Thank you." I hung up and turned to Fiona. "Sorry." I continued from where we had left off. "Art is very in. How about they steal a famous work of art?"

"You got a problem with a diamond ring?"

It was an ironic question. It floated between us. "I just think a painting or sculpture would be more current," I said. My phone rang again.

Fiona gave me a stony stare.

"It's Beth," I said.

"Give her my indifference."

I put my index finger up to Fiona. "This will only take a quick sec. I promise." Then, in a measured voice, I said to Beth, "Babe, I'm seriously in a meeting. We'll talk about it later. We'll talk about anything you want. Just later. Okay?" I hung up.

Fiona pointed to my phone and coldly said in a motherly voice, "Off."

I silenced my phone. "Right. She's only—"

"Interrupting our work." Fiona erased a note on a green index card. "They'll steal an artwork of some kind. Write it down."

"Do you really like the art thing, or are you just trying to make me feel like I'm contributing?" I asked as I typed the idea into my laptop.

"This is a collaboration. A give-and-take brainstorming," she said. "We have to be open to each other's ideas. Or we may kill each other." Then, as an aside, "We probably will anyway."

Our food came. The waitress, whose nametag read "Debbie," was a veteran server. She knew how to place plates between writers' index cards.

She knew how to be discreet. She knew how to be supportive to the creative community.

"Do you have everything?" she asked, handing me an extra napkin.

"We could use a few more days," I said to her.

"Hope your script is a big hit." She winked before rushing off.

"How are we doing so far?" I asked Fiona.

"We're almost done," she said.

"Really?"

"Sure. Let's just eat and talk about my ears."

"Cool," I said, munching on my bacon. "Did you ever have them pierced?"

She tilted her head and just glared at me.

I quickly straightened up. "What's next?" I asked.

"We'll talk to the pros. Art experts, security experts, experienced thieves, and the bad guys in the black market."

"How are we going to find them?"

She opened her phone. "Manny Lopez sent me some leads."

"Why would anyone talk to me?"

"Because you're going to tell them you're writing a movie. You'll be amazed at how fast the doors fly open."

"That's so dope."

"Showbiz, baby. Everybody wants in. They all want a piece of it." She handed me a green card with my instructions. "You'll find out how stolen art is pawned."

"Cool."

"And I'll look into the mechanics of stealing it." She fished in her purse for something. "We may have gotten our first break," she said, withdrawing an elegantly engraved card. "I was invited to attend a gallery opening this evening. We'll get some inside information there about the art world."

"Epic."

She handed me the invitation. "Meet me there at six."

"I have dinner plans."

"Had. Had dinner plans. Now you have work plans. We'll eat afterward. We start writing tonight. At my place. I live alone. We won't be disturbed."

"But, Beth—"

"Needs to learn how to be a writer's widow. Now, get the bill. I'll pick up the next one. We have a lot to do today."

"But—"

"Shave. And don't say 'epic' tonight. Or 'dope.' Or 'cool.'"

I waved down Debbie, indicating to her to bring us the check.

"You're a writer," Fiona said. "Respect the language. Don't get lazy. Don't talk like non-writers. And don't be late tonight."

"Any more 'don'ts?'"

"Yeah. Don't make me tell you again what not to do."

I had never known anyone like Fiona before. She was—uh, oh. I was going to say "epic."

Chapter 24
FIONA

I WAITED, ALONG with a smattering of others, in the dim and dank visiting room of the California State Prison in Lancaster, seventy-five miles north of Los Angeles. It was austere and smelled like a yeast infection. Through the steel door, a hefty prison guard escorted to my table Earl Anthony Bingham, a wiry convict. He wore a soiled, orange jumpsuit and an eye patch, the result of a prison yard brawl.

"I only agreed to this because, in eight years, I've never had a visitor. And the sarge said you were one hot mama," Earl panted, leering at me. "He sure wasn't lying."

"Thank you," I said. "They've only allowed me five minutes, so—"

"You'd be twice as hot if I had two eyes. But one's still hanging off a shiv."

I waited for the guard to back off and leave us alone. "I appreciate your taking the time, Mister Bingham."

"It's not like I have a busy schedule."

"I meant—"

"And call me Earl." He blinked, or winked, his only eye. "So, you're a writer? You should be in front of, not behind the camera."

I took out my notebook and pen. "The newspaper stated—"

"You must have some pictures of the warden dog-styling the governor to get in here on a day's notice."

"Let's just say a cop friend of mine pulled some strings."

"Well, maybe he can pull some for me."

"That's not going to happen," I said.

"Anyway, it's a long drive for five minutes. Fire at will."

"According to—"

"All this'll be in your script, right?" Earl asked.

"No guarantees, but some might be."

"Do I get paid?"

"No. But you might get credited as a consultant."

He smiled, revealing exactly no teeth. "Yeah. That's okay."

I carried on. "The newspaper said no one ever figured out how you entered the old mansion."

"Take a guess, purdy lady."

"Forensics didn't find any broken doors or busted windows. You must have dropped in from the roof."

"Only in the movies. You guys always get it wrong."

"Set us straight."

"Try hauling an iron safe up a chimney."

"Point taken."

"You wanna come up *under* the goods. Pry a few floorboards, grab the shit, and tunnel the fuck out."

"Perfect. That's why I came to the source. Worth every mile."

He shook his head side to side. "I bet you were a swimsuit model."

I ignored that. "Did you need a saw? A drill? A—"

"Just one crowbar and two cojones the size of cantaloupes." He spat a wad of chewing tobacco to the side. "I pushed that safe out the crawl space."

"Then, you drove to the desert."

He nodded. "One stick of dynamite, and that safe's door was blown to Barstow. I stuffed twenty-mil of crack in the Toyota and headed toward Frisco."

"Nice score."

"You want your characters to pull this job off?"

"That's the idea."

"Then, make sure they don't do what I did."

"Get caught?"

"That's the idea."

The steel door swung open, and the prison guard called out, "Time's up, Bingham."

Earl flipped him the bird. "Anything else you need to know?" he asked me.

"What would you have done differently?"

"Not gotten caught."

"The burned-out taillight?"

He bobbed his head. "I'm one offramp away from my first sale. Highway Patrol pulls me over, offers to fix the light, and asks me to pop the trunk. That's when I shot the cop through his badge." He smiles at the memory. "Then, his partner tackled me, cuffed me, and helped himself to a couple bags of blow before taking me in."

"Earl. Now," yelled the guard.

Earl leaned forward. His breath took mine away. "I'll give you one more big tip, for one little French kiss."

My stomach lurched. "That's all right, Earl. I've got what I need."

He spat between his legs, rose slowly, and started toward the guard. At the steel door, Earl turned. "Can you believe it? I'm doing life 'cuz of a fuckin' fifty-cent bulb. And the only ones I get to kiss these days have beards."

ON THE WAY home from the prison, I stopped off at Safeguard Security Supplies, which was housed in a nondescript, one-story building in the industrial area of Canoga Park. Numerous spy and surveillance gadgets were on display. I had no doubt that my every move was being monitored and recorded. A few customers drifted throughout the store.

It felt good being out in the field, digging up dirt, studying characters, extracting the inside scoop. I felt like a writer once again. Maybe that's why I had a smile on my face when I approached a slouching salesman wearing a wide paisley tie and an off-center toupee.

"Hello. I'm Fiona Logan. I'm doing some information gathering for a movie."

His job was to be suspicious, so he looked me over like I was a KGB spy. "Lemme guess. You're an actress researching a role."

"No. I'm a writer researching a story."

He apparently didn't like to be wrong. "You *were* an actress though, right?"

"I was a lima bean in the world premiere of *The Photosynthesis Follies*."

"Experimental theater? Off-Broadway?"

"Kindergarten. Roosevelt Elementary. Closed after one night."

He laughed. "I think I like you." He circled around my body, sizing me up like a prize bull. "Didn't know they made good-looking writers."

Couldn't I meet a man who *didn't* make a fool of himself? But I needed this loon's help, so I played the coquette card. "Didn't know male models worked in retail."

"You have good taste." He smoothed back his so-called hair. "So, tell me. This movie, is it for one of the majors?"

"Major studios?"

"Or streamers? Which is it? Warners, Universal, Fox, Amazon?"

Everyone in Los Angeles knows something about or someone in show business. It's a company town. "We're not working with a studio," I said.

"Indie financing?"

"Roger Bowman's the producer."

"Roger. Sure. Good man. Anything for Roger." It was obvious this guy didn't know who I was talking about. "What do you need to know?"

"So, I—"

"Just don't let on in front of the boss." He jerked his head toward the far counter. "He's a dick."

"Okay."

"I don't get bonuses for giving out free advice. But we Hollywood types have to stick together, right?" he said with an oily smirk.

"Hey, I'd do it for you," I said without conviction.

"I wanted to be an actor. Came west right out of the Army." He picked at a scab on his chin. "I auditioned for the cartoon voice of *Stinky the Skunk*," he said, in the shrill voice of Stinky the Skunk. "They said I stunk." He extended his hand. "Daniel Gibson."

I gave his eczema-encrusted hand a quick pump. "Fiona Logan."

"Where was I?"

"About to help me," I said.

"Right, right. So, what's this movie about?" He sniffed, adjusting his clip-on tie.

"It's about two hours." I couldn't resist the old joke. He laughed. "It's about this couple who steals some valuable art."

"Art's the way to go. Way better than jewelry."

Somewhere, Jack was gloating.

"I want to make the crime as authentic as possible," I said.

"I can help you there." Mr. Gibson directed me out of earshot of his co-workers. His hand on my elbow made me queasy. "Guess who was the technical advisor on *The Gangsters' Getaway*?" he boasted, poking his thumb into his chest. "It bombed. Went straight to video. But it was one-hundred percent accurate. Ask anybody."

"I wish I could pay you."

"No worries. I'll bring a couple clients to the premier, and we'll call it even," said the sad sack whose own Hollywood dream sank long ago.

"Fair enough. So, how do my characters beat the most modern, most sophisticated security system?"

He looked around. Then, in soft tones, "Heat sensors, motion detectors, surveillance cameras, all that shit? I don't care how high-tech your security, there's nothing a pair of wire cutters and molasses can't defeat."

I looked up from my notepad. "Molasses?"

"Any syrup will do. Have your characters pour it inside the central alarm system. It coats the conductors and fouls up everything. Just to be sure, though, clip the cables, too. Red is communications. Yellow is power. White are the backup generators. Do all that, and your characters could stroll through Fort Knox."

"This is excellent, Mister Gibson."

"If you want this heist to go down for real,"—he looked around, then quietly added—"wrap your robbers in tin foil. It scrambles electronic signals and throws police dogs off the scent." He nervously looked over his shoulder. "They could fire my ass for what I just told you."

"Nobody will ever know." I turned toward the front doors, eager to free myself of him. "Any other tips?"

"If your characters encounter guard dogs, make sure their weapons have silencers. And that they always aim between the ears."

I shuddered at the thought of anyone harming an animal. "Good advice. I can't thank you enough."

"Yes, you can. Let me tell you more over drinks." He grabbed my elbow again. "It's near closing time."

"Thanks, but I'm running late for a meeting."

"You couldn't buy what I just told you. So, what do I get in return?" he said with a spiteful edge, pulling me closer.

"You're making a major contribution to the culture of cinema." Let him gnaw on that.

I left, knowing that he would review the security footage of our encounter over and over in his mother's basement, naked on a bug-infested mattress, under a bare swinging lightbulb.

A writer's imagination never rests.

Chapter 25
JACK

I was about to experience one of the special luxuries of being a screenwriter, the privilege of entering a world foreign to most people, gaining access to a place most people will never go, seeing things most people will never see. Saying you're a screenwriter, I would learn, was a license to the unknown. An all-access pass to peek behind the curtain. The key to any door.

I was escorted through a VIP gate toward a private hanger at Van Nuys Airport. The giant shelter was sealed shut. A Gulfstream jet glistened out front, book-ended by two Rolls-Royces, and guarded by a group of gorillas wearing Prada suits.

"Are you the writer?" the alpha ape grunted.

"Yes, I am."

He spoke into his walkie-talkie. "The writer's here." Then, he turned to me. "What have you written?"

"Oh, lots of things."

"Name one."

"*The Godfather*."

"No shit?"

"A little shit."

His comrades giggled like Girl Scouts.

He opened his coat, revealing a Desert Eagle handgun tucked in his waistband. "Get going, you little shit."

If we were in a bar, he would have taken a swing at me. I lettered in Division 1 football and wrestling. Nothing about him, except for his pistol, scared me.

The hangar's huge doors opened just wide enough for me to enter before sliding close and locking. The hanger served as an enormous storage unit. On the cement floor were a fleet of exotic boats, motorcycles, and cars. There were rows of racks, floor to ceiling, filled with high-end merchandise—stolen merchandise—of all kinds, including objects of art.

A menacing Italian appeared wearing an all-pink suit, a pink fedora, and pink slippers. He looked like Barbie's grandfather. "*Benvenuto.* Welcome, welcome," he said, embracing me, kissing each of my cheeks.

"*Grazie, grazie,*" I chirped.

"Any friend of Lieutenant Lopez is an enemy of mine," he said without a hint of an accent or sense of humor.

"We're not really friends, just—"

"I'm joking," he said, breaking into a smile, cauliflower ear to cauliflower ear. "I'm Carlo De Luca. And I don't particularly care for spending time with strangers who aren't offering me something in exchange."

"I won't take much of your time. I'm a writer. I'm doing research. I need to know—"

"Do you have a name?"

"Jack Reynolds. But you can call me anything you want."

"Tell me, Mister Reynolds, what films have I seen of yours?"

"Oh, gee, everyone is asking me that today. Where to begin, where to begin," I vamped.

"I like movies starring women without clothes. Have you written any of those?"

"Funny you should ask. My current project contains a large number of nipples."

"You'll let me visit the set?"

"Anytime. Or you could just take a figure drawing class. They have nude models at Santa Monica Community College."

He had lost all interest in me. "The lieutenant told me to be polite, give you the tour, and answer your questions."

"That would be awesome."

Carlo took me by the arm and led me around the massive warehouse-like building.

"So, this is what a black market looks like," I said.

"Did you think it would be painted black?" he said, laughing hard, twisting his pinky ring.

"I didn't know what to think. This is all so new."

He stopped at a long, glass showcase to point out a jadeite-laden necklace. "This is just a small sample of my merchandise. What else do you wish to know?"

I looked around. "The secrets."

"Why not? The good lieutenant will never bust me. I'm worth more to him as a snitch."

"He said you were a great informant, but a better middle man. An expert fence."

"I prefer the term 'broker.' But yes, I service buyers and sellers alike. I'm an equal opportunity accomplice."

"So, how does it all work?" I followed him down an aisle that was packed with electronic items, shelf after shelf. I could have been browsing in one of Amazon's fulfillment centers.

"Okay. One 'Black Market for Dummies' tutorial coming up," he said with a maniacal grin. "By the master Italian fencer, Carlo De Luca. Let's say you steal something, like a thirty-five-million-dollar yacht. You want to unload it fast, at a profit, of course. You come to the best in the business, me. 'How much do you want for your little dinghy?' I ask. You say, 'Thirty million.' I find a buyer who pays thirty-one million. The buyer gets the yacht, you get your asking price, and I get a small fee for facilitating the deal. The buyer got a great deal, you got a great deal, and I got a great deal."

"Win, win, win."

"It's not always that simple. Sometimes people end up in a refrigerator, sliced and diced. But mostly, it's the ideal business model. Long live capitalism. This is a great country. Never forget it."

Our walk came to a stop alongside a baby grand piano painted candy apple red. I checked my notes. "How about art, stolen art? How does one sell that?"

"In your script, you will use my name?"

"Absolutely not. I promise."

"I *want* you to use my name."

"Oh. In that case, by all means."

He smiled, proud to be in the movie business. "Art thieves are a turnkey operation," he said. "They rob museums, galleries, private collectors, then sometimes bypass the great Carlo De Luca by ransoming their booty back to the insurance company or to the owner." He took a step toward me. "Maybe there's a small part in your movie for a good-looking WOP?"

I smiled nervously. "I'll talk to my people."

With shifty eyes, he said, "The tour is over."

"It's been so educational, so illuminating, and so—"

He turned into a stone killer. "You were never here. We never met. This never happened. Is that clear?"

"Who are you? Where am I? What happened?"

"*Ciao*," he said, withdrawing and brandishing a gold dagger from his shoulder scabbard. "If you tell anyone anything I told you"—he dragged the point of his dagger across his throat—"I'll remove your voice box. Now, get outta here."

I scampered like a scalded cat down the tarmac to my car. Fiona never warned this cat that research could cost me one of my nine lives.

BETH AND I sat at a picnic table on the hospital's patio as evening approached. We swirled hot coffee in our cups, barely speaking, like the elderly couples you see at restaurants who just sip their wine and look off, remembering the early years when they had so much to talk about.

I always wondered if old folks tried to keep their relationship fresh as they aged, but ran out of ideas. Or interest. What do you say when you know that the other person knows what you're going to say? What new information is there to exchange after so many years together? Do you discuss bowel movements? The recent drought? A new bunion? Or do you just sip your wine and look across the restaurant at others engaged in lively conversation? When do you talk about how you feel about not talking? What do you do about a marriage vanishing like smoke from a snuffed-out candle?

I had to break the silence. "This guy had bodyguards. And the bodyguards had bodyguards. It was insane."

"Sounds interesting," Beth said, warming her hands around the coffee cup.

"Does it?"

"Yeah."

"You don't sound like it sounds interesting."

"Sorry. I'm tired. I was on call all night."

We sipped. And looked off. After a while, I said, "Well, it *was* interesting. It's all been interesting. She's taught me a lot."

"I held a child's heart in my hand today," she said.

"It's not a contest, Beth." More silence. Then, "I've been working at a fucking bakery. A meaningless, mindless, moronic, miserable job. But today, *today*, I was a *real* writer doing *real* research for a *real* movie. I'm kind of stoked about it, and I kind of wanted you to be, too."

"Because you're going to be out again tonight?"

"Because I want you to be happy for me."

"You sound like a girl."

"That helps."

Silence.

"I *am* happy for you," she finally said. "Happy now?"

"It's not solving the debt crisis, it's not brokering a Middle East peace accord, it's not open-heart surgery on a newborn, but it's what I want to do with my life."

"Then, go to your art party with your new girlfriend."

"It's research for my work. And Fiona has generously taken me under her wing. It's an honor."

"I thought her name was Professor Logan."

More silence. Painful silence. Louder silence. I looked at a bald woman slumped over in a wheelchair. She wasn't very old. In one hand, instead of carrying a purse, she held her urine drainage pouch. In the other hand, instead of holding a smart phone, she held a cigarette inches away from her oxygen tank. She just sat there smoking, dying. I'd take silence over dying any day. That gave me some needed perspective.

I turned to Beth.

At the same time, we said, "I'm sorry."

We gazed at each other.

"Does this tie go with this shirt?" I asked.

"They both should go in the trash."

"What do you wear to an art opening? A drop cloth?"

"You could wear a muumuu and still be the best-looking man in the room." She smiled. "I just miss you. That's all. I miss *us*. Between my internship and your internship, we're two intern ships passing in the night, missing each other."

I laughed for the first time that day. "Intern ships. That's good. You're a better writer than me."

"Than I," she said.

We fought over who was going to have the final word.

"You win," I conceded.

"That helps." Beth drew my hand to her lips and kissed it softly. "Go research. Comb your hair. Don't knock over any antiques. Do no harm." She grabbed her coffee and stood. "My body misses yours. I don't know how much longer it can hold out."

"You sound like a boy."

She managed a chortle, turned, and marched away.

Cancer girl across the way looked at me and grimaced, blinking in slow motion, puffing smoke into the air. I put on my black blazer and set off for Rodeo Drive.

Chapter 26
FIONA

AFTER A DAY of driving through three sprawling counties and talking to two repulsive men, I had to take a long, hot bubble bath. And drink a tall glass of ice-cold ginger-peach soda. I closed my eyes and let the steam cleanse my pores. I tried to tune out the sounds of tenants arguing, kids squealing, and radios blaring. I tried to calm my senses. I meditated in the glossy water.

In an hour, I would meet Jack at the gallery. Afterward, we would start writing together. I guess this was actually happening.

What was I doing? Really, what was I thinking? Why was I now second-guessing myself? And why hadn't Eddie called me, damn it? I thought he would have thrown himself at my feet by now. And if he had, how would I have reacted? Did I want him? Was I able to love again? Or was I merely tempted to dip my toe in the dating waters to test my readiness?

More importantly, what should I wear to the art opening? I had to go for a look that made me feel confident and comfortable, while showing my own artistic flair. The white pantsuit made my hips look too big. The lacy camisole made my breasts look too small. And the jeans with the suede bomber jacket made me look like I was trying to be thirty again. Maybe I should play it safe with the smart Navy-blue skirt suit and my frilly white blouse.

"Yeah. How about that, Rathbone?" My furry fashion consultant slobbered a bit, then trotted out of the bathroom, chomping on his squawking chew toy.

Why was I so nervous? It was just a little cocktail party. I certainly wasn't dressing for Jack. Was I?

I tried on six outfits and four combinations before asking the eternal question. What would Betty Davis do? No doubt about it, she would take a risk. Stand out. Steal the show.

I posed before the full-length mirror in my bedroom, examining my chosen ensemble from head to toe. It was a bold commitment. I had squeezed into my beige jodhpurs, knee-high boots, and silk tuxedo shirt. Did I kill? Was I an original? Would Betty have been envious? More questions than answers. I broke the no-weekday-contact rule by FaceTiming my daughter for an expert's opinion.

She appeared on my iPhone with a moan.

"Did I wake you?" I asked.

"Is it Sunday?"

"I need your advice."

"What time is it?"

"Just open your eyes and say yes or no. Then, you can go back to sleep." I held my phone at arm's distance so Charlotte could have a full view of my getup.

She opened one eye half way. Good enough for me. *"Are you going skeet shooting?"* she whispered.

"An art opening."

"Are horses going to be there?"

"I want to make a statement."

"That loud?"

"It's a simple statement. Strong. Self-assured. Doesn't need a man," I said.

"Two out of three are true."

"Is it really too much?"

"Lose the spurs. Think simpler. Make an understatement." She rolled over on her side.

I was happy to see that Olé-the-matador wasn't there.

"Where did you get those hideous earrings?" I heard her say.

"From your jewelry box."

"Bury them with the jodhpurs."

"Charlotte?"

"I'm asleep."

"What should I do?"

"Go classic. Go black. Go find a man. Love you, Mumsie."
"Honey?"
She was deep in dreamland.
To her back, I said, "Love you, Char."

Chapter 27

JACK

Living off a cake decorator's wages, money and I had an on-again, off-again relationship. I'd pay dearly for a frosted mug of German beer. I'd tip a waiter twenty percent, a waitress twenty-five. And I'd never drive past a lemonade stand without buying out the kid's supply. But I'd never pay for parking. I wouldn't pay to park in a lot. I wouldn't pay to park at a meter. And I certainly wouldn't pay twenty dollars to have a valet park my car fifteen feet away for an hour. So, I found free "after six p.m." street parking in a residential area just north of Marcia Yang's Art Gallery in Beverly Hills.

I walked through a ritzy neighborhood on the palm tree-lined street, marveling at the size of the mansions, and imagining the size of the staff needed to keep them up. The scent of exotic vegetation and freshly manicured lawns perfumed the air. If I were a wealthy screenwriter, would I want to live there, next door to studio tycoons? Or would I prefer the Malibu colony among the movie stars? Or Bel Air with the prosperous producers? Or in Toluca Lake amid the living-large directors, adjacent to the city's snootiest country club? Would success change me? Would I forget my Midwest upbringing? Was I getting a little ahead of myself?

A catered, upscale gallery opening was in full swanky swing. The small space was packed with an elite crowd of art dealers and collectors, as well as an array of artsy groupies who had come mainly to pirouette for the paparazzi. A sleek woman with a live kingsnake wrapped around her neck was chatting up an obese goateed man wearing a Moroccan Kaftan. An albino transvestite laughed it up with a shirtless dwarf. Gaunt supermodels rubbed up against their doddery sugar daddies. Socialites gave interviews to social media reporters. Well-known influencers meandered about with selfie sticks. A soccer star had a YouTube singing sensation on his arm. Waiters wearing veils served sautéed shrimp and chilled Dom Perignon off silver trays. I grabbed a prawn and wandered around examining pieces of art, acting like I appreciated what I was looking at, pretending like I didn't hate everything I saw. I stopped to examine a large, gold dragon sculpture, squinted my eyes, and stroked my chin in an erudite manner.

"Just in. Impressive, isn't he?" a female voice shouted over the crowd noise.

I turned to acknowledge the porcelain face of a chic woman dressed in canary yellow, from satin headscarf to open-toe sandals.

"Impressive indeed." I tried to sound urbane.

"Song Period, Yuan Dynasty. But you knew that."

"My favorite Dynasty. I had a crush on Heather Locklear."

"One of a kind." She sensually fondled the sculpture. "Priced to sell."

"You're—?"

"Marcia Yang. And you're—?"

"I'm writing a movie," I said proudly, expecting her to be enthralled. She was. "Oh, my. Lots of money in that field."

"I hope so."

She glided her long, yellow fingernail across the dragon's snout. "Pristine condition. No chips, no cracks, not one blemish."

"I'm not buying. I'm researching."

"Researching? We call that slumming," she said. "Gate crashing for free hors d'oeuvres. Being seen with the in-crowd." Her mood had completely changed. It was chilling.

"No, really. I'm here with my writing partner. She was invited."

"Where? I don't see a partner."

"She's on her way. We're writing a movie. I'm a movie writer," I stuttered. "This is movie research."

"Either leave now, or I'll have security escort you. Believe me, you don't want to make a scene."

I noticed Fiona emerging through the throng, wearing a low-cut black dress—a little too short and a little too tight—and way too alluring red stiletto heels. She certainly didn't look like a professor or an apartment manager. For an instant, I actually lost my breath. And swallowed a shrimp tail.

It was like that scene from *West Side Story*, when Tony and Maria lock eyes from across the dance floor at the gym. Time stops. The other dancers dissolve away. Maria floats straight toward Tony as in a trance, like Fiona was now moving toward me. Inside my head, I heard a song. *Fiona. The most beautiful sound I ever heard. Fiona, Fiona, Fee-oh-naaaa....*

Ms. Yang followed my gaze.

"There." I pointed to Fiona. "That's my date." I caught Fiona's eye. We took in each other's formal attire. We had both transformed into movie stars.

"Fiona. I'm delighted you could come," Ms. Yang said as Fiona reached for her hand.

"Wouldn't miss it, Marcia."

"How do you two—" I started to say.

"Yoga class," Fiona said, gawking at me. Then, she added, "Nice tie."

"Nice everything," I answered back, awed by her magnificence.

Ms. Yang turned to me, "Mister—?"

"It's Reynolds. Jack Reynolds. Movie writer."

"I'm sorry, Mister Reynolds, for our earlier misunderstanding." She stepped back to consider us as a couple. "My goodness. Together, you look like a stunning work of art."

"We're here on business," Fiona said, trying to deflect the compliment.

"So I've heard," Ms. Yang replied. "Writers. You paint with words, sculpt with ingenuity, and bring beauty into the world."

"Just trying to make a buck," Fiona said.

"You are an *artiste*, my dear. And I support the arts in all its forms."

"So, you'll help us?" Fiona asked.

"It would be an honor."

"We need to get some ideas," I said, grabbing a crab cake off a passing tray.

"About what?" Ms. Yang asked.

"About which art objects move best through the black market," Fiona said.

There was a long silence, and then Ms. Yang said, "Relax. Have something to drink. Then, we'll talk."

AFTER THE LAST guest stumbled out, the party planners had left, and Ms. Yang bolted the front doors, she took us into her cramped office, poured green tea, and gave us a lesson in the illegal trafficking of art. She knew way too much not to be behind bars.

I WALKED FIONA to the valet stand, and she drove me to my car. We would meet at her place. I would stop on the way to pick up food, and she would stop on the way to pick up wine. Dinner and drinks at Fiona's. The ex-teacher and her ex-student had come a long way. What had I gotten myself into?

Chapter 28

FIONA

It was nearly midnight by the time I returned from the gallery to my apartment. I trudged down the hall carrying my high heels in one hand and my notebook in the other.

Jack was sitting on his ragged backpack on the porch, his head resting against my door, fast asleep. He had cartons of take-out Chinese food and a little blue box in his lap.

I paused at my door to watch him sleep. He was a sweet young man and as good-looking as a man of any age could be. His girlfriend was a lucky lady. What was I getting myself into?

I woke him with, "It's time to write."

Jack stirred, glanced around, and struggled to his feet. "Yeah. I was just resting my eyes. No big deal. I can go all night. Let's get this party started." He yawned.

I unlocked the front door. Rathbone welcomed me home, eager to be fed.

"I hope you like beef and broccoli," Jack said, entering my apartment. "And a ton of rice. That's all they had left."

"I'm a strict vegetarian. Until it comes to things I like." I carried the food to the kitchen, while a groggy Jack loosened his tie and took a self-guided tour around the living room of my quaint, two-bedroom apartment. "Welcome to the convent," I said.

He stood in front of my grandfather's grandfather clock, taking in the vibe of my modest dwelling. "This is a great place. Lots of character," he said. "Lots of warmth."

"It's nothing like our house in the hills above the valley. We could see to the North Pole." I stopped to reflect. "From a mountaintop on Mulholland to a hovel in Hollywood. Beware of life's little land mines."

"You should be a writer."

"You should clear the table off."

He stopped to study a small photograph in a silver frame on the mantelpiece.

"Charlotte, my one and only," I said, letting my hair down. "She's in Europe, doing her junior year abroad. I miss her terribly."

Jack picked up another frame. "And this must be your husband."

"Marvin. My rudder. My everything. I miss him beyond words. And I'm a writer."

"Great smile," Jack said softly.

"Great man."

"How—"

"ALS. And the irony? He owned a signed Lou Gehrig baseball card. We sold it on eBay to pay medical bills."

Jack placed the picture back carefully. "I'm sorry."

"If you're not going to clear the table off, you can light a fire. Preferably in the fireplace."

He wandered to the corner of the room where I hung my birdwatching binoculars, fishing pole, and a vintage wicker shoulder basket, known as an angler's creel. He held up the basket. "Hobby?" he asked.

"Birding is my hobby. Fly fishing is my addiction." I handed Rathbone his nightly treat. "Whenever I can get away, which is never."

He moved to a bookshelf stuffed with scripts and lingered there. "Did you write all these?"

"That's about half of them," I said. "Wine?"

"Where are the others?"

"They make great kindling. Gets cold in here at night."

"You destroy your life's work?"

"I've toasted marshmallows over them," I said, pouring two glasses of red wine. "Put that paper to good use."

"Your work reduced to ashes? I hope you have copies."

"They're just words, Jack. Expendable words."

He flipped through the pages of one of my scripts. "You make something out of nothing. You create what others can't even imagine. An empty page, then presto. A whole world comes to life."

"Good job on getting that fire started," I said sarcastically, handing him a glass of Merlot.

We were face to face, in my living room, holding wine.

"Really, Fiona. You make magic. You shouldn't—"

I cranked my neck toward his Bliffer's Bakery box. "What evil lurks in tonight's blue box, asked the strict vegetarian?"

He didn't want to talk about dessert. He wanted to talk about what we leave and what we don't leave behind. He wanted to believe what writers write is worth keeping. That what we write makes a difference. Has lasting value. That we don't just sell words for a living.

"Listen, Jack. Just like in life, as a writer, you can't look back. Only forward. What's written is written. What is yet to be written is all that matters."

He had a look in his eyes that showed he understood my true meaning. That he understood me. That he understood I was trying to move forward, for which he, this young man, was partly responsible.

He nodded and pointed to the blue box. "Cake. I swung by the bakery on my way here."

"Details."

"Pecan caramel double fudge."

"Why not? I've had a good life."

He continued his sightseeing trip around the room. Coming to the giant movie poster of *With Guns Blazing*, the film I had showed in class. "Burn this," he said. "It's big enough to keep you warm all winter."

"Chopsticks or fork? Purist or pragmatist?" I asked, clearing the table off.

"Dealer's choice." He moseyed to the far wall and looked at the picture Marvin had painted of me fishing in a rushing mountain stream, flanked by a cluster of majestic Ponderosa Pine trees. "That's you?" he guessed.

"A lifetime ago. Marvin painted it. He didn't believe in cameras."

"Where is this place?"

"If I told you, it would no longer be a secret."

"I won't tell. I swear."

"Crystal Cove. Lone River, Colorado. Quietest place on earth. A fly fisherman's paradise, a birder's utopia."

"My idea of camping is room service and a spa."

"I'm retiring there," I said. "The day I win the lottery."

Jack stacked logs on the grate and ignited a low and inviting flame.

I sipped my wine and watched the firelight flicker across his face. It was nice having a man in my apartment, at night, around a cozy fire. So much better than re-reading another chapter of *Sense and Sensibility*. It was also nice having a man look at me, not as, or only as, a sex object. This particular man, I thought, saw me. The real me. And that felt good. If only I were younger.

I shook my hair out and set down my wine, banishing the foolish thoughts that had slipped into my head of their own accord. "Get it while it's cold, Jack."

He came to the table and stood behind his chair. "Fiona?"

"Speaking," I said, dishing out dinner.

"They're not just words. They're *your* words. Your heart and soul." His voice was tender. "It's a way of saying, 'I was here.'"

I looked into his green eyes, tempted to tell him my life story, my hopes, my fears, my aspirations. Instead, I said, "Sit down and eat your vegetables."

Chapter 29

JACK

For a moment, Fiona looked like she might want to open up. Like she might be tempted to drop her guard. With her wine glass in her hand and the firelight dancing across the room, she looked softer, needier than I'd seen her before. But the moment passed. We sat down to eat.

During dinner, I couldn't keep my eyes from following her curves in that little black dress she wore. I don't care what men say, they *all* look. Most of them fantasize about what they're looking at, and some aggressive ones act out their cravings. It doesn't matter if the woman is young or not so young, short or tall, Nigerian or Amish, married or single, we look. We try to engage their eyes. We hope to receive a smile of appreciation in return. As we walk pass these charismatic creatures on the street, we play out a dream sequence in our minds. We pretend that we turn around at the same time. Stop in our tracks, walk toward each other—*West Side Story*-style—take each other's hands, and head to the closest hotel room. Men. We're no higher than ferrets on the food chain. Our mental bumper stickers read *Lust Never Sleeps. Sex Drive Never Takes A Holiday. Desire Never Dies.* And nothing, I mean nothing, arouses a man's senses like a little black dress. No matter who is in it. Or who just turned on some soft jazz from her playlist.

I had better stop staring, thinking, envisaging, projecting. It wasn't right, appropriate, or possible. I had to be better than my gender. In matters of the heart and groin, I had to think only of Beth.

But beyond her beauty, I found Fiona thoroughly captivating. A real woman in every way.

Stop already.

Four chimes rang from the grandfather clock. The fire was out. The wine was finished. Fiona was in her bare feet, studying dozens of three by five cards taped to the dining room wall.

I stopped taking notes on my laptop and stared at my own bare feet. "We're never gonna make our deadline."

"Not with that attitude," she said, pacing back and forth like General Patton in black lace stockings.

Rathbone watched his master teach a master class.

"Don't worry about the end. Focus on the now. Take it one word at a time, one page at a time, one day at—"

"Okay, I get it."

"Enjoy the process. The end comes soon enough." Fiona returned to the wall and stared at the cards. "Everybody likes to see the rich get their comeuppance," she said.

"Comeuppance? That's how my parents talk."

She winced. "So, we'll commit this perfect crime against the upper class."

"Okay," I said with my eyes closed.

"The middle-aged maid and the young butler conspire to steal from their abusive employer," she continued to extemporize.

"Okay," I mumbled. But suddenly, I perked up. "Wait. Maid and butler?"

"Pretty good, uh?"

"It sounds so old fashioned. Kind of like 'comeuppance.'"

She bristled. "Sit up."

"I'm tired."

"Have some more coffee."

"I had some more coffee. I just can't go on. I'm outta gas."

"Stop complaining and keep working."

Rathbone gave a worried woof. Exhaustion had set in. We were all becoming short-tempered.

A morning spent convincing Fiona to write with me, time learning the perfect crime from Lieutenant Lopez, an afternoon touring Carlo's warehouse, an evening's tense cup of coffee with Beth, and a posh party with Ms. Yang had finally caught up with me. Although I was sapped, Fiona was just getting fired up. She had the energy of a woman far younger, however old she was.

"I'm sorry. I'm done in. We have to quit," I said.

"Quitters never win, and winners never quit," she said.

"Who said that?"

"Vince Lombardi. And *my* writing teacher."

"It's been a long day, Fiona," I said, rising to my bare feet. "I have to get home."

"We only have a few days to write a hundred and twenty pages. It takes me at least six months to write a bad script."

"I called in sick yesterday. I have to be at the bakery by nine this morning. Or I'll lose my job."

"This is your job. C'mon, we're on a roll here."

"I'll come back tonight after my shift."

"So, I do all the work, and you get half the money?"

"I'll be thinking all day."

"Of what?"

"Of a nanny and a pool man." I didn't realize how loud I had become. How exasperated I was. How the muse had just paid me a timely and surprise visit.

"A nanny? And a pool man?" Fiona said slowly and mockingly.

"It's more contemporary."

"Splendid. Let me get my quill and jot that down."

I let that slide. We were both worn out. Our nerves were raw. I folded my laptop. "The office is closed. Good night. We'll continue later."

"We haven't developed our characters," she boomed. "We have no idea who they are, what they think, how they talk, where they—"

"Elsa!" I exploded.

Rathbone growled.

"She's the nanny." I had no idea where these thoughts were coming from. "Older woman, smokin' hot, wears a sexy, little black dress. Um, uniform. Did I say dress?" I was on the far side of fatigue.

Fiona's face was frozen.

"Black uniform dress. Like a maid. Only she's a nanny," I added, fumbling my recovery. "She's a dare devil from Denmark." I was a dolt from Dayton.

Fiona said nothing.

I put one of my shoes on. "The pool man, Ethan, twenty-something, surf 'n ski bum, rides a pearl-white Harley." More ideas kept flooding in. "The filthy rich family they work for?" I searched for the perfect surname as I put on my other shoe. "The Rathbones. They are ungrateful, mean, and chintzy. Elsa and Ethan want out. They want money. They want each other." I stood. "They steal a fourteenth century gold dragon from the Rathbone's mansion. And sell it on the black market for a million bucks." I put on my blazer. "The upper class gets its upcomeance or whatever you called it. Elsa and Ethan get each other. And I get to go home to sleep for maybe three hours tops." As a punctuation mark, I flamboyantly zipped my backpack closed. "The. Freakin'. End." I finally inhaled.

The room went quiet. Fiona's face remained expressionless. But I think I astonished her. I know I astonished myself.

"Well then, sit down and write it with me," she said.

"I'm drained. I'm out of ideas. It's four-something in the morning." I staggered to the front door.

"It's four-something in the morning for me, too."

I opened the front door. "Get some rest," I said. "Good night, partner." And I left.

I felt pretty good about everything. After all, I had just invented Elsa and Ethan, the Rathbones, and the crime. I'm not saying I could have done it without Fiona, but I was certainly getting the hang of a job my screenwriting teacher once described as "making stuff up."

I LITERALLY WAS asleep on my stool. If Shanelle hadn't awakened me, my head would have fallen into the birthday cake I was assigned to decorate.

"Dude. You have frosting on your face," Shanelle said.

"Helps cover the circles under my eyes."

Shanelle wiped some icing off my cheek.

"Kevin left his blender," I said.

"It's a parting gift. He left it for you. I've got one." She wrapped her arm around my shoulder. "I'm feeling guilty. How long can you stay there?"

"Don't worry. In a few days, I'm getting twenty grand. I might buy a tropical island."

Benny approached, examined the cake, and then pointed to the counter area where a corpulent man stood waiting. "That's Kyle O'Shea over there. A good Irishman. A great customer," Benny said, keeping his voice low.

"I know, Benny. I'm almost done," I said.

"This cake is for his wife, Patty," Benny said.

"Patty cake, patty cake, baker's man," I sang in my drowsy state of mind.

Benny found the work order on my table and handed it to me. "Read the order."

"'Happy Birthday Patty,'" I read out loud.

"Now, read your cake." Benny fumed.

I looked down at my cake and read aloud the words I had sleepily scripted in icing. "'Happy Birthday Fatty.'"

Shanelle turned away, muffling a laugh.

I struggled to keep it together. "Uh, oh. Typo. Kinda funny, if you think about it."

"That's not your first screw up this week," Benny said, just as Eleanor passed by.

"Leave him alone," she said. "He's going to be famous."

"Patty O'Shea is obese," Benny said in a loud whisper. "You think she'll find 'Fatty' funny?"

I rushed to repair my error. "Here, look. I'm fixing. Nothing's easier than turning an *F* into a *P*." And then sleep deprivation overtook my senses. I was overwhelmed by the absurdity of it all. I was overcome by a wave of inappropriate laughter. That didn't help my overall cause. Or lower Benny's over-the-top heart rate.

"We all want you to write your Academy Award winning movie," Benny said.

Shanelle lost it, bursting into howls of laughter. She had to lean against a wall just to remain upright.

"We want you to shatter all the box office records," Benny continued.

A couple salesladies came from behind the counter, congregating around me to read the cake and join in the hilarity.

Benny plowed on. "And I'm looking forward to walking down the red carpet at the super-duper premiere." That sent me into more fits of hysterics, until little Benny delivered his big finish. "But *my* writing comes first. With no big fat typos."

I sobered up fast. So did the others, including Shanelle. As our boss glared at them, they scurried back to work.

"Let me see it after you're done," Benny said.

"I'm done," I said.

"Your *script*. I know a thing or two about the picture business. I may have some ideas for making it better." He waddled off.

I called after him, "I love you, Benny." Then, I broke into more gales of uncontainable laughter.

Chapter 30
FIONA

I WAS SURE at any moment, Eddie would turn a corner and bump his shopping basket into mine. After all, this was the scene of the crime, Gelson's supermarket, the lonely heart's best hope for a non-saloon, non-gym, non-dental office chance encounter.

This time, I had Jack at my side, texting notes to himself while I tried to dictate the specifics of a tight story. I quietly pushed the cart as I thought aloud. Some writers do their best creative thinking on the toilet. My best thoughts come to me in the dairy section, not coincidentally near the frozen desserts' display.

"Elsa and what's-his-name—"

"Ethan," Jack said.

"Have to be likable," I said, studying my choices of ice cream flavors. "Stealing isn't likable. We have to justify their crime so that the audience will sympathize with them. Identify with them. Care about them. Root for them. Understand and approve of their motives."

Jack did his best impersonation of me, speaking in a high octave. "If you learn nothing else in this class, remember this. Emotional motivation."

"Someone was actually listening," I said.

"Someone still is."

We had instituted a temporary truce.

I grabbed a carton of pistachio Haagen-Dazs. "Are you a fan of pistachio?" I asked.

"Who isn't?"

I tossed the ice cream into the cart and continued to work out our story. "So, why do the nanny and pool man steal from their employers, the...."

"The Rathbones," Jack reminded me.

"Because the Rathbones—" I stopped pushing the cart and pondered hard, lost in thought. What the hell did the Rathbones do to cause their most-trusted staff to steal from them? I couldn't think of a damn thing. Drawing blanks. Too much pressure. I was stumped.

"Because Elsa and—" Jack said.

"Quiet. I'm thinking." But I wasn't coming up with anything. The supermarket's background music was interrupted by a call for a price check on papaya. After a long moment, I looked at Jack hopelessly.

He jumped in. "Because Elsa and Ethan have discovered that the Rathbones are art thieves."

I rolled that around in my head. "Bad guys?"

Jack scrolled through his notes. "The Double Steal. The perfect crime. Rob from robbers."

"Okay, okay. But we also need a personal reason, the emotional motivation. Something that drives Elsa and what's-his-name—"

"Ethan."

"Something that provokes these good people to steal from their employers."

I pushed the cart toward the fruit and vegetables section.

"Got it," Jack said. "The Rathbones treat their help like dirt."

"That's not enough."

"Okay. The Rathbones forbid our couple from fraternizing."

"We need more."

"The Rathbones are irrational and heartless."

"How?" I demanded.

"They don't give Ethan and what's-her-name—"

"Elsa," I said.

"Christmas off."

"Bigger."

"They stiff them at Christmas. No time off, no gift, no bonus."

"Bigger."

"They FIRE them on Christmas Day."

"YES," I yelled, as if I had climaxed right there surrounded by cucumbers and zucchinis.

Jack impulsively gave me a giant bear hug, lifting me high off the floor, twirling me in circles as if he were an infantryman returning from the frontline, and I was his steady gal. Around and around he whirled me. My feet knocked a few tomatoes onto the floor, bouncing them down the aisle.

I was laughing into Jack's face. And he was laughing into mine. Until we heard, "Do you mind?" from an old woman standing by the persimmons, glaring at us.

As if he suddenly realized the length of our embrace, his awkward crossing of the line, and my awkward lack of resistance, Jack set me down gently. *Swan Lake*, in between the onions and the avocadoes, was over. Being held in the arms of a man had sadly come to an end.

I slowly disentangled, cleared my throat, straightened my blouse, and pointed to his iPhone. "Fired on Christmas. Write it down."

THAT NIGHT, WE dug in for another writing marathon. Rathbone watched as I prepared a salad in the kitchen, and Jack set the table in the dining room. We moved around each other with grace and ease. We read each other like an old married couple. And I was clicking artistically on all cylinders for the first time in years.

"Fired on Christmas, action. Reaction? They steal from the Rathbones," I said.

"Cause. Effect," Jack said. "What side does the fork go on?"

"They know the house, they know the security system, they take the—what do they take?" I asked.

Jack referred to notes on his iPhone. "A gold dragon. Yuan Dynasty."

"Worth one million dollars," I recalled. "They sell the dragon on the black market."

"A once-in-a-lifetime payday."

"They run away," I said.

"And get married," Jack said. "Farewell, Elsa. So long, Ethan. Fade out, movie."

"Not quite."

"Oh, quite. We're through, teacher," Jack said. "Roll credits. It's a wrap."

"No, something's off."

"No, everything's on."
"Not yet," I said.
"Why?"
"It's not working."
"Why?"
"I don't know why," I sighed.
"It just doesn't *feel* right," he said, looking at the table.
"Exactly."
"I meant the fork. It looks better on the left side."
"We need a twist. Something the audience won't expect," I said.

Jack looked for drinking glasses in the cupboards. "A twist, a twist," he mumbled to himself. "Maybe they're attacked by zombies."

"It will come to me. It always does," I said.

Jack discovered a scrap of paper on the kitchen counter and skimmed it. "I didn't know you liked poetry."

"I don't. I just write it." Then, it hit me. "That's what this story needs. Some poetic justice."

Jack read the scrap of paper out loud. "'May sweet memories mend your soul and everlasting love sustain your heart.'" He was genuinely moved. "Wow."

"Look for it in the greeting card section of your local pharmacy, under 'condolences,'" I said, putting a half bottle of Cabernet Sauvignon on the table. "Come on. We have to nail this story."

Jack reverentially put the scrap of paper back down.

Chapter 31

JACK

After dinner, to clear our heads, we took a top-down drive to the beach in the Mercedes convertible. An offshore breeze warmed the night air. Armed with lemonade and key lime pie, Fiona and I continued our writing session at Figtree's, a popular outdoor cafe on the Venice Boardwalk. Rathbone obediently remained at Fiona's feet, ogling a procession of beach dogs parading by.

"We'll worry about the lovey-dovey business after we figure out the ending," Fiona belted, growing more and more agitated.

"But the lovey-dovey business *affects* the ending," I said, returning fire.

"It can wait."

"It's the only reason they steal the dragon. It's what the whole movie's about."

"I'll get to it when I get to it."

Our debate was becoming louder and hotter. The Canadian tourists sitting next to us got up and moved to a faraway table. Fiona and I were absorbed in a battle of wills and wits, creative combat at its most animated and passionate. And I loved every bloody sparring second. I was mixing it up with a true expert, taking on a veteran, going toe to toe with a heavyweight champion. Giving as well as getting. What a wonderful way to fight. What an intellectual turn on. What a profession.

"Out of all the people on earth," I said. "An older nanny from Denmark and a younger pool man from Denver discover they are made for each other. It doesn't matter if they pull off the crime. They found each other. This is a pivotal story point."

"That's why we have to get it right."

"They've got the hots for each other. What's more right than that?"

"Our nanny doesn't just jump the pool man's bones because he's sexy. She has to fall in love with him. Love, Jack. Not hots. She has to fall in love with his mind, his heart, his idea of love."

"His idea of love is her," I said.

She shook her head. "He has so much to learn about love." Who was she talking about?

"All he has to know is how he feels," I said.

"How would you feel if you were Ethan?" she asked. "Ask yourself that."

"Ethan is one of the lucky ones. He's found someone who makes him happy. Don't you want Ethan to be happy?" I leaned forward. "Happiness. Isn't that what we all want?"

She leaned forward. "It's just a stupid little script for a miserable, slimeball chauvinist."

"For your information, I googled your 'slimeball chauvinist.' He happens to be a very legitimate and successful businessman, who hires mostly women."

"Yeah. Women who mostly work in the nude."

"What are you so angry about?"

"That's it. We're done for the night." Seething, Fiona started to put her index cards away, when out of nowhere, Beth, wearing shorts, a tank top, gloves, and kneepads rollerbladed to a stop at our table, catching us both by surprise.

"Well, look who I found," Beth said merrily.

A rush of guilt pulsated through me. Why was I feeling so caught? I wasn't doing anything wrong. "Guilty as charged," I foolishly said, delivering no hug, no kiss. "You're here. And I'm here. I mean, wow. We're all here. Just look at us. All at the same place, all at the same time. Don't ever underestimate the powers of the Universe. Right?"

"Is this a work thing, or can I join you?" Beth asked, removing her helmet, intending to stay.

"It's a work thing," I said, flustered, inflaming matters. "But allow me to make some long overdue introductions." For some unfathomable reason, my anxiety had caused me to become a British envoy, complete with a cockney accent.

Beth and Fiona looked at me like I was a Martian.

"Beth, this is Miss Fiona Logan, my superior writing instructor." Somehow, I came up with "superior," but couldn't say the word "partner," nor could I look either woman in the eye. Why was I so unnerved? And acting so bizarrely? "And Miss Fiona Logan, this is Miss Doctor Elizabeth Watson, my medical intern love interest of almost one year's time. It seems like only yesterday," said the village idiot.

They shook hands and scanned one another, head to toe, as women do.

"I didn't mean to disturb the creative process," Beth said. "If that's what this is."

"What else could it possibly be?" blurted her disturbed boyfriend.

"No worries," Fiona said. "It's a welcomed disruption. We had hit an impasse. One of us is pig-headed." She stretched her arms in an exaggerated fashion. "I needed a break anyway."

Fiona, too, was acting weird. What was going on here?

"Great meeting you, and so forth and so on." She untied Rathbone's leash from the table leg. "You two chat. I'm going to, uh, walk my dog." Fiona scooted her chair back, shoved the rest of her index cards in her purse, and strolled away with Rathbone.

I felt badly that we hadn't resolved our clash. And that she felt driven from the table.

"Like my grandma Gretta," Beth said to me. "They can't sit in the same position too long. Restless leg syndrome. Not uncommon."

"Thanks, Doc, but she's in better shape than I am."

Beth watched Fiona and Rathbone saunter off. "The way you described her, I thought she was a lot younger." Beth sat down, put her elbows on the table, and cradled her chin in her palms. "So," she said. "It's been a few days. Are we moving forward? Am I moving in? Am I moving on? Where are we?"

"I haven't had a moment," I said, watching Fiona and Rathbone amble farther down the boardwalk. "And I don't think we want to talk about this here and now."

"If not now, when? If not here, where?"

"Damn, you're a good writer." I reached for her hand, but she withdrew it.

"Seriously, Jack. It bewilders me that you haven't found the time to deal with something this important."

"It is important. But it can wait," I said. "My script is also important. But it can't wait."

"Your sperm can wait. My ovaries can't."

A bolt of electricity shot through my body. Beth had suddenly catapulted our relationship several steps into the future. She had never invoked the biological clock argument before. This was getting serious. She was pulling out all the stops, sending us down the aisle toward the altar, toward pacifiers, toward T-ball, toward a minivan. A game changer faced us.

"We can't have this conversation now. There're people around. I'm in the middle of a business meeting. You're wearing knee protectors."

"Breathe," she said, touching my foot with hers.

I liked Beth. I even thought I loved her. But with talk of having children, I'm afraid the ante had now been raised beyond my limit. "You've been so patient and understanding and—" I said.

"Because here's the deal," Beth interjected, tired of being so patient and understanding. "We have to be practical and honest with each other. If we're going to do this thing, we have to know, as best we can, that the mechanics are in place."

What was she talking about? What did mechanics have to do with our minds, our hearts, our idea of love? Why was my chest pounding? Why was my stomach turning? And why did I feel like I was suffocating?

Breathe, Jack.

I not-very-subtly dropped my head between my legs. Everyone was looking. Why couldn't I figure out women? This woman? Clocks? Babies? Mechanics?

Breathe.

Where did all the lovey-dovey stuff go?

Breathe.

"I can afford to pay my student loans and half your rent," Beth said. "We can split household expenses and chores evenly. And we should turn Kevin's room into an office for your writing. I won't charge you a dime for the extra square footage."

I lifted my dizzy head. "You've really thought this through."

"Someone had to."

"I just haven't had a moment," I chanted.

"We'll give it six months, then reevaluate. If it's working, we carry on. If it's not working, I can move in with my cousin within a day."

"Do we sign something in blood?"

"I'm just saying that we have to be real. You know the statistics. No reason to plod through month after month if it's all going to turn to shit. But I don't see that happening, Jack. I don't see a problem here. I see a wonderful life together. That's this doctor's prognosis."

An entire life together? I flashed on those elderly couples in restaurants who sip wine, look off, content to sit in silence, resigned to the fact that their original spark had long been extinguished. Was I not ready for this move with anyone, or was I not ready for this move with Beth?

"You get an *A* in mechanics," I said. "Now, can I say something?"

"Let me finish." She crossed her arms and legs at the same time. "I'm doing everything I can to make this transition as painless and as unthreatening for you as possible, including a twenty-four-hour escape clause. This isn't easy for me either, Jack. And I know it scares the hell out of you. But I'm not going to hang around forever. And I'm certainly not going to beg."

I listened for a moment to a street musician on the boardwalk singing *Danny Boy* in Farsi.

"My turn?" I asked.

"Go ahead."

I didn't know where to start. So, of course, I started in the wrong place. "I've never lived with a girl before."

She moaned. "I'm not a girl. I'm the woman you sleep with."

"Just let me finish this script," I said. "Then, we can talk about *our* script."

"What will you know then that you don't know now?"

She was right. It was time for me to get off the pot. Why couldn't I commit to this good woman at that very moment, babies and all? On paper, she was everything I ever wanted, *plus* being a doctor.

I took her hand. "We'll make the right decision," I said.

"I already have. I never thought it would be this difficult for you."

"Commitments aren't easy to commit to."

She stood. I stood. We held hands.

"Jack, this change should feel as natural and right to you as it does to me," she said. Our hands parted. "I won't harass you anymore. Just know that I love you. I want to live with you. And I want a future with you." The stoic doctor's big hazel eyes were turning red. "And, yes, I want your children." With the sound of crashing waves in the background, she ended with, "And there's no greater love than that."

Although I should have been overjoyed, instead all my major organs seized up and shut down. She waited, probably for me to say that I felt exactly the same way about her as she did about me. That I didn't need one more second to make this life-transforming decision, that we were meant to be together, like Elsa and Ethan, that I wanted her to be the mother of my children. That I had made my decision. That she was the one for me. The future for me. That I loved her, too.

But I couldn't move my lips. Or even take her in my arms. Our opposites weren't attracting.

She put her helmet back on. "This isn't an ultimatum, Jack. But it is my best and final offer." She turned and skated away.

I stood there feeling very much alone. And pissed off. My potential life partner had pushed me into the last corner. My work partner had pushed me into saying things that came out wrong. I don't believe it's enough to just have the hots for someone. Hell, I had plenty of hots for Beth. But I would hold out for love—true love—like the pig-headed guy I was.

Fiona, who stood under a distant streetlamp, caught my eye, and offered a sympathetic smile. She proudly held up a waste bag full of Rathbone's poop. Her mood had lightened, but mine had only darkened. I felt like a bag of poop.

Breathe.

Chapter 32
FIONA

JACK SAT IN the worn bucket seat next to me as I drove him from Figtree's back to his place. Neither of us spoke. I tuned the radio to a classical music station, letting it fill the silence and calm our nerves. In a short period of time, this nice young man and I had evolved from a formal student/teacher relationship into something inexplicable, indefinable, and perhaps way too informal. I didn't know who we were to him. Or to me, for that matter. As with Eddie and my dentist, I wondered whether Jack thought about me when we were apart. I wondered if he was becoming as confused as I was. I wondered if I was beginning to think of Jack as a contender for my heart. I wondered whether continuing this project together was healthy, proper, wise? I wondered where this partnership was leading. And whether he was wondering the same thing? I wondered if this man, who had been hidden in my emotional blind spot, liked me. Lastly, I wondered why I was just as insecure in my late forties as I was in my early teens.

I stopped the Mercedes at the curb in front of Palm Gardens, Jack's apartment building in Culver City. He made no effort to get out of the car. He just sat there, distraught, his eyes staring blankly ahead.

"I'll pick you up at the bakery tomorrow at one," I finally said. "We'll work through your lunch hour."

Jack made no attempt to respond. Or to leave. So, we just continued sitting there.

"Writing partners disagree. They argue. They make up. That's how it works." He didn't react.

"Collaborations are expected to collapse every so often. But an hour goes by, and it's like it never happened. As with any good relationship, a writing partnership is based on respect and honesty and, dare I say, a dollop of affection."

Still not a peep, nor did he flinch.

So, I ventured out. "Or is this about something else?"

He stayed quiet, frustrating the hell out of me.

"Writers are a strange breed. We're mentally deformed, in a good way," I said. "Our senses are on high alert around the clock. It's a basic liability and an essential asset. We feel things more intensely than the average John and Jane Doe. We get our feelings hurt more easily."

Still no reaction.

I ventured out even further, into treacherous terrain. "Do you want to talk about what's bothering you?"

He obviously didn't.

I turned off the engine, but kept Vivaldi playing in the background. "Writing partners, it's like a marriage," I said. "Except we get to go our separate ways at the end of the day. It's the best of both worlds." I leaned across Jack's body and opened his door. The handle came off in my hand. "So, go. We'll live to fight another day."

He didn't move a muscle.

After a long silence, I decided to let him into my life a little closer, a little deeper. Maybe it would help to uncork his silence. "I was fresh out of college when I started writing. First for a small newspaper in Boston, then for a big magazine in New York. My Brooklyn boyfriend at the time broke up with me because I was, in his words, a ghost. He said I floated in and out of his life, but I mostly drifted to my keyboard. He didn't want to compete with a computer. He concluded that I loved my writing more than I loved him. He concluded correctly."

I checked to see if Jack's face had registered any change of expression. It hadn't.

I continued. "In the phone banks of a PBS fundraiser, I met a fellow volunteer, Marvin, an obsessed artist. We were inseparable after that night. I loved him a whole lot more than my computer. He loved me a whole lot more than his canvas. We had a child, way too soon, but who we loved a whole lot more than anything on earth." I was rowing gently down the stream of consciousness late at night in the rusty red Mercedes with Vivaldi scoring my saga. "Hollywood called. They liked a short story

I had written and wanted to buy the rights to make it into a movie. Too naïve to know any better, I insisted that I be the one to write the script, having never written one. Of course, they said no. But so did I. It went back and forth. I'll never know why they agreed in the end. Marvin and I drove across the country, set up shop in Encino in an apartment smaller than this car, and did exactly what we had always dreamed of doing. Write and paint, side by side, and watch a little girl morph into a young woman overnight. What none of us ever imagined was the avalanche. I was buried for five years nursing my husband, raising Charlotte, living off royalties and residuals, unaware that our highly-recommended and scrupulous business manager was secretly draining our savings dry. After Marvin died, when I thawed out, I tried to write again. I couldn't get it back. Marvin had taken my mojo with him." I turned the radio off when that annoying jingle for *Kars4Kids* came on. "If you learn nothing else from me, remember this. Don't take a five-year leave from this town and expect to come back from where you left off. There are no open arms to greet you when you return. It's like starting all over, except you're an eternity older. Ancient, as some would say."

"You're far from 'thawed out,'" Jack said in a low voice. "Or 'ancient.'"

I was pleased to see he had rejoined the living. "No one had my back," I said. "I had to get tough to survive it all. I sewed myself a suit of thick armor and reentered the world."

"Where's that toughness getting you?"

"It gets me through one day at a time. But it takes its toll." I let that settle in. "Better to live a life that's devoid of toxins, but one that's open, that's trusting, that's loving. Wouldn't you agree?"

Again, he clammed up.

"Talk to me, Jack. Look at me. Scream at me. Anything."

Nothing. He just gazed out the front window.

"PLEASE."

"I wanted you to meet Beth, get to know each other, let me know what you thought of her. But no, you had to bolt from the table without giving her a chance."

"I was giving you space, a little privacy. Besides, you don't need my blessing, not in that department."

"She wants to move in. She wants to get married. She wants to have kids."

"Nothing unreasonable about that."

"She wants it all now."

"What do you want?"

He withdrew back inside his shell.

A night jogger ran by my car window, singing *Dancing Queen*, scaring the hell out of me.

I took a moment to regroup. "Beth is very pretty," I said. "I once had her thighs."

Jack pulled himself together, pushed open the car door, and stepped out. "See you tomorrow," he said. Then, he turned and leaned back into the car. "I'm good at the lovey-dovey stuff."

"I'm sure you are," I said.

"You know, writing it," he added hastily.

"You'll have your shot, when we get there," I said, looking into his eyes. "You know, writing it," I added hastily.

He closed the car door and walked heavily away.

I started the engine. It coughed and died. On the fourth attempt, it caught, and I puttered off, leaving a trail of thick black smoke in my wake.

Although the freeway would have been faster, I drove on surface streets back to my home in the Hollywood Hills. It took nearly an hour. I needed the extra time to figure out how to tell Jack our partnership was over. He would have to finish the script alone. And keep all the money.

Whatever I had got myself into, I had to get out of. Again, never use a preposition to end a sentence with.

I WAS TOO upset that night to sleep. I tried everything. I medicated. I meditated. I paced. I read. I watched TV. I ate. I drank. I took Rathbone for a walk. I ate. I scrubbed my tub. I brushed my hair. I ate. I wrote a poem. I did yoga. I painted my toenails. I even thought of calling Eddie. I'm not known for making the best choices. I ended up back in bed at three in the morning, wide awake, watching the movie *Sense and*

Sensibility with Rathbone snoring next to me. On the other side of me, I had a large, now-empty bag of caramel popcorn.

At five-thirty in the morning, my phone rang, waking me from a deep slumber. My TV was still on at full volume. I reached for my phone.

"Speaking," I murmured.

Jack's voice was on the other end. *"They ransom the dragon back to the Rathbones, who pay them a million dollars."*

"Where are you?" I said in my feeble attempt to be coherent.

"I'm sitting on the beach, thinking, working, watching the most beautiful sunrise."

"The sun doesn't rise over the Pacific."

"I'm facing east, damn it," he said. *"They take the money, then call the police with an anonymous tip about some stolen goods, turning in the Rathbones."*

"Poetic justice," I said sleepily.

"Poetic justice," he said. *"Now, Elsa and Ethan are heroes."*

"And the audience will like them," I said.

"End of story. With a twist."

Silence.

"Write it down," I whispered, confirming that our partnership was still intact.

"I did."

I could hear seagulls crooning in the background. "This couldn't wait until tomorrow?"

"It is tomorrow."

Our partnership had survived its first quarrel. I'm glad my partner couldn't see me smile. Or dab a tear away. "I'll see you later, Jack," I said softly.

I hung up, feeling reborn. Feeling vindicated that poetic justice had been served.

Chapter 33
JACK

I WAS WORKING on a party cake at my decorating station when Fiona glided into the bakery. She looked like a supermodel in her white capris pants and green silk blouse. Everyone stared. She walked, in her neon orange sneakers, straight to me. Looking at the top of the cake where a toy golfer was teeing off, she read the inscription aloud.

"'Goodbye tension. Hello pension.'"

"What do you think?" I asked.

"I think you're too young to retire."

"I was about to last night."

"Me, too."

Peace. Collaborators once again.

She looked around. "Nice office."

"If you like sugar."

"My longest relationship has been with sugar."

I noticed my co-workers were waiting to be introduced. I took my cue. "Benny. Come here. I want Mister Bliffer, the boss himself, to meet the mentor herself, Fiona Logan."

Benny shuffled over. "Take our picture together, Jack. To put up on the wall of fame. I need to be standing next to a beautiful woman, or at least someone still alive."

I accommodated, whipping out my phone and snapping a shot of tiny Benny with his arm wrapped around Fiona's tiny waist.

Eleanor joined us. "Hello, dear," she said to Fiona. "Don't get any ideas about my husband. He's taken. For fifty-seven years. Fifty-seven *long* years."

Everyone laughed.

Except Shanelle. She approached cautiously as Eleanor led Benny back to work.

"And this is Shanelle, my number one ally here. She protects me from blunt force trauma. You know, a pumpernickel to the side of the head."

"Nice to meet you," Shanelle said. "Jack has told us so little about you."

I didn't know whether Shanelle meant it as a joke or as an insult, but I swiftly went into my neurotic crisis management. "I try not to mix my work with my work." I turned to Fiona. "Shanelle is my roommate's fiancé. His name is Kevin. You would like him. Great guy. Moves well to his left, amazing outside shot. Well, he *used* to be my roommate." I was starting to spin out of control again. "Now, they're living together. Isn't that great? Remember? That's why I needed the money from our script, to pay Kevin's portion of rent on my two-bedroom apartment until either I become a gainfully employed screenwriter, or I move into some place less expensive, or I get a new roommate, or—"

"Or his spectacular girlfriend moves in with him and pays half the rent, which she's offered," Shanelle said. "Did you know Jack had a girlfriend?"

"We met briefly last night," Fiona said. She turned to me. "I think we should get to work before your lunch break is over."

"Yes. That's precisely what we shall do." Once again, I went overboard trying to defuse the tension. "Perhaps all of us could have dinner together sometime. Beth and me, or as she would say 'Beth and I,' the scintillating Shanelle and Kevin, and Fiona and whoever—or is it *whomever*—she would like to bring. How fun would that be?"

"Fun-nomenal," Fiona said.

"Enjoy your afternoon delight," Shanelle said, returning to work.

When Shanelle was out of ear shot, Fiona asked, "What was that all about?"

"Too much sugar."

"Seriously."

"You tell me. It's a woman thing. Trust issues. Fear of abandonment. Probably goes back to the womb." I had become deranged. I had no idea what I was saying. "Eve should never have bitten into that apple. Swans mate for life. So, why can't—"

"Everyone realizes that there's no reason for jealousy here, right?"
"Oh, my gosh, of course. Why in the world would—"
"We just write together."
"That's all. Write, write, write. Sometimes we eat a little."
"When we finish the script, we go our separate ways."
"Yes, that's the deal," I said definitively. "Let's go eat a little."
I took off my apron and hastily escorted Fiona out the door.

Chapter 34

FIONA

JACK HAD NEVER been to L.A.'s famed Pink's Hot Dog stand on the corner of La Brea and Melrose, a local treasure. I took great pride in dragging out-of-state relatives to this modest but legendary eatery. There was always a mile-long line, limousines idling out front, and celebrities milling inside.

We sat at a two-person round table in the patio. I nursed a tame veggie dog, while Jack wolfed down the first of two gargantuan chilidogs. Across from us, a few Dodger relief pitchers were having a friendly food fight. It's that kind of place.

Jack devoured his hot dog as if he had just survived a hundred days in a life raft. I spread out the index cards and opened my laptop. This was to be a no-small-talk working lunch. As Jack took monstrous bites, I raised my bottle of Dr. Brown's cream soda and offered a toast to his Dr. Brown's root beer.

"The heavy lifting is over. We've done the research. We've created our story, invented our characters, defined the relationships, designed the—"

"Now? Now, can we actually put pencil to paper? Fingertips to keyboard?"

"Yes." We clinked bottles. "Here's to a great script."

"I've been waiting forever for this moment," he said.

"It's time to face the natural enemy of the writer, the daunting blank page."

"Let's bang this puppy out, turn it in early, and cash that fat check," Jack said, taking a sloppy bite of his second dog.

He had such zest. Such gusto. Such an appetite for living. And eating. I gave Jack the other half of my veggie dog.

"I ike diss pace," he said with his mouth full.

"I'll wait."

He swallowed and translated. "I like this place. I wonder if we can make it one of our locations in the script."

"We can do whatever we want. That's the power of being a writer."

Jack stopped chewing for the first time since we sat down. "Wouldn't it be great if we really *could* do whatever we wanted, that we could write our own life story? What would you write for yourself?"

His question rattled me. "I would start writing this script that we're so behind on."

"Seriously. What would you do, Fiona?"

"Seriously. You're wasting time."

"I really want to know." He was looking through me.

"You're really stalling," I said.

"Tell me." He leaned forward. "If you could do anything, off paper, what would it be?"

Was he testing me?

"Let yourself go," he coaxed.

Was he teasing me?

"Anything. Come on. Get selfish. Be a writer. Play God."

What the hell was he doing?

"Fantasizzzze," he growled.

I blushed. I couldn't look at him anymore. "We have writing to do. That's why we're here."

"Go a little crazy."

"You're avoiding," I said.

"*You're* avoiding. I'm warming up. Flexing my creative muscles, getting in the mood."

"How long does that usually take?"

"I'm almost there. I just need to get us on the same wavelength, so that we'll work well as a team. The better I know you, the better we'll write together."

"That's not how it works."

"It does on the basketball court. Kevin and I can crush anyone two-on-two. It's because we know each other so well. We trust each other."

"That's very nice. And has nothing to do with writing."

"You've told me about your past, but I don't know anything about your present life or future dreams. You know all about my business. It's only fair, as partners, that you share something of the current you. We can't write together if we're just two strangers sharing a wiener."

"Fine." I caved in. "On hot summer days, I put my pillow in the freezer."

"Something more intimate."

"I sleep with that pillow between my knees."

"Lucky pillow." He smiled.

I scowled. "That's it. That's all you get," I said.

"Do you have a boyfriend?"

"We're not discussing my personal life."

"A girlfriend?"

"Stop."

"It's a simple yes or no. Do you have someone special in your life?"

We looked at each other. Unless I broke the stalemate, we wouldn't get any work done. If I said "yes," I could eliminate much of our magnetism, construct boundaries between us, separating any further thought of crossing the proverbial line of propriety. If I said "no," it could open the floodgates and make me available to a taken man—if he harbored any attraction to me—complicating my life in ways I'd rather not contemplate.

"Yes," I said with great confidence. "I have someone special."

Jack seemed a bit disappointed. Or was I reading that into it?

"He's a strong, faithful, affectionate guy."

"You've never talked about him. What's his name?"

"Mister Bone," I said.

"That's cringey. What's his first name?"

"Rath."

He smiled.

"Nobody loves me more," I said.

"So, you're a single lady with an affectionate dog."

"Flying solo. Free as a bird. Lots of fun on Valentine's Day."

"Being single isn't so bad," Jack said, gauging my response. "You can do anything you want. You can play God."

We let the conversation simmer down as an afternoon breeze cooled us.

After a fair amount of silence, Jack asked, "What do we write first?" He seemed content to end his inquisition.

"Fade In."

"What do we write after that?"

"About twenty-thousand more words."

"Well, we've already built the house. Now, all we have to do is furnish the rooms," he said.

"It's not that simple. We'll write some of it together, some of it apart. You'll take one scene, I'll tackle another. We'll exchange our work and edit each other. We don't necessarily have to write the scenes in the order they appear in the movie. We can bounce around."

"Nothing wrong with bouncing around."

I loved that image. "We'll work day and night to meet our deadline. Don't expect to sleep. And don't complain about it. We've got five days before we type the words Fade Out."

"Let's do it."

In my head, I was hearing a double meaning to everything he said. I had trespassed into dangerous territory. Jack had thrown me off my game. Making me say things I would never say. Making me think of doing things I would never do. Or was that the old me? Was I willing to live in the now, now?

I shook it off. After all, I was a professional. We had a job at hand. We were writing partners. No more, no less. Soon to go our separate ways. Sitting just two miles from Hollywood and Vine, I spoke those two sacred words as I tapped them into my laptop, "Fade In."

"Nice work, God," Jack said.

LATER THAT NIGHT, this God was in bed. Eyes shut. Half asleep. In the twilight zone. Going a little crazy in my head. Wondering if Jack would take me up on my silly little dare, a farcical game that I had invented in a lightheaded moment and suggested we play after our long working supper at a crowded diner around the corner from Jack's apartment. After he had walked me outside, and I had steadied myself against a dry, gusting Santa Ana wind, below a brooding sky, under the purple canape of a Jacaranda tree. After the cognac, which was after the wine, which was before the weed. I was so stoned. And drunk. And randy.

"You're all Jack, talk," I had said in my blitzed state. "Take two. You're all talk, Jack."

"I suggest you take a giant aspirin when you get home," advised the one who had imbibed just enough not to drive. "Some say eating a banana before bed can help a hangover."

"What if one night you found the key I hid under my doormat?" I had asked.

"Uh?"

"It would be dark. No streetlamp. No porchlight. You wouldn't be able to see a thing," I had said. "A night like tonight. Just like tonight," I had hinted. "In fact, tonight," I had unashamedly proposed.

"I also recommend some coffee," he had said. "Maybe an entire urn."

"Will you unlock the front door to my apartment? If you do, you'll discover that wrapped around the inside door handle will be a string, a very long string, the other end of which will be found in my bedroom, at the foot of my bed, tied around my left toe."

"You're making no sense," he had said in his charming way. "Take two bananas and call me in the morning." He wasn't making much sense either.

"Don't worry. Rathbone knows you. He won't bark. He won't bite. There will be no lights left on for you in my apartment. Pitch black darkness. That's part of the fun, the mystery, the erotism. Be careful. Watch your step. I strung the string to lead you clear of all the furniture. Move slowly. Trust the string. Follow it, hand over hand, through the living room, down the hall, past Charlotte's room, into mine."

Jack had been working his phone. "Your Uber's a block away."

"Once in my room, you're not to speak. I'm not to speak. Only our bodies can communicate." Where had I found the nerve to proposition him so audaciously? Must have been from the cognac. Must be why I never drink cognac.

"Are you being serious or just being un-sober? Either way, it's kind of kinky."

"Slide your fingertips along the string until you've reached the end of my bed and felt my foot and touched my toe."

"Feet. Toes. It's all getting very fetishy." He had looked down the street, catching sight of an approaching Honda. "Ah, here it is. Driver's name is Amir." Jack had waved down the car.

"Then, undress," I had said. "Then, come onto my bed. Then, let me make love to you."

There it was. A seismic suggestion. Out in the open. Out loud. Outrageous.

He had just stood there, incredulous, holding open the back door of the Honda. He was speechless. Motionless. But if he had the guts to accept my offer, he would learn what I already knew. That this blustery summer night would be the greatest night of either of our lives. It would be downright awesomely epic.

Jack had folded my legs into the back of the Honda. Amir drove me away. Had I embarrassed myself beyond repair? Had God totally lost her mind? Had I gotten myself into something great?

I HAD A hard time finding the keyhole. The summer windstorm had caused a power outage in the Hollywood Hills, in my neighborhood. At the Casa del Sol, everything was black. No streetlights. No porchlights. It was deliciously dark.

I washed down two aspirins with a pot of coffee and went to bed, where I now lay, knowing Jack would never walk through my door. It was too late, too wildly windy, too soon. Too loony. Too extreme. Too wrong. I would actually lose respect for him if he *did* appear. I had already lost respect for myself. It was all a crazy, pot-liquor-induced, out of the blue idea. Entirely unlike me, other than the demented inventiveness of it all.

If he opened my front door, it would completely disrupt our lives. He was too smart, too encumbered, and too honorable to play my uncharacteristically capricious game. One thing was for certain, though. I'd never smoke a joint or drink cognac again. Never.

IT WAS ALREADY three in the morning. I was jittery. I had consumed too much caffeine. I couldn't sleep. I would apologize later that day at our writing session. He would laugh and say he knew I was kidding about that silly string seduction scheme. He would write it off to my whimsical imagination. And the dope and alcohol. He would understand and forgive this older lady's advances. He might even suggest we write the zany notion into our script.

But, as I lay naked in my bed listening to the wind chimes jingle, I couldn't help but wonder if he ever, even for a nanosecond, considered coming over and following the string, which stretched from the front door to my big toe, from innocent to guilty, from my hope to my heart.

That was my last thought before a heavy sleep finally stole my out-of-control mind.

THE SOUND OF the front door squeaking open and the warm wind whistling through awoke me. I sat up in the darkness. All I could hear was the beating in my chest. Had my prince valiantly come? I was stunned but thrilled. Rathbone knew Jack's scent. There was no cause for alarm. My hound dog merely jumped off my bed and moved to the kitchen for a sip of water.

The slack in the string pulled taut. There was a slight tug on my toe. I shivered. I tingled. My nipples hardened. My deep yearning would soon be over. My long-locked libido was about to be unleashed. Jack was steps away from the best sex of his life, if I don't mind saying so myself.

I heard slow, quiet footsteps approaching. I heard Jack rest his backpack against the doorframe as he entered my bedroom, obeying the rules of silence. In the blackness, I couldn't distinguish the contours of his build. But I didn't need the sense of sight to enhance my soaring exhilaration.

I felt Jack's hand caress my foot and lightly uncoil the string from my toe. He had arrived. He had found me. My body vibrated in anticipation. I heard him disrobe. I lay back, drawing the satin sheet aside, parting my legs, and offering myself. He paused to relish the moment.

No need to rush now. We had waited so long. Been so patient. Shown such restraint. Acted so ethically. We had been good. We were about to be bad. On the verge of being phenomenal.

His tongue started at the sole of my foot, curled around my heel, and licked unhurriedly up my body, lingering to explore every trembling inch, every crevice, until finding my tongue.

Soon, he was on top of me with enveloping heat. Naked body on naked body. Mouth on mouth. Cognac breath on cognac breath. Our bodies instinctively knew how to move in rhythm, as if we had been lovers from the beginning. My hands were everywhere, enjoying his every curve and sinew. His sculpted body was flawless.

It felt so right. My head was spinning. The wind whirled outside, snapping tree branches against the windowpane. His fingers moved with the proficiency and sensitivity of a masseur. Tenderly. Expertly. He knew where and when to touch and the right amount of pressure to apply. A gentle fondle. A harmless bite. A painless slap. He knew precisely how to elicit the most intense response. A hard sucking. A soft pinch. What had grown into a gale force wind whipped the window screens. My body writhed under his weight, screaming to be entered. Every nerve ending was on fire. I couldn't catch my breath. I was deliciously wet. I was ready.

I wanted him that instant. I couldn't control myself any longer. I shattered my own insistence on silence when I cried out, "Love me, Jack. Love me, now."

As he became part of me, plunging deep within, I heard a recognizable but out of place sound. At first, I thought it was Jack's skull banging repeatably against the headboard. But soon I realized it was a pounding at my front door. I tried to disregard it, bracing for our rapidly approaching, mind-blowing, simultaneous orgasm. My body twisted and convulsed in spasms of elation. But the rapping on the door only became louder, more persistent, more infuriating, so piercing that it drummed out the hot swirling winds, the rattling four-poster, and our escalating cries of rapture. Finally, Rathbone's barking and the incessant hammering on the door woke me.

Woke me? What? Had I been sleeping? Had I dreamt the whole toe escapade the whole time? Had the screenwriter's God-like mind been fantasizzzzing? Had my dream state really played another ruthless, pitiful prank on me?

What in the hell was my subconscious thinking? As creative as I might be, I would never have made such a sick and preposterous overture to Jack, nor to anyone else. And drunk on cognac? No way. Just wasn't me. And pot? I'd never even tried the stuff.

Again, there was a deafening knocking on my front door.

Breathless and perspiring, I struggled out of bed, noticed I was still wearing my clothes from the night before, threw my robe over them, and staggered to the living room. My head was throbbing. "Who is it?" I called out.

"Your phone's off."

"Jack?"

"We agreed to meet at six," Jack shouted. "Come on."

I had to pull myself together. This wasn't how I imagined our first post-coital moment. I cracked open the door. Daylight rudely rushed in. "Don't look at me," I said, turning away.

"Big night?"

"You know how it is. Dinner, dancing, drinking, crawling from club to club," I said. "Come in."

"Are you sure?" Jack asked, peeking past my shoulder into my apartment.

"Yes. Why?"

"Well, you look like you might have been entertaining."

"Nobody's here, Jack," I said sharply, gathering my wild, sweaty hair into a low bun. "Not that it would be out of the question, mind you."

Jack entered. "I'm sure you have a very active social life."

"Canasta on Tuesdays. Bingo on Thursdays—"

"I wasn't implying—"

"That I didn't have plenty of suitors down at the senior center?"

"That's not what—"

"You can make yourself something to eat while I get dressed," I said. "Oh, I just remembered."

"What?"

"Shuffleboard on Sundays." I started to walk down the hall but stopped under the archway. "Last night."

"What about it?"

"Did I fizzle out?"

"After the pizza and wine, after a long game of Scrabble and more wine, after we wrote 'til two in the morning. After you put your shoes in the microwave, yeah, you were out on your bare feet and tootled off to bed. Didn't even say 'see ya at the movies.'"

How about see ya in my dreams? I said to myself. "Sorry," I said to Jack.

I toddled back to my bedroom, feeling relieved. It *was* just a dream. I *hadn't* made a fool of myself by luring Jack to my bed in such a lascivious way. True, I desired him. But next time, it would have to be with no strings attached.

Chapter 35

JACK

Fiona, with little notebook in hand, let me walk Rathbone on a long leash as we climbed the switchback trails of Runyon Canyon at sunrise. Early morning runners, professional dog walkers, and gossiping mountaineers trudged up and down one of Tinseltown's more fashionable hikes. You couldn't go fifty feet without spotting some ingénue jogging on the path alongside her personal trainer and diamond-collared Labradoodle.

Fiona, whose shapely legs looked great in cut offs, was lecturing me on the importance of having a broad outline and detailed treatment before launching into the script stage.

"There are no shortcuts," she said. "Every film student wants to just jump in and start writing a script. That's like jumping into your car and driving to Milwaukee without a roadmap."

"They've got something new now called GPS."

"The point is, that's why I made us take the time to lockdown the outline. It's our blueprint. Now, we can fill in the blanks."

"Well, so far so good. We've written all but no pages," I said. "That ain't gonna get the job done."

"We had to be sure that every beat of every scene was absolutely right before we even thought of writing the dialogue."

"When do you know it's absolutely right?" I asked.

"When it feels right."

"How do you know when it feels right?"

"When it stops keeping you up at night."

Rathbone tried to take off after a squirrel.

I pulled his leash tight. "So, if I'm still thinking about something, it's not right?"

"Are we still talking about our outline?"

"Yeah," I said. "And Beth."

We stopped walking. "Is she keeping you up at night?"

"I have some decisions to make about her."

"Well, you can deal with that in a few days. For now, we're going to remain on task, stay on schedule, and knock out at least twenty pages today and—"

"You're right. I'm sorry. We're here to work."

Fiona walked ahead of me, so I barely heard her say, "Do you want her to move in?"

"I keep thinking I do," I said to the back of her head.

"Maybe it's the words 'I do' that keep you thinking."

"What do you mean?" I said, sprinting to catch up.

We continued to follow the rocky trail up the mountain. "I'm good at outlines, Jack. I don't give relationship advice. Ask your therapist."

"I don't have one."

"You live in L.A. and don't have a therapist? What, are you crazy?"

"She wants to get married."

"Women her age don't cohabitate for convenience."

"When did you know that it was right with Marvin?"

"I'm not comfortable talking about this."

"Was it at first sight, or did it take time?"

"Both."

"And when you had to decide—"

"I didn't have to think about it. I didn't lose one second of a night's sleep."

An elderly couple passed us. They weren't sipping wine and looking off. They were still ascending the mountain together, step by step, hand in hand.

"It felt right?" I asked Fiona.

"It felt right," she answered.

"No thinking?"

"No thinking."

We hiked farther up the trail. Rathbone was in heaven. So many smells to smell. So many celebrity dog butts to sniff.

"So, you easily got married," I said.

"'Til death did we part," she said. "Not even then."

"What do you mean?"

"He's never left."

I observed a moment of silence. It was the reverential thing to do. We walked to the top of the next rise, a lookout point just under the Hollywood sign. I followed Fiona's eyes up to the huge white, historic cutout letters.

"It's a sign," she said, "that it's time to write the dialogue."

Chapter 36
FIONA

I was on my hands and knees, not a very sultry position, painting the wood picket fence that separated the front of Casa del Sol from the street.

Jack sat on the curb with his laptop balanced on his knees.

Rathbone looked on, listening in.

"The language has to be unique to the characters," I said. "The voices need to be distinct and consistent."

"How do we do that?" Jack asked.

"When what's-his-name—"

"Ethan."

"When Ethan speaks, he has to sound different from what's-her-name—"

"Elsa," he said. "Ethan would probably have a deeper voice."

I tried not to roll my eyes. "They are of different genders and ages. They come from different countries and backgrounds. It must all be reflected in their choice of words, the way they talk, what they say, how they say it. That's the art of writing dialogue."

"Let's write some already."

"First, we need to improv."

"Great," Jack said. "What does that mean?"

"Writers use the actor's technique of improvisation to explore their characters. We act out the scene."

"Sounds like fun."

"You play the role of 'him' and I play the part of 'her.'"

"I'm tall, dark, and handsome," Jack said. "And you're Danish, but with red hair."

"You forgot drop-dead gorgeous."

"Young, handsome pool man and older, drop-dead gorgeous nanny," he said. "I can't wait to do this."

"Pick a scene, any scene," I said, dipping my brush into the paint can.

Jack scrolled through our treatment on his computer. "Scene thirty-two. The one where they first discover they're attracted to each other."

"You would select that one," I said under my breath.

"I've been waiting a long time to write the lovey-dovey stuff."

"I know, I know. But jot down what we say as we say it. That's the writing part," I stressed. "We'll clean it up later."

"Great, here I go." Jack read from the document on his screen. "Ethan and Elsa are outside, around the swimming pool in the enormous backyard of the Rathbone's mansion. Ethan is cleaning the leaves out of the water with a skimmer. The Rathbones are away at their country club. Elsa has put the children down for a nap and is coming to give Ethan a glass of orange juice. Ethan wears shorts but has his shirt off." He hesitated a beat and turned to me. "Should I take my shirt off?"

"Not necessary." Though I would have enjoyed that.

Jack closed his eyes, shook out his arms, rolled his head, and drew a deep contemplative breath like an actor does before he goes into character. "Hi," he said as Ethan.

"It's so hot," I said in a poor Scandinavian accent, portraying Elsa, while continuing to paint the fence. "I thought you might want something cold to drink."

"Thank you."

"I squeezed the oranges myself."

"Thank you."

"Added a mint leaf to make it look special," I said.

"Thank you."

I became slightly exasperated. "Jack, you're supposed to be feeling something here."

"I'm feeling grateful. You know, for the juice. And that was so nice of you to include the mint."

"'Thank you, thank you, thank you,' isn't interesting writing. This scene is about their unspoken attraction. It has to move the story along, bring the relationship closer, show the characters' suppressed desire for one another. That's the purpose of the scene."

"Right."

"Do you think you can do that?"

"Yeah, I got this. Let me try again."

"Think clever, witty, with a soupcon of sexual tension."

"Soupcon?"

"Just a touch. It's the subtext."

"All these fancy words."

"Put yourself in the moment. Act the part. Become Ethan," I said. "Be attracted to me."

"I'll try."

"I know it's a stretch."

"What is?"

"Just give it another go."

There we were, outside on the street, performing a little play, trying to portray a little romance, as the aggravating sound of a leaf blower blasted through the neighborhood.

Jack typed the words we spoke as we spoke them.

"Hi," he said.

I kept slapping paint on the slats of the fence. "Hi."

"Is that juice for me?" he asked.

"I thought you might need something to cool yourself off."

"What time are the Rathbones coming home?" he asked.

"Why?"

"Just wondering."

"Not for a couple hours."

"I know what will cool us off."

"Us?"

"Your cheeks are red," Jack said. "A little dip will do ya."

I looked up from my brushwork. "I can't. I'm working."

"This is America. Land of the free."

"I'll get in trouble."

"Home of the brave." Jack took a moment. I noticed that he had stopped typing. He was slowly transforming into his character or vice versa. Cars drove back and forth on the street as he read from the treatment. "'Ethan puts down his pool skimmer, takes off his sneakers, and eases into the water,'" Jack said. "Join me."

"I could be fired," I said.

"Nobody will know," he said.

"They have cameras everywhere," I said.

"It's not like we're committing a crime." Jack referred to the treatment. "'Elsa looks at Ethan.'"

"I'm afraid," I said, expressing some real feelings.

Jack got up off the curb and moved closer to me. He brought his laptop with him.

I forced myself to keep painting.

"I come to this mansion once a week, Elsa," Jack said. "Once a week we say hi, and you kindly bring me something to eat or drink. And I say thank you. That's all we are to each other. Two well-mannered employees exchanging pleasantries. 'Elsa is feeling nervous, conflicted.' But we both know there's something else happening here between us. You've felt it. I know by the way you look at me. I've felt it when I look at you, when I think about you. You keep me up at night thinking about you. How about today, right now, we start telling the truth, say what we're really thinking, what we're really feeling? How about we do that, Elsa?"

"I can't," I said. "Not now. Not here."

Jack snapped his fingers like he had just remembered something. "If not now, when? If not here, where?"

I was rendered wordless. This innocent exercise had evolved into something perilously close to our own situation. I shouldn't have suggested it. My mouth was dry. My palms were wet. My neckline began to blotch. Rathbone was entranced.

Jack paused. "Fiona?"

I couldn't speak.

He tried again. This time with, "Elsa?"

"What?" I clucked.

"It's your turn."

"Uh, sure," I said, emerging out of my stupor. "Go ahead. Say what you're feeling, Ethan." I stopped painting. "*Klaphesten.*"

"What was that last word?"

"It means 'please' in Danish."

"Wow. Is that really the word?" Jack asked.

"I made it up," I said too harshly. "Stay in character, Jack. Just keep talking."

He resumed his spontaneous speech. "That you and I are here, at this very moment in time, spinning on this tiny spec in space, is a miracle beyond belief. Something, some benevolent force, brought us together. That's what I think. We just have to embrace it. Then, it will be ours. That's how I feel. Despite our age difference." Jack was looking into my eyes. "'Ethan drifts slowly in the pool toward Elsa.' Life is too short to put off doing what you want. As my old pal Lucky once said, 'One has to maximize every fleeting moment. Because, well, tick, tick, tick.' 'Ethan opens his arms to Elsa.' Dive in. Take a chance. You'll never know how good it feels if you stay where you are, stuck in your thoughts, playing safe, unwilling to take the leap." Jack stepped forward toward me with his arms extended, inviting an embrace. "Take the plunge, Elsa. Just jump in."

A single engine plane flew overhead towing a banner that read *Marry Me, Meagan*.

The automatic sprinklers went on across the street. And the sparrows watched us from the phone wires above.

I was in a heightened state of awareness. I was hiding behind the character of Elsa. Her reality and my reality had intersected. All I could think to say was, "I can't."

"Why not?"

"I can't swim."

"I'll catch you."

"I'm scared."

"Trust me. 'Elsa looks around, deep in thought.'"

There was a long pause.

"Then what happened?" I said like a six-year-old being read a bedtime story.

Jack read on. "The drop-dead gorgeous nanny removes her sandals, sensually takes off her uniform, and stands before Ethan in her bra and panties."

"And then?"

"We wrote this. You know what happens next," Jack said.

"Don't stop. Keep saying things. Invent more dialogue," I stuttered. "Sometimes, when I hear the words, I think of better ways to write them." I didn't want the mood to wane. "Just keep talking. Improvise. Say what you feel. I mean what Ethan feels. Just dive in."

"Okay," Jack said, getting back in character. "Jump, Elsa. Change your life. Swim away with me." He looked back at the treatment. "'Elsa smiles timidly, pinches her nose, steps off the edge of the pool, and drops in the water, into the waiting arms of Ethan.'"

My brush was frozen in the air, white paint dripping off the handle down my arm. "And then?"

"And then, Ethan gently takes off her bra."

"He does?"

"Exposing two impeccably erect nipples."

"What?"

"Two impeccably erect—"

"Nipples?" I shrieked.

"That's right."

"You were doing so well. Why would you spoil everything by throwing in nipples?"

"I promised Bowman nipples. We forgot to put them in the outline, so I thought I'd add a couple now."

"It's not always about nipples."

"You keep saying nipples."

"These two people care about each other," I said. "Sure, there's a physical attraction. But there's also an emotional one. The nipples can wait. We'll get to them when we get to them." I stabbed my brush into the paint can. "You don't have to race into the sex stuff. Let them pace themselves. Give them time to acknowledge the love, to bask in it, to celebrate it. Have the sex be the end result of love, not the other way around. In other words, make Ethan different from every other goddamn man on earth."

Jack stepped back. "Okay. Geez," he said, then continued reading. "'They bob around in the water.' I mean Ethan and Elsa, not the nipples. 'And, for the first time, the older woman and the younger man embrace, resisting all temptation to go any farther.'" Jack added, "Despite the fact that they both want to get it on."

I held my tongue. "I'm just saying that we have to give their love time to develop. Remember, enjoy the journey. Don't rush to the end."

He sat down and began entering our dialogue in his laptop. Without looking up, he said, "By the way, Tom Sawyer, there's more paint on your face than on your fence."

Chapter 37

JACK

Rosco's House of Chicken and Waffles on west Pico Boulevard was, according to actuarial tables, the place to go to lower your life expectancy. I loved having breakfast there for dinner, but I'd advise you to leave your major arteries at the door. Rosco's was also Kevin's favorite place, so we all met there at eight. I hadn't seen Beth for a few days, since the Venice Boardwalk incident, and was nervous about having to face her. She wore her formal ER scrubs, the dark blue ones. Shanelle was all dolled up in sequins for a night on the town.

I was halfway through my Big Mamma Special when Beth turned to me and smiled. "I'm glad your teacher gave you the night off."

"Not quite. She had to fix a busted waterpipe. We're meeting again at midnight."

"That's just crazy."

We ate quietly.

Then, Beth asked, "So, how are you, Jack?"

"I'm eating my weight in waffles, but sitting next to someone who knows CPR. How bad could I be?" I took a big bite. It needed just another pint of syrup, which I poured on. "Did you know that syrup can destroy a home security system?" I said. "We learned that tasty little factoid by researching our script."

"Fascinating. How's the writing coming?" Beth asked.

"We've been going around the clock, working like coalminers."

"Sitting in a chair is back-breaking work?"

"Brutal. But we're getting closer to the end. We turn it in the day after tomorrow."

"Not to be too selfish, but I'll be glad when it's over."

"Me, too."

"Is that true?" she asked.

"Well, Benny will be. I've been in, but mostly out this week."

Shanelle entered the conversation. "Yeah, yesterday you left me with five miles of vanilla piping to do."

"When I make it big as a screenwriter, I'll bequeath you my most cherished icing nozzle."

"I'll be long gone from there by then," Shanelle said.

"Thanks for your vote of confidence," I said.

"Summer weddings. Not the best time to take off," Shanelle scolded. "The overtime pay will come in handy, but you killed me this week. Just sayin'."

"Speaking of weddings." Shanelle leaned over to talk to Kevin, leaving our conversation.

Beth turned to me. "There's talk that I'm up for some big international research project."

"That's great news," I said.

"It's not for certain yet, but it would entail some travel."

"Really great."

"That wasn't the response I was looking for." She sighed.

"I said 'great news.' What do you want?"

"It's not all about your script, you know."

"Where's that coming from?"

"We could be separated for weeks at a time. Do you have any feelings about that?"

"I'm just trying to eat dinner here."

Thankfully, Kevin threw his arm around me. "Who wants to split something called a Banana Cream Bonanza with chocolate sauce?" he asked, holding the dessert menu. "It's the size of a Macy's balloon."

"I might have a bite or three," I said. "But hold the chocolate sauce. I'm trying to watch my figure."

Beth's phone played the first bars of "Hello Zepp," the theme from *Saw*, signaling an incoming message. "Well, it's been fun," she said, reading the text.

"No. Don't go," Shanelle begged.

"A shootout in downtown." Beth snatched her keys off the table. "Friday night. Paychecks and booze. Bad combo."

"I thought we were going dancing," Kevin said.

"At least I almost made it through dinner this time."

I helped Beth on with her sweater.

"Four years of med school, and now the good times begin. Murders, killings, and assaults."

"Stabbings and gunshots and rapes. Oh, my," I added.

"Shit. I was really looking forward to tonight." Beth got up from the table. "Sorry, guys. Time to stop the bleeding."

I ESCORTED BETH out of the restaurant and walked her to her car. "Drive carefully," I said. "Sorry we didn't get to—"

"To what, Jack? Eat? Talk? Dance? Finish our fight?"

"All the above."

"See ya when I see ya," she said. "Story of my life. Our life."

"The research thing. That's so good. I'm really proud of you."

"Yeah. Thanks."

We exchanged a quick kiss, and she sped off, disappearing down Pico Boulevard in her burgundy mini coup. And oddly, I wasn't sorry our night had been shortened. I realized that I didn't want to go dancing. And I didn't want to go back into the restaurant. I wanted to be with my writing partner, to be working side by side at midnight. That's what I truly wanted.

Chapter 38

FIONA

SINCE HER THYROID operation, my therapist Dr. Aaronson only practiced two days a week. I didn't see her on a regular basis anymore anyway. She had released me back into the wild a year earlier, after I had shed years of tears in her office over Marvin's passing. From time to time, crisis to crisis, setback to setback, I had popped in for a psychological tune-up. A mental reboot. A spiritual booster shot.

Dr. Aaronson didn't want to be my friend, despite the energy I put out to have her like me. She was kind, but all business. And, at age seventy-two, she knew all the tricks that patients played clamoring to be her favorite client.

Her fourth-floor office overlooked the collegiate streets of Westwood Village. You could hear the chatter of UCLA coeds outside hustling to class below. The interior walls of the office were made of old brick and lined with calming lithographs of landscapes and an antique clock to remind everyone of when their fast fifty minutes had elapsed. Next to the window sat a cushy leather chair, which I called a womb with a view. I sank into it and brought my knees to my chest, holding on tight for what I predicted was going to be an internal breakdown. Knowing me all too well, Deana—I never called her Dr. Aaronson—slid a newly opened box of Kleenex closer to me.

"Your Boston Fern is doing well," I said, pointing out her corner plant. "Indirect light is the key." I fiddled with my pendant. Interlocking silver hearts. A no-special-occasion gift from Marvin.

Deana smiled and got comfortable in her pricey wicker armchair.

"My daughter is good. That's the main thing, right?" I said. "She's in Spain, having a ball and sometimes studying." I snapped the fingers of both hands, castanet-style, over my head. "*Olé*."

Deana was not amused.

We sat there, listening to the hissing of a busses' air brakes out the open window.

"Have you ever been to Madrid?" I asked.

She wasn't biting. "Let's talk about you. How are you, Fiona?"

"Me? Oh, I'm good. Thank you for asking." I listened to the clock tick. At four dollars a minute. "It's nothing serious," I said. "Just a nasty case of...."

"Yes?"

"I guess I'd call it 'decidophobia.' Fear of making—"

"A decision. I get it. Tell me more."

"There's not much to say."

"Then, why are you here?"

"I wouldn't be here if Marvin was still here." I burst into tears. Head in lap, whole body trembling, hand groping for tissues. I had made so many breakthroughs in that office. I may have been on the threshold of another, if I could only stop crying.

Deana waited patiently for me to compose myself, at four dollars a minute.

"Am I backsliding?" I sniffled.

"No. You're human."

With that, I bawled once more. It felt good. I needed the catharsis, the cleansing. In forty-six minutes, Deana would send me into the world again feeling, at the very least, human. "I haven't opened my heart to anyone else," I said, choking on my tears, clutching my pendant. "I can't seem to leave Marvin."

"You will when you're ready."

"It's been four years, Deana. Four effin' years."

"When you're ready."

"It's not that I'm looking for anyone, or that I need anyone. I'm perfectly happy being alone." Contradicting that statement came another therapeutic tsunami of tears. I tugged a train of tissues out of the Kleenex box.

"Don't worry," Deana said. "When that one's gone, there's toilet paper down the hall."

I managed to pull myself together long enough to ask, "Double ply?"

Deana waited for my bottom lip to stop quivering. "What would you like from me today?"

I took out a blue, three by five index card, and read my list of grievances. "I got fired from my teaching job."

"I'm sorry. Why did you get fired?"

"Because I stink at teaching."

"I doubt that," she said.

"But I seem to be a natural at changing lightbulbs and snaking toilets. I'm still the empress of Casa del Shithole."

"A small price for living rent-free."

"It helps me afford you." A distant car alarm distracted me. "I still can't get any real writing work."

"I'm sure you're trying."

"Thank you, Deana. Thank you for saying that," I said. "I know the meter's running, but I'd like to cry some more, if you don't mind."

"You can use the time however you want. It's your session."

"Great. I'll be with you in just a moment." At which time, I cried again, emptying the Kleenex box. After a big blow of my little nose, I said, "A man picked me up at the supermarket."

"Up? Like off the floor?"

"He made a pass at me."

"Oh, I see. And how did that turn out?"

"I ended it."

"Why?"

"Because he drinks too much."

"That's a good reason."

"He was very good-looking."

"You made the right decision. What else?" she inquired.

"He was rich."

"I meant on your list."

I consulted my card. "My roots are gray."

"Use a red Sharpie. Next?"

"I'm thinking of having my boobs done."

"How come?"

"They're going south on me."

"Okay."

"But I probably won't. These will have to do."

"Then, why did you bring them up, so to speak?"

"Because the next item is harder." I put the blue index card back in my handbag and sucked in a mouthful of potpourri-scented air. This was why I made the appointment. This is why I fought the traffic, took a half-hour to find sixteen dollar parking, walked up four flights to sit in this safe space. "I met a guy," I said haltingly.

"Supermarket guy?"

"No. Sober guy. Nice guy. The kind of guy I'd want my daughter to marry."

"You're smiling."

"He's younger."

"Is that why you're smiling?"

"Much younger."

"How does that make you feel?"

"Much older."

I was getting it out. It was time to face my feelings. And to face someone who could help. This was good. I was glad I was sitting there. Minute by minute, I was feeling the stress and strain decrease, along with my personal savings.

"It's not a romantic relationship. Nothing like that. I just like his company. We're working together on a writing project. He's pleasant to be with."

She nodded. "So, where does the indecision come in?"

I bowed my head, stared at my lavender tennis shoes. "He's been good for me. He makes me happy."

To hear myself say that out loud was also good for me. I felt more weight lift off. My breathing returned to normal. It was a revealing and important admission.

"Yeah, happy. Isn't that what we all want?" I said, celebrating with another crying jag. When I recovered, Deana poured me a glass of water. And handed me several sheets of paper towel.

"Maybe you're ready," she said.

"How would I know?"
"By that smile."
"But he's so young."
"You said that. Three times now." Deana straightened her skirt. "Is he old enough to vote?"
"I could take him across state lines, if that's what you mean."
"I had to ask," she said.
I took a sip of water. "Does age matter?"
"Does it to you?"
"It doesn't seem right."
"By whose standards?"
"Mine. I mean, I wouldn't let any of my friends get into something like that. And more to the point, I'm sure he doesn't think about me in amorous terms."
"Do you know that?"
"Carnal terms maybe. But I don't think he views me as romantic fodder. Did I just refer to myself as 'fodder?'"
"But if he *did* have romantic feelings, then what?"
I entertained the concept. My smile returned.
"What then?" Deana asked. "Would you decide to—"
"Did I mention he has a girlfriend? A serious girlfriend?"
Deana, who never made any judgments in that small room, remained stone-faced. And waited for me to hang myself.
"Too young. Only wants to get in my pants. Has a girlfriend, practically a fiancé," I said. "Ideal prospect, right? Do I sound ready?"
"Obviously, this young man has had a positive effect on you. Whatever happens, you're making emotional progress. And that, for you, Fiona, is a significant leap forward."
I spent the rest of my session doing what I wanted to do, crying.
Deana credited me a quarter hour.

I LEFT THAT office feeling validated and somewhat whole again. A two-hundred-dollar facial wouldn't have made me feel as good. Though I certainly could have used one after that uplifting yet depleting hour.

BETH AND BENNY had agreed to let me own Jack over the next three days and nights. We wrote nonstop. It was the final sprint. We argued, we laughed, we walked, we talked about movies, and we wrote and wrote. And ate and ate, taking catnaps in between. He was a good student, sponging up everything I taught him. He was a real trouper, standing shoulder to shoulder with me during the long nights. He was creative. He was committed. He was a writer.

Our first draft was nearly finished and was due to the sleazy producer the next day. Just a couple scenes left to write. Just a few more pages. Somehow, we had endured the ordeal. We took a break by walking Rathbone through the midnight fog that had shrouded my Hollywood Hills neighborhood.

I held Rathbone's leash firmly because of his habit of chasing after anything that moved, including skunks.

Jack collected litter in the street and put it into trash bins along our stroll. He said someone had to do it. He reminded me at times of a young Marvin. Responsible, dependable, conscientious. The essence of a decent person.

"I watched and studied every film I could," Jack said as we wandered the empty streets. "My dream was to move to Los Angeles and write movies."

"And now your dream has come true."

"Maybe if Bowman likes this one, he'll order more. Sequel after sequel, like *Saw*."

"Doubtful."

"I could quit the bakery," he said.

"Inadvisable."

"Would you write another script with me?"

"Let's finish this one first."

"You're not being very optimistic."

"I'll be optimistic when I see the money."

"Is there anyone you trust?" He waited for an answer. "Do you trust me?"

I stopped walking. "I don't trust myself," I said, wanting to take him to bed. My God, I actually gave in to that feeling.

After a moment, Jack raised his arms as if to embrace me, but let his hands fall to his sides, perhaps thinking a hug was a bridge too far. "Thank you," he said.

"You're welcome. For what?"

"For teaching me."

We shared a small, bittersweet smile. Then, Rathbone led us back to my apartment.

Chapter 39
JACK

It was daybreak at Casa del Sol. I squinted against the white light streaming through the lace curtains.

Fiona and Rathbone were asleep on one end of her couch as I, sitting on the other end, typed the final sentences of our script into my laptop.

I looked over at Fiona. Although her makeup had faded hours ago, she looked like a holy work of art. A Botticelli. Her wavy mane of red hair spilled over the black throw pillow. Her cheek rested on hands folded in prayer. Her heavenly lips allowed silent wisps of air in and out.

I wondered how many men had stroked that hair, kissed those lips, felt those long fingernails on their back. How many had seen the sleeping beauty I was seeing, had heard the purring I was hearing, had the privilege of knowing this very special lady? I felt blessed. I felt feelings beyond blessed that I probably shouldn't have. And should never express.

I gently nudged her. "Fiona."

She didn't budge, but Rathbone did. He pranced to his food bowl in the kitchen.

I tried again, whispering, "Fifi."

She stirred.

"We have two words left. Wanna help?"

"Uh?" she said, rubbing her eyes.

"Wanna co-write 'em?"

"Did you call me Fifi, or did I dream that?"

"You dreamed that."

"I'm not a French poodle."

"C'mon. Wake up. It's our big day."

"I must look terrible," she said, turning her face away.

"Better than a certain hound dog, worse than a French poodle."

She sat up, attempting to orient herself.

"Even your breath smells good," I said. "How do you do that?"

"How long have I been sleeping?"

"Since you said, 'Don't you dare fall asleep on me, Jack.'"

"Oops. Sorry."

"I went ahead and finished the last scene."

"Is it any good?"

"You'll make it better."

We sat in silence for a spell.

"I can't believe you called me Fifi," she said.

"We turn the script in today. I told Benny I'd be in by eight this morning. I owe it to him. He's been so good about all this. You can print it out while I'm at the bakery. We can drive it to Bowman's after I leave work. Get our money. Celebrate over dinner, somewhere with cloth napkins."

"I think we owe ourselves at least that," she said.

Was she suggesting we owed ourselves more? I looked off. "Can someone be happy and a little depressed at the same time? I mean, it's over. Went by so fast. I think it's kinda sad."

"It won't be your last rodeo. Or whatever that expression is."

I grabbed the laptop, slid my butt over to Fiona's side of the sofa, and showed her the last page of our script on the screen. I centered the curser on the page and typed, "*The.*"

Fiona grinned and typed, "*End.*"

"Fini, Fifi. Fini," I said. "The Eagle has landed. Mission accomplished."

"With a few hours to spare," she said. "I'm starting to like the Fifi thing."

We searched each other's face. The room became very still. A younger man and an older woman sat beside each other, knees touching, eyes locking, heat rising. The elephant in the room was trumpeting. In that moment, the little bubble we had been living in burst. It had become apparent to me that our partnership, our relationship, was moving toward romance, toward her bedroom. Was it apparent to Fiona? Or was I misreading the whole situation?

"It's sad. Right?" I asked, wanting to touch her.

"It's difficult to hand your firstborn over," she said.

"We still need a title," I said, losing myself in her eyes.

"We have a title. *Happily Ever Laughter.*"

"Think of something that has to do with 'stealing' and 'art.'"

Fiona spoke slowly, just going through the motions. *"The Fine Art of Stealing Fine Art."*

"I'll write it down." I spoke slowly, just going through the motions. "And type it in."

The air was sizzling with sexual electricity.

"There," she said. "That's it. We're done."

I wondered who was going to make the first move. I wondered who was going to take the other in their arms?

"I wonder what we do now," I said, wondering if she wanted to kiss me. Or wanted me to kiss her. I wondered if she wanted to make love right there on the couch, with Rathbone finishing his kibble, and doves cooing their morning melody outside the window. I wanted to stop wondering. I wanted to take action. I wanted—

"Do you want some coffee?" she inquired, rising abruptly and walking nervously toward the kitchen, breaking our mood.

I literally slapped my face to return to reality. I *had* misinterpreted all her signals. "No," I said. "No coffee, thank you. No tea. No breakfast. No kibble. I guess I should go. Yeah, I should go. I should really go."

"Are you okay?" Fiona asked.

"I should stand up, collect my things, walk to the door, turn the handle, and open the door."

Fiona was just watching me squirm.

"I should walk out, close the door, go to my car, and leave for work. No? I should go, yes?"

I was trying to buy time, but not very artfully. Maybe, just maybe, she would hold me back. She would take my hand and lead me to her bed. I didn't have to be at the bakery for another two hours. We had lots of time to explore this new dynamic. We could—

"I'll see you after work," she said, interrupting my seizure.

"Okay," I called out, opening the front door, taking a baby step outside. "I'll see you later. Bye. I'm going now. This is me leaving. Hi-yo, Silver. Awayyyy."

She didn't try to stop me, so I closed the door and walked into the courtyard. I stood there, surrounded by roses, and robins, and the promise of a new day. Was I imagining sparks between us? Did Fiona care about me in that way? Should I have been looking at and thinking about Fiona that way when I was supposed to be getting closer to Beth in every way? Was any of this real? Was any of this possible? Was I trapped in a soap opera triangle with a blue-eyed redhead, whom I had childishly dubbed Fifi?

Chapter 40
FIONA

It was nightfall by the time my Mercedes drove into the House of Skin parking lot. As sleep-deprived as he was, Jack seemed to be feeling euphoric. He was whistling the bubbly tune from *The Andy Griffith Show*.

He carried the script, around which he had tied a blue Bliffer's ribbon. We both had an energetic spring in our step until we noticed several moving trucks parked at the front entrance. Husky moving men hauled furniture, lighting equipment, and boxes of cutlery from the building.

Jack approached one of the movers. "What's going on?"

"What does it look like?" the neckless brute said.

"Looks like you're auditioning for the ballet."

The burley mover stepped toward us, fists clenched. "Are you looking for trouble?"

"Actually, I'm looking for Roger Bowman," Jack said, unruffled.

"All it says on the work order is, 'everything goes,'" he snarled.

Jack and I exchanged a puzzled look.

"I don't know your Mister Bowman."

"Mind if we look inside?" Jack asked.

"Do I look like I care?"

We entered the club. It was gutted. The fixtures, mirrors, carpeting, and stripper pole were gone. Everything. The strip club was stripped bare. We dashed across the empty stage and ran up the staircase. Bowman's nameplate had been pried off his office door. Inside the office, two perspiring thugs were packing Bowman's things into boxes. One of the men was Steve, the bouncer from the club.

"Is Roger Bowman here?" I asked.

"Do you see him?" Steve replied.

"Is this National Smartass Day?" Jack fired back.

"You're on private property. What do you want?"

"Do you know where Mister Bowman is?" Jack asked.

"Yeah. We packed him in one of these boxes."

The goons chuckled like chipmunks.

I put a hand on Jack's arm, more to steady myself than to keep him from doing something stupid. "When will he be back?" I asked.

"A week from never. Now, move out of the way."

They lifted the sofa Jack and I had sat on three tumultuous weeks before and lugged it out of the office.

We followed them down the hall.

"What happened here?" I asked.

"Are you cops?" Steve asked.

"No," I said.

"Reporters?"

"We're screenwriters," Jack said. "We work for Mister Bowman."

"Not anymore," the other thug said. "He went outta business."

Jack stopped dead. "What? He owes us money."

"Get in line, sucker."

"Can you tell us where he lives?" I asked as calmly as I could.

The thugs entered the freight elevator and set the couch down on its end. "Yeah," said Steve. "On the corner of Too-Many-Questions and No-More-Answers." The doors slid closed in our faces.

"We have to find him," Jack yelled at me. "We have to give him the script. He has to give us the money. We have a deal."

I had my phone out and was already punching in Lieutenant Lopez's private number.

"What's up, doll?" the lieutenant asked.

"Manny, I need an address."

Chapter 41
JACK

Our headlights guided us through the dark onto the luxurious grounds of a once-lavish 1930s country chateau in Pacific Palisades. In contrast to the decrepit mansion, a fresh "For Sale" sign was posted on the overgrown front lawn. On the estate stood several ornate but crumbling statues. An algae-encrusted Italian fountain was situated a short distance from a dried-up koi pond. Weeds grew in the cracks of a netless tennis court.

We pulled into the gravel parking area in front of the three-story manor. Looking out of place was a fleet of flashy cars, including a modified gold Escalade. We jumped out of the Mercedes and marched to the carved oak front door.

I held the script.

Fiona rang the bell.

A uniformed housekeeper cracked opened the door. "Yes?" she said.

"I'm Fiona Logan, and this is Jack Reynolds."

"Yes?"

"We're here to see Mister Bowman," I said.

"I'm sorry, no visitors. No solicitors."

"We're associates. We have an appointment with Mister Bowman," Fiona said. "He's expecting us."

"Señor Bowman isn't here right now," she said. "So, I guess he wasn't expecting you."

I had to bluff. "Really? Lieutenant Lopez of the LAPD just told us he *was* here," I said defiantly. "Should we call him to confirm?"

The housekeeper considered that and decided to unlatch the safety chain. "This way." We entered. She gestured toward a set of double doors. "You can wait in the study."

She disappeared, and we took a moment to look around the grand foyer. At one time, it must have been spectacular, where I imagined raucous Hollywood soirees would have taken place. Errol Flynn swinging naked from the chandelier. That kind of party. Nothing like it in Dayton, Ohio.

I marveled at Bowman's extensive and dust-covered collection of movie memorabilia. I peered into illuminated alcoves showcasing such relics as Wilson the volleyball from *Cast Away*, Julie Andrews's guitar pick from *The Sound of Music*, a feather from the headdress worn by Elizabeth Taylor in *Cleopatra*, and one of Harpo Marx's blond, curly wigs.

We slid open the double doors the housekeeper had indicated and entered what looked more like a small, dark museum than a study. The hardwood floor was so old and cracked that it creaked and bowed under our weight. I thought we might fall through.

"Whoa. This guy is some sort of Hollywood hoarder," I said.

We browsed the wood-paneled room featuring several more one-of-a-kind objects from old Hollywood. The spats George Raft wore in *Some Like it Hot* sat on a pedestal with a descriptive label. I crossed to a tall, custom-built cabinet against the far wall.

"Oh, man, Fiona. I can't believe it. Here's Indiana Jones's whip." I looked at the next shelf down. "Rocky's boxing gloves."

Fiona joined me.

"Luke Skywalker's light saber," I shouted jubilantly, like a yokel tourist.

Fiona pointed to the top shelf. "Dorothy's ruby slippers," she said, matching my excitement. "Those must be worth a fortune."

The surrounding walls and credenzas exhibited other priceless props, posters, and photos. It was altogether amazing.

"This place is unreal," Fiona said.

"I wonder where the gift shop is," I joked. At a display table, I picked up the renowned cane from *The Kid*. "Look. Charlie Chaplain's cane." I imitated Chaplain's penguin walk and nifty cane twirl.

"Careful. We're being monitored," Fiona whispered, pointing to a security camera mounted in the vaulted ceiling.

I was putting the cane back just as Bowman barged in. He wore a silk smoking jacket and carried a fireplace poker. "Were you playing with that?"

"I just—"

"There're signs everywhere saying 'Don't Touch.' Why would you touch anything? And what are you doing here?"

"We've brought you our script. *Your* script. It's due today," Fiona said. "Remember?"

"No," he said. "I don't."

"The romantic comedy with the nipples," I said to Bowman, holding the script out. "The blue ribbon was my idea."

Bowman pushed my hand away. "I don't want your script. And I don't want you in my house."

Fiona took a bold footstep forward. "You hired us to write a movie. We wrote it. Now, you owe us our money."

"Forty thousand dollars," I said.

"Show me the contract," he shot back. "A deal memo, a letter of agreement. Show me one iota of proof."

My fingers curled into a fist. "You gave us your word."

"Guess what," he said, tightening his grip on the poker. "An oral agreement isn't worth the paper it isn't written on."

"You're not going to pay us?" I asked, my voice cracking like a Bar Mitzvah boy.

"I don't know what you're talkin' about," he said, then bellowed, "Dolores."

"Mister Bowman—" Fiona interjected.

"You don't know me. I don't know you," said Bowman. "But I do know that if I shoot a couple of intruders inside my home, no court will convict me."

I was ready to twist this cretin's head off when Dolores appeared in the doorway.

He turned to her. "What the fuck? You let any fuckin' strangers walk the fuck in."

"They said—"

"Shut up," Bowman roared.

Where I come from, you never talk to a lady that way. I cocked my arm.

Bowman turned to me, raising the poker above his head. "I want you out." He turned to Fiona. "I want you out." He turned to Dolores. "And I want *you* out. For good."

BOWMAN SLAMMED AND bolted the front door to the mansion behind us. We walked Delores to her car.

"I'm so sorry," Fiona said to her.

"I'm not. I'm happy. He's *el Diablo*. I pray they kill him."

"They who?" I asked.

"Señor Bowman is in trouble. He can't pay back a loan."

"Why doesn't he just give them some of his stuff?" I asked.

"A *big* loan. He could sell the cars, the house, and everything in it. Still wouldn't make a dent."

"This is so wrong," I griped. "He's a liar and a cheat."

"He cheated the wrong people this time. I hope they bury him alive," Delores said, getting into her Nissan.

"I'm going back in there and telling him if he doesn't pay us right now, we'll call the police," I said.

"He has a gun." Delores started her car. "He's used it before."

"This is so totally shitty," I whined.

"He ripped off a lot of folks. I won't see my last paycheck either," Delores said. "But, if there's a God in Heaven, that devil will burn in hell."

And off she sped into the night.

Chapter 42
FIONA

THE WINDING DRIVE down the Pacific Coast Highway at night was one of L.A.'s most beautiful rides. You can see the reflection of lights from the seaside restaurants dancing off the dark sea. You can see the multimillion-dollar homes of the world's richest and most powerful people squeezed together on the exclusive shoreline of finite beachfront property. You can see the oil rigs just off the coast. You can see the 175,000 LED lights of the giant Ferris wheel spinning on the Santa Monica Pier.

But, if your fickle Mercedes has stalled on the westside shoulder of said historic highway, you can't see anything but white smoke belching from its stubborn engine. I fed it my bottle of Evian spring water, while Jack leaned against the fender, belching his own hot fumes. I gently closed the hood and tried to make eye contact with him. We hadn't exchanged a word since driving away from Bowman's impressive property.

"It needs to cool down," I said. "We all just need to cool down."

Jack looked out over the charcoal ocean, an angry vacant stare.

"It's a good car." I drank the rest of the bottled water. "A little temperamental, but it always—almost always—gets me to where I'm going."

Jack remained detached.

"Marvin named it Sadie, short for Mercedes. He loved this old buggy. On Sundays, he'd put the top down, turn up the radio, and just sit in it, doing the crossword puzzle, getting a tan, parked in our driveway."

Jack was unresponsive. A club of colorful motorcycle enthusiasts raced past us.

"As writers, we're communicators," I said. "I'd like to communicate with you anytime now."

"Before you say it, I know you told me so," Jack finally moaned. "Okay?"

At least he was communicating again. "One way or the other," I said.

"The writer always gets screwed," Jack conceded.

"Without fail. Write it down. If you remember anything, never forget that."

"All that work. The research, the interviews, the sleepless nights, the arguments. All down the drain, all for no money, all for nothing."

"Chalk it up to a learning experience," I said.

He took a gulp of salt air. "We'll sell this script to someone else then."

"Jack, we slapped some words together in record time for a low-budget film. It's passable for a few days' work. But it's no *Butch Cassidy and the Sundance Kid*."

"It's our work. Our words. Our future."

"It's nothing special. Nobody will read it. No one will buy it."

"So, it's a total loss?" he asked plaintively.

"No, I'll use it for kindling."

"That's it? It's dead?"

"You could spend a few years adapting it into a novel and watch that never sell."

Jack exploded. "Bowman can't do this to us."

"He already has."

"Well, we've been swindled, and that outlaw ain't gettin' away with it," he snorted.

"You reckon, Sheriff?"

"What?"

"Sounds like bad dialogue from an old western."

"I'm not in the mood for a writing lesson."

"It's a life lesson. Always listen to your gut. Mine told me from the beginning that Bowman was a phony and a con man. We should have walked away then. I take full responsibility."

Cars whooshed by us, sending a needed breeze swishing across the highway, blowing our hair.

I rested against the fender next to Jack. "It sucks. It bites. It blows."

"You said none of us would ever sell a screenplay," Jack said. "I should've believed you."

"Look at it this way. We're a thousand bucks richer than we were three weeks ago, you got a free course in how to write a feature film, and I put on six pounds. All in all, good times."

Jack abruptly turned and hiked his way down the bluff toward the sand. I followed, trying to navigate the pathway through a dense mist. He stomped across the empty beach, stopping at the water's edge. I parked behind him. I felt terrible. His dream had been dashed. I wanted to console him, to comfort him, to hug him.

"It's my fault," I said. "I knew he was a quack, that it was all a sham."

Jack had shut down. And shut me out. Who taught men to do that?

I started up again. "I'm sorry, Jack. I'm sorry that Bowman popped your Hollywood balloon." I hesitantly placed a hand on his shoulder. "I'm really sorry, kid."

Jack spun around. "Don't call me that. Don't ever call me that." He kicked at the sand. He kicked at the water. He cursed at the heavens. When he had calmed down, he turned to me. "Thank you for taking a chance on me. For all your time. All your help." He faced the sea again and spoke over his shoulder. "I'm not a kid. You're not ancient. We were partners. Equals."

In the dark, listening to the waves smash at our feet, I felt a deep connection to nature. Maybe Jack and I *were* meant to meet, to write together, to prove to us that kindred souls like Ethan and Elsa do exist and can find each other. The cosmos had now decided that we were meant to part. We had achieved what providence had planned. We had come, thanks to that wretched Roger Bowman, full circle.

I was the older one. I was the one who was expected to know what to say, what to do. Provide the answers. But I just stood there staring up at the brightest star, wishing for enlightenment. Jack and I were both hurting and vulnerable. He wasn't a kid. And he didn't see me as a geezer. We wanted each other, I thought. We should have made love right there on the beach, *From Here to Eternity*-style. But then what? Why would I enter or escalate a relationship with a taken man? Why would I breach my own code of ethics? Why would I begin a love affair that I knew could never last? These feelings would pass. I knew how to grieve. I would recover. And, when I relapsed, I'd call Dr. Aaronson's private number. I would survive this. Chalk it up to a learning experience.

I walked up behind Jack and very quietly said, "I think it's time we go our separate ways."

RATHBONE KNEW WHEN I was particularly depressed. It was when I wore my shabby sweatpants all day. When I read *Sense and Sensibility* all night. When I took a long bubble bath all morning. But mostly when I manically sorted out my bedroom closet, tossing worn out tennis shoes and old bras into a big bag for the Goodwill. It was so obviously symbolic. Out with the old. Purify. Begin over. Clean up your act. In with the new. New, like buy a racquetball racquet and a pushup bra.

When I had finished purging my closet of clothes, I scrubbed the kitchen floor and cupboards, then the shelves, drawers, and cabinets throughout the rest of my apartment, followed by a full-on dusting, vacuuming, and polishing campaign.

I even found myself attacking the garage—better known as my workshop—throwing out empty paint cans, dead batteries, and used "Yard Sale" signs. I had just tossed a full load of junk into the dumpster when I sat on a stack of three spare tires and broke down crying.

Rathbone rambled over and rubbed his head against my shin. He knew when I needed to be petted. I knew when it was time to call Dr. Aaronson. She knew to answer on the first ring.

"*Hello, Fiona,*" she said.

"Hi, Deana. Are you able to talk?"

"*I'm washing my car.*"

"I hate to bother you."

"*What's going on?*"

"Oh, not much. Except...." I felt my eyes getting hot and my voice beginning to crackle. "I'm having a terrible, horrible, no good, very bad day."

"*Do you want to cry? I can hold. I'm just hosing the hubcaps.*"

"No. I'll wait until later."

A beat of silence.

"*What's the problem, Fiona?*" she asked.

I rose and shuffled around the garage, the depository of my past. I had to step over gardening tools, earthquake provisions, a bin holding Charlotte's teddy bear collection, skis, suitcases, canned goods, firewood, camping equipment, and the last of Marvin's unsold paintings. "Do you remember that man I told you about? The young one?"

"He helped open you up."

"It's over."

"I thought it never began."

"We were writing partners. But the project ended. It's done. He's gone."

"Sounds like you wanted him to be more than a writing partner."

I inhaled, exhaled. "I did."

"It's difficult to lose someone like that."

"It's devastating."

"I'm sorry."

"I have feelings for him, Deana."

"I can tell."

"I know the difference between emotion and infatuation and lust."

"Would you like to meet me at my office and talk about it?"

"I'm too depressed to operate a motor vehicle."

"Where are you?"

A moth buzzed my head. "I'm in my garage, at my workbench, where I can fix anything. Anything but a broken heart."

Deana went gently. *"That young man was involved with someone else, if I recall."* I didn't respond. *"Is he still unavailable?"*

"He's still young and still unavailable, yes. And he's still gorgeous and smart and quirky and kind."

"Let's stay with 'unavailable.' You have to deal with what's real, what you can and cannot control."

"What's real is that he's the first man, since my husband, who has made me feel like a woman again." Rathbone sat on my feet. "I can't control my emotions."

"But you can control your actions."

"He and his girlfriend. They're wrong for each other, Deana."

"She's real. You need to accept it."

"And if I can do that, then what do I do?"

"You mourn the loss."

I picked up a dusty self-portrait of Marvin's. "I'm an expert at that."

"Then, you move on. He's helped you to do that. So, be grateful for having known this man and bring your renewed openness to the next relationship."

"I have one in the wings, chilling on ice. Supermarket guy."

"I thought he had a problem with alcohol."

"He's a mess. But I could do worse."

"How?"

"He could also be wanted for murder."

"There will be others, Fiona. You're a very attractive and bright woman. You don't have to settle for anyone less than who you want. But stick to the available ones."

"Deana?"

"Yes?"

"Could you say that again?"

"Which part?" she asked.

"'Attractive and bright.' Sometimes I need to hear a pinch me moment twice. Just to know it was real."

"We'll deal with that idiosyncrasy another time. But, for now, I repeat, you're very attractive and bright."

"Thank you for saying that. Twice."

"It's true. Both times."

"And thank you for being there. Send me a bill."

"This one's on me. Be good to yourself today."

"What should I do?" God, I was needy.

"Wash your car. It's very therapeutic."

"What else?"

"Surround yourself with friends who love you."

We hung up. I walked back to my apartment, went into my bedroom, got into bed with the friends who loved me. Rathbone and Jane Austen.

And, of course, I cried myself to sleep.

Chapter 43

JACK

I sat on my stool, squeezing my icing applicator, making small swirls and curlicues on cupcakes for a kindergarten's open house. So brilliant. Soon I would add multicolored sprinkles. Oh, boy. And plant on the top a tiny toothpick flag. Yippee. What a stupid job for a grown man. For the man who aspired to write the Great American Screenplay. Now, this man was facing a future of painting flowers with frosting on fudge cakes. How pathetic.

My colleagues at the bakery were sensitive enough to leave me alone. They knew that Bowman had stiffed me, that Fiona and I had ended our partnership, and that my plan to become a movie writer had faded to black.

Decorating those cupcakes had forced me to reflect. And to reconsider keeping my Polynesian apartment, rethink hoping to become a writer, reevaluate saying farewell to California and moving back to Ohio, being sentenced for life to hard labor in a hardware store. And more immediately, to reexamine everything about Beth, about us as roommates, as a couple, as spouses. As parents.

It was time to get off the potty.

The lighting in the cafeteria at Santa Monica Hospital made everyone look sick, staff alike. Or maybe it was because they were sick from the food. The buffet that night featured an ironic choice for a healthcare facility, the undisputed cholesterol champion of the world, macaroni and cheese. Forget the middleman—paramedics—just race down the hall to the ER.

Although Beth and I sat as far away as we could from the other doctors, nurses, and visitors, every once in a while, a patient passed by us wheeling an I.V. stand and flashing a bare, dappled ass through the split in their hospital gown. Hardly an appetizing eyeful.

"Can I get you another Jell-O?" I asked Beth, who fiddled with the stethoscope hanging around her neck.

"No."

"Do you have time to take a walk?"

"No."

"Can we go outside? Maybe sit on the patio?"

"Just tell me why you're here, Jack," she said, fidgeting with the prescription pad poking out of her breast pocket.

Beth knew why I was there, why she was so anxious. Why I couldn't tell her over the phone. And why she couldn't look me in the eye. She knew we were one patient she couldn't save. She toyed with her ID badge lanyard throughout a doomful hush. Then....

"You know I don't cry. Tears are an occupational hazard," she said with a heaviness in her voice. "But that doesn't mean I'm not in a lot of pain."

"I know. I'm sorry."

She looked at her hands, her ringless engagement finger. "Time's the best medicine, said the doctor."

"This was the hardest decision I've ever had to make," I said to my plate of uneaten mac and cheese.

"Spare me."

"I mean it, Beth. I've agonized over this. I've lost weight."

"Am I supposed to feel sorry for you?"

"You're not the only one who has invested a lot into this relationship."

"You're right. So did my mom and dad. They've waited a long time to be grandparents." She stared at the ceiling. "None of us are getting any younger. Certainly not my eggs."

We sat there listening to announcements and pages over the PA system. I saw Beth summon the strength to ask me the dreaded break-up question, "Is there someone else?"

I looked up from my dish. "No," I said without hesitation.

"It's her, isn't it?" Beth posed, her face tightening.

"There is no 'her.'"

"She's witty and pretty—"

"Beth—"

"And bright. That's from *West Side Story*," she said, reminding me why I fell for her in the first place. It was one of our favorite films.

I felt guilty about using it as a reference to Fiona entering the art gallery. I felt unfaithful. I was about to feel worse.

"You both love the movies—"

"Stop. Turn back. You're going down the wrong road."

"Then what? Why?"

I didn't know how to respond. I needed to be honest, but I didn't want to be thoughtless and unnecessarily hurtful. There was a likely chance that I would come to regret this night for the rest of my life. I wouldn't be able to crawl back to Beth either. She'd be taken. There were a dozen residents in that very room who would marry her tomorrow. And make her parents grandparents in nine months. "I'm not ready," I said. "That's what it all comes down to. I'm just not ready."

"Will you ever be?"

"Yes."

"When?"

"When my gut tells me."

I suppose that statement left the door open just enough for Beth to make her final plea. "At the risk of being totally humiliated, I'd stick around if I knew things with us would change. I can hold on—not forever, but for a little longer—until your gut tells you I'm the one." She waited for me to give her a greater glimmer of hope. "It's worth it for me to take that chance."

I said nothing, which said everything.

Beth apparently needed to salvage some measure of self-respect. "I need someone who loves me at least as much as I love them."

"All I can say is that I'm sorry, Beth. I'm so, so sorry."

She turned away.

So, I started up again. "You'll find that person. You deserve that person." It wasn't much consolation, but it seemed to comfort her. "Because you're a spectacular person."

That last unnecessary tag, however, ignited a vigorous rant. "I know what I am. I'm everything every man wants, blah, blah, blah. On paper, nobody scores higher. I know all that. And don't play the we-can-still-be-friends card," she said, rising from the table. "Because we can't." Her hands were shaking. "Happy goddamn Thanksgiving, Jack."

I rose and let loose a small but relationship-ending, "Welllll…."

We stood there looking at each other for what we knew was the last time as a couple.

She broke the silence. "I'm great. You're great. We'll both end up with someone great."

I pulled her close to me.

Beth buried her head in my chest, and for the first time in my presence, let alone in public among her peers, she sobbed.

That was it. We were through. One year. Over and out. It would be part of our respective histories. Each of us was instantly alone again. Neither of us wanted to be the first to break free from that farewell embrace. Eventually, the stronger of us did.

Beth gently pushed away from me. "Don't stay in touch." She walked away without a single backward glance.

I left the cafeteria with a deep sense of sadness. And relief.

Chapter 44
FIONA

I HAD SPENT the day listening to Pink Floyd and rewriting an essay for Colleen, my hairdresser's daughter, who was applying to college. We bargained. I'd write about "What Makes Me Unique" in exchange for three free hair blowouts.

I needed to break out of my prison. I needed exercise and fresh air. I needed to do something that Makes *Me* Unique. I needed to continue my rebirth, my restart. So, I jumped on my sparkly red Schwinn Cruiser, named Winnie, and headed down the hill to make amends with an old friend, my ex-agent Kim Fleishman. It did my ego little good to pedal through West Hollywood receiving harmless catcalls from the male gay community.

Kim and I had been too close for too long to have let my back-lot meltdown demolish our relationship. I rode up North King's Road and into the driveway of Kim's modest duplex. Setting the kickstand, I grabbed a large shipping envelope out of Winnie's basket.

I snagged the morning newspaper enroute to Kim's front door. His shades were drawn. Nobody responded to the doorbell or my hard knocking. As I was about to deposit my delivery on his welcome mat, the door suddenly swung opened. Kim stood there in the fuzzy, monogramed, canary-yellow bathrobe he had swiped from a Palm Springs hotel suite. His eyes were glassy, and his nostrils were running.

"Jesus, it's three in the morning." He sniffled.

"It's five in the afternoon."

"You scared the shit out of me," he said through his nose. "Not that I have any left. I've got diarrhea. Been on the can for days. *Explosive* diarrhea. Stand back."

"Lovely." I handed him the newspaper. "Here. In case you run out of toilet paper."

"Are you delivering newspapers now?"

"It's a living."

Kim looked at the envelope in my hand. "Do you have an olive branch in there?"

"One of your mercy meetings paid off. I got an advance of a thousand bucks." I handed him the envelope. "There's a check for a hundred dollars inside. Your hard-earned ten percent."

"You didn't have to come here for a hundred dollars. I never would've known about it."

"I would've."

He sneezed. "I have a cold. A nasty, snotty cold." He held my hand against his forehead. "Do I have a temperature? I think it could be the flu. Or pneumonia. Or I'm dying of Covid all alone here."

"You have a mild case of hypochondria. You'll see another Christmas."

A trio of fire trucks screamed down the street, sirens wailing. We waited for them to pass. We waited until we could hear the blue jays chirping again. We waited until we thought of something remorseful to say to each other.

Kim pressed my envelope to his bosom. "So, do you think a hundred clams will bring peace to two warring factions?"

"I hope so," I said. "I'm sorry for being—"

"Such an ungrateful ingrate?"

"I wasn't going to be that specific."

"We have a love/hate relationship, don't we, Fiona?"

"Yeah. You love me. And I hate you."

"I'm just going to say this once, so pay attention. That business about you being the world's biggest loser, I'm sorry I said what I said. There, I've said it."

"Enough said."

"While we're at it, I'm also sorry I called you an ungrateful ingrate." He extended his hand. I shook it. "Does this mean I'm unfired?"

"Only if you withdraw your resignation."

We both smiled. We were old friends again.

"Want some breakfast?" he offered with his nose dripping.

"No, thanks. I had breakfast ten hours ago."

He inspected me up and down. "You look good."

"I'm not."

"Anything I can do?"

"Yeah. Inside that envelope, along with your commission and an original poem of apology, you'll find a script. Something I dashed off with a student of mine. See what you can do."

He tore open the envelope as if it contained raw diamonds and pulled out the screenplay. "This is wonderful." He read the cover page, "'By Fiona Logan and Jack Reynolds.' So *that's* Jack Reynolds."

"Do you know him?"

"Not until his agent called me."

"He has an agent?" I gasped.

"Benjamin Bliffer. He said he looked your name up and got my number."

"Why in the world would Benny call?"

"He wanted to make sure that if I ever sold this script, his client would get fifty percent. I didn't know what the hell he was talking about. Anyway, the point is sweetie, you're writing again. How did you get out of the slump?"

"I was inspired by Benny's only client."

"I was going to call you tomorrow," Kim said. "I couldn't wait any longer. I can't handle these breakups of ours. Promise that you'll never leave me again."

"No. But I promise I'll always come back."

He pulled my body toward him, smooshing me against his sunny, yellow bathrobe in a snug embrace. "I'm so proud of you. I'd cry, but I don't want to run my mascara."

"Too late for that." I kissed Kim on his moist forehead and walked back down the driveway. Stopping at my bike, I turned and blew him another kiss. "See ya at the movies, Big Bird."

Chapter 45
JACK

Two weeks had passed since Bowman screwed us. Kevin and I were shooting hoops after work on a cloudy day at Roxbury Park. Playing basketball. It's how men talk. We need an activity in order to relate in a real and honest way. Some guys play poker or shoot pool. Some watch football together. The rich ones play golf. The brainy ones play chess. We shot baskets and scored talking points. Our gender didn't get the complete communication gene. We aren't emotionally fluent. Our fathers didn't teach us how to talk about the real stuff because their fathers didn't teach them. But in the twenty-first century, we're trying to express our feelings by bouncing a rubber ball and throwing it through a metal hoop while talking about, well, how we feel. About the real stuff.

"So, how're you doing?" Kevin asked, passing me the ball.

"Great," I lied. That's how men talk. Feelings are locked in a wordless vault.

"Do you miss her?" he asked.

"Of course." I took a jump shot from the top of the key. Air ball all the way. "You get used to somebody. The way they argue. The way they plan a scene. The way they see the world through their writing."

"I was talking about Beth."

I should have known that. "I'm kidding. Sure, I miss her." What was wrong with me?

"So, what happened?" Kevin gathered the ball. Threw an errant hook shot.

"I don't know. The last few months, I was having doubts. We had drifted apart." I took a twelve-foot shot. My ball fell short.

"What was missing?" Kevin asked, chasing down the ball.

"Call it chemistry. Call it bad timing. Call it the X factor."

I watched an old man discourage his dachshund from taking a dump under the slide in the playground. I watched a pregnant mother run with a kite, trying to send it aloft to the delight of her little daughter. I watched a middle-aged man push his sleeping father in a wheelchair, crossing paths with a young father pushing his sleeping newborn in a stroller.

"Beth is a great catch," Kevin said, flubbing a dunk.

"I may have blown it like you just blew that easy lay-up." We continued to shoot around, setting a new Roxbury record—no baskets in four minutes.

"You were in love, though, right?" he asked me.

"I don't know. I don't think so. That was the problem. Otherwise, Beth is amazing. I really thought she might be the one. She'll go down as a near miss. Or should I say a near Missus?"

"Misses. That would describe your shooting today," Kevin said.

"Anyway, Beth will be hard to beat. She set a high bar going forward."

"Damn shame," Kevin said.

"Damn straight." I tried a bank shot from under the basket. Blew it. "You and Shanelle," I said. "How's that working?"

"We're buying furniture."

"Great."

"For the baby's room."

I stopped. "Are you shitting me?"

"I shit you not."

"A baby. Wow. Congratulations, bro."

"Yep. Got me an instant family."

"Did you know right away? Did your gut tell you Shanelle was the one? The best one?"

"Everything told me. Not a single doubt."

I took another shot. The ball hit the rim, bounced over the backboard and rolled onto the grass.

"Nice shot," Kevin said, retrieving the ball.

"I was trying to do that."

He carried the ball back to me, but held on to it. "Shanelle said your writing partner came by the bakery a few weeks back. She thought something was going on with you two."

"There wasn't."

"I'm your best friend. I'll support you either way. And won't tell a soul. I'm just curious."

"I repeat, there wasn't."

"And now?"

"There isn't."

"In the future?"

"When we finished the script, we finished seeing each other."

"Shanelle cares about Beth. They've become good friends, you know."

"It was strictly a professional relationship," I said. "I'm sorry you never met her. She's really something."

"Can I ask you a strictly personal question?"

"These haven't been?"

"Did you think your writing partner—"

"Yes," I answered. "I thought she was sexy and smart and sassy."

"I was going to ask if you thought she was kinda old for you. Again, either way, I'm in your corner."

"I told you, it wasn't like that," I said.

"Answer the question."

"Not an issue. With her, I never thought about age."

"One more question. Did what's-her-name…?"

"Elsa?"

"Elsa? I don't know an Elsa." He shook his head. "The writing lady."

"Fiona."

"Did Fiona have anything missing on the X factor scale?"

"Tell you what," I said, stealing the ball out of his hands and setting up for a three-point shot from the corner. "If I sink this one, you get to ask exactly no more questions about what's-her-name."

"Considering you're zero for infinity, I'll take that bet."

I lined up the shot, fired, and swish. Nothing but net. End of discussion. My heart's secret remained safely locked in the man vault, even out of my best friend's reach. I turned to him and said, "And that, my beloved black brother, is how you put the lime in the coconut."

Neither of us knew what the hell that meant.

THAT NIGHT, I dreamt that Beth and I were married, living in Bowman's mansion with our two children, Ethan and Elsa. We had returned from the movie premiere of *The Fine Art of Stealing Fine Art* only to find the front door wide open and our nanny Delores missing. In a panic, I charged upstairs to the children's room. It was empty. Ethan was gone. Elsa had vanished. Rathbone, too, had disappeared.

Princess Fiona rode bareback into the foyer on Night Mare, a pearl-white horse, then galloped up the grand staircase. She scooped me up. I sat behind her on that stallion, my arms wrapped around Fiona's waist. She had an *X* tattooed on the back of her neck. We bolted down the stairs, out of the manor, across the estate, leaving Beth alone in the motor court bawling, with a dogless leash in one hand, and in her other hand, an infant's beating heart.

Fiona and I cantered atop that powerful steed down the streets of Pacific Palisades to the beach, over powder blue sand, through the tide, into the open sea, passing a floating basketball and the bloated body of Bowman. We stroked and splashed our way toward the horizon and a huge sign with purple, cutout letters that spelled HOLLYWEIRD.

I awoke in a cold sweat that tasted like salt water.

Chapter 46
FIONA

I GREW ACCUSTOMED to hearing phantom knocks at my front door during all hours of the day and night, hoping it would be Jack. On several occasions, I opened the door only to find no one there. So, I thought it was my imagination when I heard a tentative tap early on a Sunday morning.

Rathbone dutifully barked, "Hello."

I opened the door.

Standing there looking like a male model in a sharp tennis outfit was Eddie holding a dozen red roses. "Please don't throw acid in my face," he said.

"Hello, Eddie."

"May I come in?"

"I'll come out," I said, shutting the door behind me.

"Do you have company?"

"Yeah. We're just winding up an orgy. What's up?"

"Can we sit down?"

"No. That would suggest this is going to take longer than I want."

"Do I sense a hint of hostility?" he asked.

"I'm not a fan of 'I was just in the neighborhood and thought I'd drop by.'"

"I had to see you in person. So, I took the liberty of—"

"Not calling."

He shrugged. "My bad."

"Why me, Eddie? I'm sure you could have any woman out there, a sweet-talking, good-looking, Hah-vard man like yourself."

"Not to toot my own horn, but yes, I can, and have. Toot, toot."

"Then, what is it? Do women who turn you down turn you on? Must you always win? Is it a lawyer thing?"

"I trust my instincts. That's what's made me a rich attorney. And I trust my instincts about women, who will make me rich in love." He turned serious. Real serious. "I don't love you."

"That's a relief."

"I don't even know you. I admit that. So, it must seem peculiar that I haven't given up. I'm going on instinct. I see the possibility of something great. Something I've been looking for. I'm willing to stand here, Ladybug, and humble myself because my instincts tell me not to let you go."

"I was right. This is taking way too long."

"I think you and I should play this, whatever it is, out. Because something deep inside"—he thumped his chest—"tells me we could be much more than a weekend fling."

I fanned my face with my hand. "My, oh my, Mister Harper. You do know how to flatter a girl."

"Will you at least listen to what I have written, memorized, and rehearsed at AA many times for this moment?"

"Why must you torture yourself?"

"This doesn't have to be a conversation. You don't have to say a word. I'll do all the work."

Here was a well-educated and charming man, my age, willing to embarrass himself once again so as to bed me. This time, however, I was susceptible. And my bed was a mere fifty feet away. And, in my vulnerable condition, I could use some validation through a harmless, good ol' recreational roll in the hay. "Hit it," I said.

"Thanks, I really appreciate the opportunity to—"

"Eddie, just say what you want."

"You. I want you."

"I know."

"So, what's the problem?" he asked.

"You. I don't want you."

"Let me just quote a small portion of my speech."

I sighed.

He restarted. "When I first saw you in the market, I knew I had met my match. Then, I stupidly allowed my demons to destroy any hope with you. Though our candle burned only briefly, it burned brightly." He smiled. "Did you like that line, you being a writer and all?"

"I'm getting drowsy. Is there more?"

"I realized that if I were ever going to change my evil ways, it would have to be now, for I had found my reason, my incentive, my motivation, my inspiration. I had found you." He handed me the roses. "With hair so red and eyes so blue, I give my heart to only you. Came up with that little ditty on the Peloton this morning."

"Pulitzer Prize material."

"And so, Ladybug, I ask that you give me one final chance. If I disappoint you in any way, I swear I'll leave forever." He was all but down on one knee.

"Finished?" I asked, devoid of any emotion.

"One footnote. You need to understand that I've given up booze and yoga forever. Neither were good for me."

"Is the show over?"

"Yes. I rest my case. Except for this…."

He continued to blather on. I never blinked, but I tuned out his voice. I asked myself, "Do I want Eddie Harper in my life?" That's what it boiled down to. He was fun and funny. And relentlessly persistent, which made me feel needed and desired. I could make things much easier on myself if I just put a hand over his mouth and said, "Shut up. I'm yours."

Instead, I said, "Thank you for the flowers. And the kind words. Next time, call before you knock."

"So, there will be a next time?"

I folded. "Seems inescapable."

"Let's mark you down as a resounding yes." Eddie flashed his irresistible matinee idol smile. "This is truly very good news," he said victoriously. "Not to press my luck, but are you free tonight?"

"You're pressing your luck."

"Right," he said backing off. "Well, I think we made substantial strides on this beautiful Sunday morning, which could be extended into brunch at my country club if—"

"I have to go home now," I said.

"You are home."

"Then, *you* have to go home."

He tipped his imaginary hat, turned, and joyously sprinted toward his sportscar. Halfway down the walkway, he actually jumped to the side and clicked his heels.

I went back into my apartment. While I arranged Eddie's roses in a ceramic vase, I contemplated the nagging questions. Why didn't I feel better about myself? Why didn't I look forward to Eddie's next call? Why did I say yes when my gut said no? Why couldn't Eddie be Jack?

I also contemplated calling Deana, but instead took her sage advice. I filled a bucket with hot water and dish soap, grabbed a sponge, and washed my old Mercedes.

Chapter 47

JACK

THE BAKERY WAS crowded. Benny was giving away day-old rye bread, and the line snaked out the front door. I was putting the finishing touches on a five-tier wedding cake when a poker-faced Shanelle glided by, checking out my work. She was glowing.

"Will you do that good a job for me?" she asked.

My eyes widened. "Get out."

Shanelle flashed an engagement ring. "Just now. At lunch." She gave a little squeal. "He thinks better now than to wait 'til my water breaks during our vows."

"I'm happy for you. For both of you. For all three of you. When's the wedding?"

"Tomorrow."

"So much for a Save the Date notice."

"It's a drive-thru in Vegas. Kevin wants to do it quick and dirty."

"That's what got you into this mess."

"We'll be back the following morning in time for work."

"Short honeymoon."

"After the baby comes, we'll throw a big wedding party in Pasadena."

"That's awesome, Nelle. I'm really happy for you guys." I gave her a big hug.

The free rye bread contingent pushed and shoved its way toward the counter. You would have thought we were handing out keys to free Ferraris.

"I don't know how to tell you how sorry I am that you and Beth—"

"It's okay. We're going to be fine."

"I had visions of a double wedding."

"I've got to call Kevin and congratulate him," I said, steering away from the subject.

"Can we borrow your car tomorrow?"

"Sure. Why?"

"My jalopy is in the shop, and this two-ton bride ain't riding no Harley to her nuptials."

"Does the gang here know?" I asked.

"You were the first."

"Do you mind?"

"Go ahead. Make it official."

I banged two metal trays together. "Hey, everyone. Listen up."

The patrons, the freeloaders, and the staff stopped their business.

"My best friend and ex-roommate, of his own free will and very sound mind, just popped the big question to this pretty lady. He's going to make an honest woman out of her." I turned to Shanelle. "And an honorary godfather out of me."

There was a burst of applause. Benny hobbled over to embrace Shanelle while Eleanor passed out cookies to everyone. Suddenly, the bakery was transformed into an impromptu engagement party venue. Shanelle couldn't stop smiling.

The celebration reminded me that life goes on. Mine would, too, but not without avenging the recent past.

IT WAS EARLY evening when I set foot on the grounds of Casa del Sol, in search of its manager. I hadn't seen Fiona for a few weeks, though it seemed like forever. I probably should never have seen her again, especially considering where I found her—at the swimming pool, surrounded by tall vanity hedges, wearing a turquoise one-piece swimsuit, looking like a divine mermaid.

She was propped up in a chaise lounge, sipping a margarita out of a cocktail glass. A blue ice chest sat by her side. Resting on the chest were her birding binoculars and a blender with a long extension cord leading to an outlet by the barbeque. With her fishing pole in hand, she practiced casting into the pool water, trying to place her weighted fly in the center of a child's rubber swim ring without spilling a drop of her drink.

Rathbone barked and trotted cheerfully to me for a petting.

"Hello, old dog," I said.

Fiona tilted her sunglasses down and looked up scornfully. "Who're you calling an old dog?" Her words were slurred.

"Hi, Fiona."

"Oh, no. It's Boomerang Boy. He just keeps coming back."

"Sorry I didn't call first."

"Nobody does these days."

"It's good to see you."

"Hit the road, Jack."

I couldn't take my eyes off her. "Do you really want me to leave?"

"Yes."

"All right." I started to go.

"No," she whimpered.

"Fine," I said. I wasn't going anywhere until I stated my case. And reeled Fiona back in.

She kicked one foot in the air. "I need someone to make sure the Widow Logan doesn't fall off this lounge and roll into the pool and drown. Not that anyone would care." She was running her words together. "Some handsome paramedic would try to breathe life into this old dog."

"Fiona—"

"He would do mouth-to-mouth, but declare me brain dead," she said.

"Maybe I should go," I said.

"But he'd also declare me a good kisser."

"I'm going."

"Then, the funeral. I've given this one a lot of thought. What would I wear in my coffin? Could Rathbone come? Would there be enough parking? Do they validate?"

"I'll come back later," I said. "I'll call first."

"No, stay. But only if you promise to give Rathbone a good life after mine ends." She gestured toward the pool. "And to obey the rules and regulations of Lake Inferior." She licked some salt off the rim of her glass.

"There's no running or horseplay. No food, no spitting, no smoking, no illicit drugs."

"Okay."

"And, my personal favorite, any adult who is experiencing even a mild case of a flesh-eating disease may not enter the water."

"I guess that would rule me out."

"Proper swimming attire is also required. I'll permit you to keep your khakis on, for the time being. But that shirt has to come off, or you must immediately vacate the premises."

I pulled my T-shirt off. "How's that?"

"Oh, my. That's really good," she babbled. "Tell me what that tattoo on your bulging bicep has to say?"

"Passion Rules the World," I replied.

"That's so true," she said. "Do you have any other distinctive markings you'd like to disclose to the aquatic committee at this time?" She was making a delightful fool of her intoxicated self. It was great to see her this way—unguarded, cutting loose, enticing.

I humored her. "I have a scar under my chin. Most guys do."

"Most guys have your scar under their chin?"

I didn't respond. She was far too out of it to converse rationally. Then, she sat up abruptly, waving her fishing pole above her head. "Hear yee, hear yee. The Lady of the Lake has a royal proclamation to proclaim. She hereby allows the Duke of Dayton to keep his socks on."

"That is most gracious," I said. "I wish to leave my shoes on as well, if that pleases Your Fifiness."

"You don't have to ask permission. You're no longer my student, Zack."

"Jack."

"We've gone our separate ways. You're just a man, with an incredible physique. I'm just a woman with a man standing in front of her with an incredible physique. And we're just hanging around the ol' swimming hole together. Don't try to make anything more of it."

"I won't."

"Incidentally, exactly how drunk am I?" she asked, her hands flailing like a marionette's.

"You could lose your fishing license."

"Don't ever tell my daughter about this. That's another pool rule."

"Okay."

"I don't expect you to believe this, but I don't generally over-drink. I'm not like Eddie."

"Who's Eddie?"

"It's just that today's a special occasion."

"What's today?"

"National Self-Pity Day." She gulped down the rest of her drink. "Maybe I should get out of the sun."

"Yeah. With your red hair and fair skin—"

"Aw. Is he worried about her burning up?"

"You want to look good in that casket of yours."

"I have some sunscreen. Wanna rub it on me? All over me? For about an hour?" She was obviously beyond repair.

I stepped forward. "Let's get you into the shade." I adjusted the umbrella on the patio table, casting a shadow over her lounge.

"Care for a drink?" she asked. "You'll need three to catch up."

"More like three hundred."

"You may imbibe directly from the blender. We're all friends here."

I took the blender and laid on the lounge next to Fiona. We reclined, side by side, both on our backs, as if we were in bed together.

She set her fishing rod down and held her glass up to me. "Free refills," she twinkled.

I topped off her drink.

We chugged the liquor, me out of the blender, Fiona out of her glass, looking out at the "lake." The dusk sky turned pink as I watched Fiona fall asleep beside me.

I drank alone until, without opening her eyes, Fiona sputtered, "How long have I—"

"About an hour."

"Did I talk in my sleep? Charlotte says I do."

"You asked if Mack was still here. But you meant Zack, I think. But you really meant Jack."

"Are any of them here?"

"Jack's right next to you."

"That's nice."

"I agree," I said.

"I think I may have passed out."

"You did."

"That's not very ladybug. That's what Eddie calls me. I meant ladylike."

"Who's this Eddie?"

She rolled on her side toward me. And became serious. "Why do you put up with me?"

I rolled on my side toward her. "You're talented. You're fiercely independent. You're witty."

"Pretty? Did you just say pretty?"

"Yes. And sometimes you're fun and generous. Less often, you're patient and—"

"Okay. I get the idea." She rolled to her other side with her back to me. "Your agent contacted my agent."

"That's nice. I didn't know I had an agent."

Fiona seemed to nod off, but came back to. "I gave my agent our script."

"Did he think it was good?"

"Good enough." She reached down and patted Rathbone. "But he can't get anyone to read it." Fiona tried to sit up. Big mistake. She settled for staying on her side. "Why do you want here? I mean what do you why here?" she said, turning to face me.

"I don't think you should drink anymore," I advised.

"You're right. I'll drink to that." She found her glass and took another swig. "Now, answer me. Why. Are. Here. You?"

"I want to make a proposal," I announced.

"Did you bring a ring?"

"No."

"Did you at least bring a blue bakery box?"

"No."

"Then, the marriage is off," she said.

"I propose that you and I write another script together," I said.

"Because the last one went so well?"

"Because the next one will go so much better. Because I'm going to get better," I said, feeling a little under the influence myself. "Because you make me better."

I noticed Fiona pinch the skin on the back of her hand. "Would you say that last part one more time?"

"You make me better."

She leaned toward me and whispered through tequila breath, "I don't think your doctor friend should move in with you."

"Why not?"

"Because I think you'd eventually break up."

"We never made it to 'eventually.'"

She appeared to sober up for a moment. "I'm sorry, Jack. Really. I'm sorry it didn't work out. Those things rarely do."

"What 'things?'"

"Relationships. They go rotten. They have an expiration date. Then, you have to get rid of them. Or they start to stink."

"Do you really believe that?"

She searched the darkening sky for an answer. "No. I was just trying to make you feel better. Relationships are all we've got. They're the essence of life. They rule the world."

I was starting to feel the full effects of my margarita jug. I was well on my way toward a blender bender. "I'm back to square one," I said. "In search of true love again. I hope it exists."

"I promise it does. You just have to keep looking. Sometimes, you don't have to look any farther than your own backyard," she said, her words tumbling out in a jumble of barely distinguishable syllables.

"I don't have a backyard."

We watched the sun drop behind the eucalyptus trees, and we drank some more. It wasn't long before night had crept in, and I was mixing another batch of Mexican firewater. Within a couple of hours, we had become somewhat tipsy. Make that thoroughly hammered. It was time to tell Fiona the true purpose of my visit. The hard liquor would help make it easier.

"We shouldn't let this Bowman character, that fat fuck, take advantage of us," I yelled.

"Jack, please. Kids live here. Use your indoor voice."

I stood up and swayed from the alcohol. "It's not right. I wanna go back there and shake him down. Shake him like a good margarita."

"It's over. The fat fuck has sung."

"I don't walk away that easily," I garbled, stumbling backward.

"I've noticed."

"Bowman's gotta pay."

"What're you going to do? Sue him? We have no contract. Arrest him? We have no proof. Rob him? He's bankrupt. You can't just break into his house and steal something worth forty thousand dollars and call us even."

"Well, we should."

She popped open her eyes. "It certainly would be warranted."

Both of us, at the same time, realized what she had just said. The Night-Blooming Jasmine wafted through the air.

"He owes us," I stammered.

"Darn tootin'," she blabbed.

"An eye for an eye."

"Just desserts," she said.

My idea was gaining momentum. "Break in. Steal. Get away. Like in our script."

"I can just see it," Fiona chortled. "You and me, dressed as ninjas."

"Lowered from a helicopter, dropped into his chimney, and tiptoeing out with a forty-thousand-dollar chandelier," I slobbered, sharing in the giddiness and dizziness.

Fiona laughed harder. "You're not supposed to go in from the roof, silly. You're supposed to—"

Suddenly, I stopped laughing. "Why not?"

"Because you can't get a chandelier up a chimney. That's what my convict told me."

"I mean why *not* do this?"

"Do what?" Fiona said, still laughing.

"Rip the son-of-a-bitch off. I'm telling ya, we should fucking do this."

"Jack. Come on. The children. The manager's gonna throw us out."

"You're the manager."

"Oh. In that case, we can stay," she hiccupped. She was so wasted. As was I. Rathbone, on the other hand, snored under the patio table.

"I'm from the Midwest," I blasted. "I know redneck justice. In L.A., you expect everyone to fuck you. Well, back home, you fuck me, and I'll fuck you up."

"What're you saying? And please say it quieter and keep the f-bombs to a minimum."

"Think about it. We've done the research. We've learned from the best how to get in and get out and sell the goods and get away with it."

"Your tequila is talking," she said. "Besides, we don't have a helicopter."

"We don't go in from the roof, silly," I mocked. "Your convict said to go in from under the house." I was building my case brick by brick, belch by belch. "Look, it's the perfect crime. Robbing the bad guy. And selling his stuff to another bad guy."

"Forget about it. We're the good guys. We do the right thing."

"Taking what is rightfully ours *is* the right thing," I insisted.

That little missile had impact. Fiona got up gingerly and wobbled around the edge of the pool, brooding. "The guy's a real scuzzbag. I'll give you that."

"Revenge." I walked cautiously along the opposite edge of the pool. "We deserve every cent of it."

"We can defeat the security system," she said, heading toward me on rubbery legs.

"Maple syrup," I said, heading toward her on supple ankles. "On sale at Cracker Barrel."

"We don't need no stinkin' helicopter. We go up from under the floor."

"That's the spirit."

"Then what?" she asked.

"Then, we grab one of those precious movie props," I said excitedly. "And sell it to Carlo."

Fiona and I came together on the deck at the deep end of the pool, nose to nose, Eskimo to Eskimo. "But there's Bowman, standing with his gun," she said.

"He shoots each of us in the face, and we die," I said.

Silence.

We stood there, two sloppy drunks ranting inanely and holding onto each other so as not to tumble into the water. I felt like dancing with her, if only I could've felt my feet.

"No." Fiona said, still plotting, not giving up. "We duck. And make a run for it." *Her* tequila was talking. "But then he calls his guards," she said, continuing to "write" the scenario.

"He doesn't have guards," I said.

"Just say he does. Just improvise with me."

"Okay." I impersonated Bowman, calling out, "'Oh, guards.'"

"We escape them," she yelped.

"Good work. We made it. We're free." I said.

"And we live happily—"

"Ever laughter," I said. "Galloping into the horizon."

"Two screenwriters research the perfect crime for a script, then use that script to commit the crime themselves," Fiona said, barely able to keep her eyelids open. "*That* script, we could sell. It would make a helleva movie."

"Life imitating art. Let's act out that movie." I rejoiced.

"You should have called first, Jack."

"Really? We're back there again?"

A tenant carrying a trash bag cut across the pool area on his way to the trash bins.

"Hola, Hector," Fiona said.

"My garbage disposal broke again," Hector groused. "You'll get to it when you get to it, right?"

"First thing next decade," Fiona answered.

Disgusted, Hector shook his head and kept on walking.

When he was out of sight, I turned to Fiona. "So, are we going to do this dirty deed for real?"

"What dirty deed?" she asked, rubbing her red eyes.

"Rob Bowman."

"Yes. Of course," she said.

"Really?"

"No. Of course not."

"Were you just teasing me? Because I'm serious."

"No break ins, no pilfering, no Bonnie and Clyding."

"Why not?" I asked.

"Because I'd rather live. For what? I don't know. Maybe because I don't have anything to wear to my funeral."

I realized it was pointless to continue this conversation. It was completely unrealistic to think that Fiona and I would ever attempt such a crime. It was no more than a drunken, though comical, tirade. "I need to go to bed," I said, wanting to add, "with you."

"You can't drive home in your condition. And I can't drive you home in my condition."

"Maybe the manager will rent me an apartment for the night," I said.

"Is that still me?"

"I don't remember," I stammered. "By the way, who's Betty?"

"Eddie." She shrugged. "We see the same dentist."

"Oh."

The pool party was over. I put my T-shirt back on over my head, through one of the arm holes.

Fiona took my hand and led me through the dark courtyard. Her touch was becoming less awkward, more natural, more welcomed. "If we can find my front door, you can sleep on the couch, if we can find the couch."

Rathbone followed us into the apartment.

Fiona left me stretched out on the sofa and retreated to her bedroom. That's the last I recall, until I woke up in the middle of the night, crawled off the couch with a crushing headache, grabbed Fiona's laptop, went into the kitchen, and started doing some cold sober investigating on the internet.

Chapter 48
FIONA

"Fiona," Jack hollered.

From a deep sleep to a heart-stopping fright, I sat up in bed thinking The Big One had hit, that it was time to duck and cover. "Earthquake?" I cried out. "Get in my bed. I mean under my bed."

"I couldn't sleep," he said, entering my room, sitting on the edge of my mattress.

In my bedroom? Sitting on my bed? Was I fantasizing again?

"What day is it?" I asked. "And why do I feel like I was hit by a tequila truck?"

"I did some research," he said.

"Are you starting another script?"

"No. The one we have is going to work fine. It's like a car or a ceiling fan."

I massaged my throbbing head. "What are you talking about?"

"It just needs some adjusting, just one more twist."

"Are you in my bedroom?" I asked.

"I'm sorry. I should have called first."

"And is that your body sitting on my body's bed?"

Jack sprang up like a frog as I yanked the sheet to my neck.

"What time is it?" I asked.

"Like two or three."

"In the afternoon?"

"In the morning," he said. "Just listen to me."

"My brain is broken. It's dark outside. I need to go back to sleep."

"We played by the rules. We worked hard. Then, that subhuman, Roger Fucking Bowman—"

"Please. Not so loud. My head."

"He's a crook," Jack yapped. "And we're going to punish him."

"I don't think you should be in my bedroom."

"I've been googling."

"Well, stop it. You could go blind."

Jack started to pace at the foot of my bed, back and forth like a bear in a shooting gallery. "The Smithsonian Museum has the ruby slippers from *The Wizard of Oz*. Another pair was stolen in 1939 from the wardrobe department at MGM studios."

"The ones in Bowman's house?"

"Probably. They kicked around the black market for years. Get this. They're worth two million dollars. A million smackers per slipper."

"Call Lieutenant Lopez."

"I'm calling you."

"I'm not answering."

"Bowman owes us."

"Not two million dollars," I said.

"Stealing something that was stolen. It's the perfect perfect crime."

"You're still drunk."

Jack sat back down on my bed. "Let's do it, Fiona."

There were those words again. I felt a chill and promptly pulled the sheet up to my nose. "Do what exactly?"

"Let's sneak in there and snatch those slippers."

I experienced a brief let down but recovered quickly. "I'm not a thief. Neither are you. And you're sitting on my bed again."

"MGM is no longer a studio. Dorothy's slippers no longer belong to anybody. And we no longer have to be victims."

The plan, of course, was ludicrous. Absolutely bonkers. "I have to fix Hector's garbage disposal and replace a dozen smoke alarm batteries today. I need to clean out the rain gutters and empty a bunch of rattraps. I'm a very busy businesswoman, Jack." I saw his heart sink. And it took mine with it. "But first, I have to figure out a way to ambulate from my bed to my bathroom, ideally without one of my former students watching."

"So, you're too busy to make a million dollars?"

"I'm too busy to commit a major crime."

"We kept our promise. Bowman broke his."

"Bowman has a gun," I said. "We have pastries."

"He stiffed us."

"I'm not going to die for that." I took a breath. "When you have sobered up, gotten some sleep, and revisited this ridiculous idea, you'll come to your senses."

Jack stood up, walked to my bedroom door, and spun around. "It's a brilliant plan, and when you come to *your* senses—"

"I won't change my mind."

"Well, then, I'm going to work," he said.

"It's two or three in the morning," I reminded him.

"I won't bother you anymore, ever again."

"Come on, Jack. You know it's an unrealistic idea."

"I understand your position. I really do. I don't know what came over me. I'd never risk endangering a single red hair on your—"

"Jack—"

"Thank you for everything, Fiona. Have a wonderful life, which by the way, is one of my favorite movies."

I thought he was kidding or bluffing. But he turned and ran off. I heard my front door slam, his car door bang shut, and the Prius's tires squeal away. Those head-splitting sounds didn't do much to soothe my monster hangover.

Jack had left. How was I to have a wonderful life without my wonderful former student?

Chapter 49

JACK

It was early morning. The streetlights were still on. The birds had yet to wake. I sped past the pickup truck that was delivering the L.A. Times. It was too late to see night shifters driving home from work and too early to see predawn cyclists working out.

I would need the darkness for at least another hour to complete my covert operation. I was determined not to let a putz like Bowman take advantage of me. Or my writing partner. I was going to get what was due us. Or, because of our pain and suffering, a settlement well beyond what was owed.

I admit that I've done some dumbass things in my time. In fact, my nickname in college was Jackass. It was conferred upon me after a stunt I pulled on the eve of our homecoming game against the Indiana Hoosiers. I had sneaked into the cheerleaders' field house, where they stored the flipcards for our team's cheering section, rearranged the cards, and added some new, self-made ones. At halftime the following day, our fans in the bleachers unknowingly flashed colored cards to our opponent's bleachers across the field that all together revealed an 80-foot-long sign that read *Indiana Losers*. I would never have experienced that kind of glory on the turf as a linebacker, so I wasn't that upset when the coach punted me off the team.

The Jackass was about to do another stupid thing—visit Bowman's estate to case the joint. I parked down the street and waited until the spotlight from a neighborhood private security cruiser swept past Bowman's property. Then, I scrambled up his gravel driveway toward the mansion, staying clear of the floodlight beams, and darted like a cartoon character behind garden sculptures and trees, making mental notes along the way of where any hazards lay.

As I crept toward a murky, brown-water swimming pool, I heard Bowman's voice. He was in the backyard, sitting on a stone bench beside the dirty grotto, in his silk pajamas, smoking a Black Dragon cigar, and talking on the phone. I moved closer, crouching low to the ground, avoiding motion sensor lights.

"Well, you're movin' too fuckin' slow," he said. "I want the house packed by tonight. This time tomorrow, I'll be doin' shots in Mexico, and all my creditors can go fuck themselves."

Tonight? Dorothy's slippers ship out tonight? We're screwed. I was tempted to tackle the creep and rip his Rolex off his wrist. But I needed to sort things out. And come to the right decision, one that the Jackass could live with. And one that would let the Jackass's ass live.

I ARRIVED AT work three hours early. No one else was in the bakery. I needed alone time to think things over. Bowman's pronouncement about clearing out his house that night shocked me into reality. As much as I wanted to get something in return for writing the script, I didn't want to do anything that would get me arrested or worse. My scheme of stealing from Bowman was running out of steam. Was I coming to my senses? Was Fiona right? Again?

Sitting at my decorating station, I stared at a tiny, single M&M resting on my turntable. Some socialite from San Marino was having a World Series viewing party and wanted to personalize her favorite candy by putting piping, in the color of her Boston Red Sox team, around each button-shaped bead. Naturally, only red M&Ms would do. I had to extract that color out of three five-pound bags before me. With a margarita migraine and lack of sleep, my hand wasn't all that steady. My piping lines wiggled. What were intended to be straight stripes looked like the jagged lines of an EKG. If there was a distinct moment that caused a tipping point in my life, it was that little chocolate coated eyeball staring back at me. It was trying to tell me something. I turned away. I couldn't look at it.

I couldn't continue. My mind was numb. My body was shot. My soul was dead. I couldn't do this stupid job one second longer.

I set down my icing bag, lowered my head, and wondered. I wondered how Beth was doing in the single world. How Fiona was doing in the single world. How I would do in the single world. I thought about how my script and movie career had flatlined in this world. How I would have to move back to the normal world of Ohio as one of the world's biggest failures.

I wondered if I would stop weeping before the bakery's morning shift arrived.

ON THE ACCOUNT of having punched my card three hours early that day, Benny agreed to let me punch out three hours early at the end of the day. As I left work, Shanelle stopped me at the back door.

"I'm so nervous, Jack. I've never been married before."

"May this be the last time."

"We leave at five," she beamed. "Wedding bells at midnight."

"I'll bring you the car. I'll even gas it up. Are you registered at EXXON?"

"Thanks, Jack," she said. "Wish me luck."

"You won't need it. You're perfect for each other."

Chapter 50
FIONA

I HAD ACCEPTED Eddie's offer to have coffee with an abundance of misgivings. We sat in the front patio of the ritzy Caffe Primo on the chic Sunset Strip. Eddie wore all white. I wore all black. He looked full of life. I looked like a pallbearer.

"Did you have a nice day?" he asked. He was being so careful to avoid any gaffes. He was being carefully boring.

"Let's see. I mopped up fresh vomit on the staircase and scraped off fuzzy mold in the laundry room. Just another day at the office."

He didn't know whether to smile. "How's your coffee?"

"Cold and overpriced. But the car fumes are invigorating."

We sat in silence, watching the attractive waiters whisk by. I was being a pill. I shouldn't have come. "I'm sorry, Eddie. I'm acting like a world-class brat."

"I'm just glad we're together, enjoying each other's company."

I couldn't agree less. My head was elsewhere. My heart was taken. I should've hung a sign around my neck, *Out of Order*.

"So…." he said.

"So, what?" I said.

"How's this going so far?" he asked.

"Well, the police haven't been called."

Eddie leaned across the table. "It's great to see you, Fiona. Be with you. Be seen with you. Be—"

"Eddie."

"What?"

"I'm about to call the police."

"Sorry. Am I allowed to say that you look absolutely smashing?"

"I was born this way. Can't take any credit."

He squished up his face, baffled by what I had said. "Well, I'm one lucky guy."

"Well, I'm lucky that I'm more than my looks."

I couldn't censor myself. I had to be me. But I surely wouldn't want to date me. Not on this day. Not for the last few years.

Eddie tilted back in his chair, mulling over an idea. "I want us to have a safe word or a signal of some sort."

"For what, Eddie?"

"For when I'm getting out of line, like just then. I want to know, so that I can immediately stop whatever I'm doing."

"I should send up a flare?"

"Tap your foot, wet your lips, blink your eyes. Anything."

I unconsciously took an audible sigh.

"What is it?" Eddie said. "Am I doing something now?"

"We don't need signals. You're good enough just the way you are."

"Are you quoting Mister Rogers?"

"I, on the other hand, am 'an ungrateful ingrate,' to quote one of my best friends."

"And that's coming from a best friend?"

"I should be more appreciative, more sensitive, more grateful to you."

"Don't worry. You're great just the way you are."

We sat quietly, sipping our coffee, watching the privileged class strut by on the sidewalk, the exotic foreign cars fly by on the street, and having a perfectly tedious time. Sipping coffee, looking off. Old people stuff. I think I missed Marvin more at that moment than ever before. I was being more of a jerk to poor Eddie than poor Eddie ever was to me.

I started to think about the night before. Sitting around the pool with Jack, enjoying the warm evening air, laughing over his preposterous idea of raiding Bowman's house. Getting inexcusably drunk. Waking up to his face. To his beautiful butt on my bed. Lordy, that was good.

Jack. Eddie. These two men were so different. Eddie was appealing on many levels. And was age appropriate. If I put an ounce of effort into it, we could probably dance for a long time. Maybe even finish our lives together. But Jack. Well, Jack brought something out of me that made me like myself again. He made my heart sing. He made me happy.

Happiness. Isn't that what we all want?

I couldn't spend my time with Eddie-types, now that I knew there were Jack-types inhabiting the planet. I took a pen and an index card out of my purse and jotted a note to myself.

"What're you doing?" Eddie asked.

"I'm a writer. I write."

"Is it a miniature script?"

"It's a reminder," I said.

"For what?"

"To call my therapist."

"What for?"

"I have to figure out what to do with you."

"What does that mean?"

"This isn't working. You and me. It should be, but it's not."

"Don't fire me again, Ladybug. Work with me. Try to make this happen."

"I'm in love with someone else." It just came out that way. Wow. Did I really vocalize that? Love? Someone else? Is this what they call an epiphany? Or is this what they call impractical, selfish, excruciatingly moronic? Or finally being ready?

"You never said anything about anyone else," he said.

"There wasn't anyone. There isn't anyone. I'm in love with someone who doesn't know it."

"Are you in middle school?"

"I've got a lot to process."

"Your therapist is about to get very rich," Eddie said.

"I'm sorry. It's where I am. It's who I am." I took a beat. "Yeah. I love him."

"And me?" Eddie rested his hand on mine. "Will I ever get to make love to you?"

"I have to get over him before I get under you." I tried to center myself. With a full breath, I launched in. "Here's the really tragic part. You're a sharp guy. And crazy good looking. I like you, Eddie. Almost a lot." I withdrew my hand. "But I have to heal from the relationship I never had with the guy who never knew before starting a new one with a guy with whom I shouldn't be with."

"Was that in English?"

I pitied Deana. I pitied Eddie. I pitied myself. "I've got a lot to work out. I'm just not emotionally available right now."

Eddie produced a wistful smile and snapped his fingers for the check. The man in all-white pulled out his all-black credit card. "I tried," he said in a weak voice. "But I lost the case." He stood up somberly. "Fly away, Ladybug, Ladybug."

EDDIE SPED ME to my apartment, deploying the tortuous silent treatment the entire way home. When we arrived at my place, he didn't get out of the car or open the passenger door or walk me to my front door. I couldn't blame him for being disappointed or angry. I could blame him for being unmannered.

"I'm sorry, Eddie. I'm a writer. We're not a stable species."

"I'll still be around after you finish your electroshock treatments," he said with his Eddie-licious smile. "Call me when you realize you'll never do better than me."

I had run out of words. I simply opened the door and got out of the car. His Porsche 911 blasted away, leaving me on the sidewalk in a gust of dust. In my mind, in my heart, right then and there, any hope for an Eddie Harper/Fiona Logan romance was pronounced dead at the scene.

Chapter 51

JACK

I was at my apartment in the underground garage. It was time to put my unlimited decorating talents to use. Squeezing my pastry bag, I inscribed *Getting Married* in blue icing on the rear windshield of my Prius. As I drew white doves surrounding the words, I began thinking again about my illicit concept, The Great Movie Memorabilia Heist. Was it possible? Or was it possibly suicidal?

I jumped when I heard a raspy voice reverberate through the garage, "Dude. I heard we lost Kevin to the dark side." Violette, my purple-haired, beach bum neighbor skidded her skateboard to a stop next to me.

"Yeah. Tonight, in Vegas. They're taking my car."

"Nice wedding gift," she said, stepping off her board, revealing too much skin through her torn short shorts. "I also heard you're back in circulation."

"More like hibernation."

The automatic wrought iron gate slid open to allow a tenant's Range Rover to enter. We waited until the gate closed and for its loud scraping sound to subside.

"Let's fly to Vegas tonight and surprise them," Violette said.

"I don't think so."

"C'mon, Buck. You're a free man."

"They're not having guests."

"That's the reason?"

"We have to honor their request," I said.

"Okay. We won't see them. We'll just do Vegas."

"I don't do Vegas," I said.

"I'll teach you." Two of her fingers crawled up my chest. "It'll be an X-rated lesson."

"I admire your impulsive nature, however—"

"I have a friend who can get us the Pyramid Suite at the Luxor for free."

"Truth is, I'm busy tonight." Had I just made a decision?

"You've got to take chances, Bucky. Live a little. Risk a little." She sounded like Ethan.

"Oh, I intend to." I *had* made a decision.

"The suite has a giant jacuzzi in the living room overlooking the strip," Violette said as only a temptress could. "Do you still have plans tonight?"

Lust Never Sleeps. Sex Drive Never Takes A Holiday. Desire Never Dies. I reversed my decision. I decided *not* to have plans tonight. I decided not to rob Bowman. It was an idiotic idea in the first place. Instead, I decided to live a little with a bronze, hard-bodied, surfer girl. Hey, why not? Beats getting shot in the face.

"Call your friend. Sounds like fun," I said.

Violette clapped her hands and squealed like a four-year-old.

Why did I say yes when my gut said no? Why couldn't I do Vegas with Fiona? Why couldn't I stop thinking about her? Why was I selling out to a woman who meant nothing to me? Why was I acting like every other single-minded, goddamn man? Why was I asking these questions, when I knew all the goddamn answers?

Chapter 52
FIONA

YESTERDAY WAS NINETY-ONE flesh-burning degrees, and today a freak summer thunderstorm was in the forecast. California, where nothing is as constant as change. Gloomy clouds had already gathered in the skies above Casa del Sol. On the front lawn, a group of neighborhood kids joked around, played ball, and tossed a Frisbee. With my garage door open, Rathbone and I could keep an eye on the youngsters from inside my workshop.

One of my tenant's sons, Ruben, had asked me to fix his Super Soaker, a toy water rifle. I stood at my workbench wearing protective goggles, trying to teach the boy some of the basic rules of repair.

"My dad used to tell me that anything could be fixed." I spoke in my father's deep voice, "If you just keep looking at the problem, a solution will look back at you."

"Miss Fiona?"

"Yes?"

"Can you hurry? The war's 'bout to start."

"Well, we wouldn't want to make you late for battle." I pointed out a busted part. "See this right here?"

"Uh, huh."

"That's why it's leaking. We gotta patch up the pressure-relief valve."

"Will it take long?"

"Not if we use my father's secret weapon. Duct tape."

Something outside the garage caught Rathbone's eye. He barked and charged out, down the long driveway, picking up speed.

"Rathbone," I yelled, as he raced across the grass. "Get back here."

He hurdled the fence I had painted. "Rathbone," I shouted. He was following a wayward Frisbee, which was sailing into the street.

I ripped off my goggles and ran after him as fast as I could. "Rathbone. STOP."

He leaped off the curb.

"Rathbone. NOOOOO."

It all happened so swiftly, yet in slow motion. The horn blaring. The screech of brakes. The horrific impact. His guttural wail.

I rushed into the street without looking, like he had. By then, the shaken driver was out of his car, and the kids had gathered around my unconscious, beloved companion.

I cradled Rathbone's limp body in my arms. His cowboy bandana was seeping blood. The shaken driver spoke, but his voice sounded far away, as if it were underwater. "I never saw him. He just—"

"It's okay. It's okay," I stuttered, half to the driver, half to Rathbone.

Ruben tried to keep from crying in front of the older kids, except he failed. But nobody laughed at him. Nobody made a sound. The war, on this blustery evening, was called off on the count of one canine casualty.

Chapter 53

JACK

As I drove through a light fine rain to Shanelle's apartment to drop off my car, I listened to an interview with a Chinese oyster fisherman on National Public Radio. His translator said, *"Pearls don't lie on the seashore. If you want one, you must dive for it."* It made me think. By not taking from Bowman that which was rightfully mine, was I copping out? Was I giving up my Midwestern principles? Was I stuck in the sand, not strong enough to take a stand, not daring enough to place myself in peril? Too afraid to dive for my pearls? What would Ethan do? It made me reconsider.

I decided to rob Bowman after all. Clearly, I wasn't thinking clearly.

I called Violette from my car.

"Hey, hon," she said. *"Are you ready to party?"*

"Something's come up."

"Save it for tonight," she snickered.

"I can't go."

"Why?" she asked.

"It's kind of hard to explain."

"Hard? Save it for tonight," she joked again.

"I'm really sorry about this."

"I don't get it."

"I have to visit my aunt in hospice," I said, not knowing how that came to me.

"Hospice? Is that in California?"

"She's dying. The doctors say she won't last the night."

"There're flights like every half hour to Vegas. Could we go after she dies?"

"No. I'm so sorry."

"You're making a big mistake."

"I hope not. Maybe we can get a drink next week."

She faked a cry. *"It's not like hooking up in Vegas. Boo hoo. I really wanted to go,"* she whined. *"Well, don't think I'm done with you yet, Bucky boy."* Violette hung up.

One down, one to go. I called my partner in crime. The call went to voicemail. *"You have reached the number you most recently dialed. No one answers phone calls anymore, so text me."*

Vintage Fiona. I texted her the same message I left on her voicemail, *We have to talk.*

No reply.

I tried again. *Call me.*

Nothing. *It's an emergency.*

Still no response.

The Chinese oyster fisherman had one more pearl of wisdom. He said he was determined to *"die without regrets."* For sure, my next tattoo. And my mantra for that night.

I GAVE KEVIN the key to my car and a big hug of congratulations. He gave me the key to his Harley and a big warning not to total it. We tied some tin cans to the rear bumper of the Prius, and off they drove, for richer or poorer. Shanelle waved out the car window until the white doves were swallowed by the drizzly night.

I pushed the starter button of the Harley and, for better or for worse, flew to Fiona's apartment.

I POUNDED ON her door. No answer. Not even a welcoming woof from Rathbone. I went into her garage. The Mercedes was gone.

"Miss Fiona isn't here," a small voice said.

I turned around to see a young Hispanic boy standing at the door holding a Super Soaker. "Where is she?" I asked.

"At the animal hospital. Her dog was hit by a car."

A wave of nausea washed over me. That dog meant the world to Fiona.

"There was a lot of blood," the boy said. "Real blood."

"Yeah, I bet that was tough to see."

"Do you think Rathbone's going to live?" the boy asked.

"He damn well better."

"Ooh, you said 'damn.'"

"You're right. I'm sorry."

"I'll leave my rifle here. Miss Fiona hasn't finished fixing it." The boy placed his gun on the workbench, turned, and slowly walked out.

I fired up the Harley and hurried to Animal House, the closest pet hospital according to Google, the all-night clinic on Cahuenga Boulevard. The rain had begun to fall harder.

Tears from Heaven.

Chapter 54

FIONA

THEY HAD GIVEN me a paper cup of water, which I didn't touch. They had given me a magazine, which I didn't open. Mounted on the wall was a TV screen showing funny animal videos. I never looked up. I sat dazed. Nothing would be funny ever again.

I'm a devout atheist, but I found myself praying for my dog, whose blood was still damp on my jacket. You would think the light rain tapping on the outside shutters would help to calm my nerves. But it irritated me.

Dogs. They're just mammals. They don't write. They don't read. They don't talk. They just keep you company. They snuggle with you when you need a warm body.

Rathbone made me happy on stormy nights like this one, when skies were gray. He was my sunshine.

"Dear God or Whomever," I implored. "Please don't take my sunshine away." I was singing into space like a schizophrenic hobo.

Was it *my* fault? He's usually on a leash. I'd die without him. I just knew it. He was my guy. My strong, faithful, cuddly guy. And why the hell wasn't anyone coming out to tell me how he was? It had been over an hour. Someone must know something by now. Don't they care what I'm going through out here? Don't they know I'm alone?

Jack burst through the front door. He was dripping wet. He rushed up to me. I couldn't even stand. My knight kneeled before me.

"The Super Soaker kid told me what happened. How's Rathbone?"

"I have no idea. They've had him back there forever."

"I'm so sorry."

I choked up. "This is not happening. Tell me this is not happening."

The double doors leading to the back rooms swung open. A stocky female veterinarian in surgical scrubs, smeared with blood, came out. We sprang to our feet.

"If you're going to get hit by a car," she said, peeling off her squeaky latex gloves, "that's the way to get hit. Your dog's going to pull through." She smiled. "He'll be fine."

"He'll be fine? Really? Fine?" I said, needing to verify it over and over again.

"Looked worse than it was," she said to both of us.

"But he's going to be fine?" I asked once more.

"A few cuts and bruises and one heck of a headache. But with some rest and meds, yeah, he'll be himself again."

"Can I—"

"Not now. He's pretty out of it."

"Thanks, doctor. My gosh, you have no idea how much that old—" I fell into her arms. She patted me on the back. "He's not just a dog, you know," I said, breaking away from her clinch.

"I understand."

"He's my day and night."

"I know. But considering his concussion, I want to keep him a few days, maybe longer. We'll call you when he's ready to go home," the vet said, impatient to get back to work.

"Yeah. A few days. Sure," I said. "Thank you very, very much." Then, this nonbeliever added, "God bless you."

She disappeared through the double doors.

I collapsed into my chair.

Jack plopped down in the chair next to me. The sound of rain on the roof had grown louder, but less annoying. He put his arm around me.

I burrowed my head in his soggy chest.

He held me as I broke down.

"Guess he wasn't ready to leave me," I sobbed.

"You're not that easy to leave."

I composed myself for a moment and looked up at him, searching his face. "What were you doing at my apartment?"

"I tried calling first, I swear."

"I ran out. Didn't stop to get my phone."

"It's okay. We don't have to talk about it now. You keep crying. It's good for you."

The front door opened. A hunched over, bearded man holding a cage came in from the rain. He signed in at the unattended front desk and took a seat opposite us. He whipped a beach towel off his cage, like a magician, revealing a green cockatoo with a nasty feather disease. It was like a scene out of a Fellini film.

"I thought you weren't ever going to bother me again," I said quietly to Jack.

"I did some more investigating. Some groundwork I needed to report to you."

"Don't tell me you're still—"

"Do some more crying."

"You're possessed," I said.

The cockatoo squawked, shaking off black, flakey feathers. The bearded man squawked back at his bird. They were meant for each other.

"After I left your place this morning, I went to Bowman's," Jack whispered.

"Why would you do a thing like that?"

"He has no guards. No watchdogs. No barbed wire."

"Why would you need to know things like that?"

"I walked right in. I overheard him talking. He's packing his house and fleeing to Mexico."

"Why would I want to know a thing like that?"

"Because he leaves tonight. Skipping out on all the people he owes."

"Don't do it, Jack."

"We have to," he pleaded.

"There's no 'me' in 'we.'"

"I'm doing this with or without you."

"You'll get yourself killed."

The bearded man and his cockatoo exchanged another squawk. It was such a strange spectacle.

"All we have to do is follow our script," Jack said. "We wrote it together. You get co-credit. And half the money. A million dollars."

Fortunately, the cockatoo finally stopped screeching. Unfortunately, the bearded man didn't. Such is Hollywood after dark.

"I've been through hell tonight. I'm dead," I said, rising, handing Jack my umbrella. "Walk the dead to her car, please."

He stood, faced me, and placed both his hands on my shoulders. "Right now, across town, they're emptying Bowman's house. Our window is closing. Our ruby red slippers are slipping away."

Though his hands on my shoulders felt so good, I said, "I'm not doing it. Not even for a million dollars."

The wacky cockatoo man shrieked, "I'll do it."

Jack ignored him and continued to make his case. "Let's live in the now. Let's do something exciting, bold, fun."

"Something fun like a felony?" I asked.

"Let's dive for the pearls."

"I don't even know what that means," I said, walking to the door.

"It means—"

I put my hand up. I didn't want to hear anymore. "Don't open my umbrella inside. If you're going to do something stupid tonight, you don't need any bad luck."

My last word was punctuated by a raucous squeal from across the room. And a loud clap of thunder outside.

WE RAN THROUGH the deluge to my Mercedes. I jumped behind the wheel.

Before I could close my door, Jack said, "You taught us that most writing gets rejected, that most writers enjoy little success, that when we have the chance to score, we should take the shot."

"That last one is yours. Along with that diving for pearls bit."

"The point is, Rathbone might be sending us a message, that life is fragile, that one moment we're here, the next maybe not so much. Let's take our shot tonight, Fiona. Let's change our lives." Rainwater dripped off the tip of his nose.

"Let's say good night." I closed the car door.

He stepped in front of my Mercedes, leaned against the hood, blocking my path. He looked at me through the front windshield. It was a Tiananmen Square moment.

"Help me this one last time, and I'll go my separate way," he shouted over the storm. "You'll never have to see me again. I give you my word."

It struck me that all Jack really wanted was revenge against Bowman and the money we were owed. He didn't, however, want me. He was too willing to walk away from what I thought could have been a special relationship. I had been deluding myself. An old familiar wall rose within me, the first line of emotional defense. It was replacing wishful thinking with face-the-fucking-facts, Fiona. I still had Rathbone's collar in my hand. I didn't think my heart could break any harder that night.

"No, Jack," I said.

He slowly moved aside, soaked to the bone, completely dejected. I drove past him into the thundery night, fearing I might never see that dear man again.

I HUSTLED ACROSS the footpath to my apartment.

Under the archway, out of the rain, at my door, sitting on a motorcycle helmet, was Jack. He had beaten me home and was holding a yellow rose. "I got this for you," he said, handing me the flower.

"From my garden?"

"It's the thought that counts."

"You're all wet," I said, looking down at him.

Jack's tired eyes begged that I grant him another hearing. He stood up. "What will it take to convince you to come?"

I took a deep breath. And said, "Let's dry you off."

We entered my apartment. Jack sat on the couch.

I fetched him a towel from the bathroom. I sat next to him. And rested my hand softly on his knee. "You're a good writer, Jack. And I don't mean just on birthday cakes. Your passion is writing. It rules your world. If you learn nothing else, remember this. Follow your heart." I reluctantly withdrew my hand from his knee. "Robbing Bowman is far too dangerous. If you're so desperate for money, well, it's not much, but the Fifi Film Foundation would like to loan—correction, would like to *grant* you—some funds, enough to keep you housed and fed for another year.

You can quit your job, go off and write the movies you want to write, if you don't die of pneumonia tonight."

"That's incredibly generous of you, but you don't have that kind of money, and even if you did, I wouldn't take it."

Disheartened, I went to the kitchen to get Rathbone a treat, and then remembered. Poor Rathbone.

Jack stayed on point. "Come with me, Fiona. This could be the greatest—"

There was a loud bang on my front door.

"Damn it, Eddie." I instinctively yelled through the door.

"Eddie?"

"Someone else who doesn't find me easy to leave." I faced the door. "I'm not here."

"It's Adolf," a muffled voice from the other side hollered. "Open the fucking door."

"Adolf?" Jack asked incredulously.

"The punk rocker in unit three."

"Is he friends with Eddie?" he asked. "Who are all these men?"

I opened the door. Adolf, my drugged-out, skin-headed tenant stood on the porch in a black trench coat, collar up. His neck was tattooed with words from *Mein Kampf*.

"Where the fuck have you been?" he boomed.

"I left my phone—"

"I've been calling you all fucking night."

Jack stood up and joined me at the door. "Simmer down, Sparky," he said.

He turned toward Jack. "My fucking roof is leaking. You try sleeping under a waterfall."

"I'll look at it," I said.

"Looking won't fix it. You don't do shit around here."

"We heard you," Jack said in a firm voice. "Now, go play in the puddles."

"Fuck off," Adolf shouted back.

Like a scene out of one of my bad movie scripts, Jack slammed Adolf against the porch wall, and pieces of terracotta showered down. Something else for me to fix. In a flash, Jack had pinned him with one hand, while his other was clenched in a fist, cocked, and ready to pummel.

"Two things, dickhead," Jack said coldly. "First, never swear or raise your voice in front of this woman again. Got it?"

The dickhead tried to nod, but the vice-like grip squeezing his windpipe didn't make it easy. I hadn't seen this side of Jack's personality. It was scary. But I wouldn't say I didn't like it.

"And second," Jack said. "Move out of your apartment. Got it?"

"'K," was all Adolf could croak out.

Jack let him go. Adolf trembled. He started to stagger away when Jack grabbed his coat and jerked him back. "And third—"

"Oh, fuck. There's a third?" Adolf asked.

"I want you out by Saturday."

"You can't evict me," Adolf shot back. "You're not the owner."

"I have friends downtown. They'll make it happen," Jack said, shoving Adolf into the rain. "By Saturday. Or I'll track you down and feed you your nuts." Surging with adrenalin, Jack turned to me and threw his hands up. "This is your life. What do you want to do about it? Fix a leaky roof, or make a fortune?"

That was the crucial question. "I could have handled that," I said.

"I know. I just had to let off some steam."

"You should eat more fiber."

"What's it going to be, Fiona? Manager or millionaire?"

A good ol' home invasion robbery was a chance to grow closer to Jack and an opportunity to conquer one of my demons—atychiphobia, fear of failure. Or was I just trying to rationalize committing a crime like any other well-intentioned crook would?

If I went through with this ill-advised venture, Deana would institutionalize me. Charlotte would disown me. On the bright side, Eddie might represent me. I locked eyes with Jack. "If I were stupid enough to say yes...."

"You'd be a million dollars stupider by the end of this night."

Some author once said, "Bad decisions make good stories." I was about to make a terrible decision. However, I would have—if I lived to tell it—a great story for my grandchildren. My Spanish grandchildren.

"I suppose it all comes down to this, Jack. 'It is not what we think or feel that makes us who we are. It is what we do. Or fail to do.'"

"Jane Austen," Jack said, completely capturing my heart. "*Sense and—*"

"You win." I said. "Get in the car."

Chapter 55
JACK

THE RAIN HAD increased. Bolts of lightning made a rare appearance in the L.A. heavens, etching white spiderwebs above the skyline. Fiona parked the Mercedes on a remote hillside high above Bowman's estate. While she repaired Ruben's Super Soaker, I used her birdwatching binoculars to survey the activity below. Several moving men were loading minivans and trucks.

"I count three guys. Probably more inside."

"Is it ever going to stop raining?" Fiona said fretfully.

"Always has."

"We're going to die here. You know that, right?"

"Think positively."

"Okay. I'm positive we're going to die here."

I put down the binoculars and picked up our script. "We're going to do exactly as Ethan and what's-her-name—Elsa—did. They got away with it. And so will we. Nobody's dying here tonight."

"Oh, yeah?" she said. "Try wearing a foil poncho in a lightning storm and see what happens."

We had stopped at Walgreens on the way to Bowman's to buy two cheap disposable rain ponchos, fifty feet of aluminum foil, and a jumbo roll of duct tape. We had taped the foil over every square inch of the ponchos, following the instructions of the security expert Fiona had interviewed. The foil was supposed to scramble electronic signals and throw any dogs off our scent.

I threw opened the car door. "It's time to suit up," I ordered. "Let's go."

We stepped out of the Mercedes into the rain and opened the trunk. We grabbed our foil ponchos and helped each other put them on.

I looked like a silver alien. "The Tin Man is off to get Dorothy's shoes," I said to lighten the mood.

Fiona strapped her vintage wicker fishing basket over her shoulder. "And an unarmed apartment manager and an unarmed cake decorator are off to rob a man with a gun. What could possibly go right?"

"Who's Eddie?" I asked.

"Are you trying to distract me?"

"Yes. And who is he?"

"He's a rather smitten and tenacious gentleman caller, if you must know."

"Is that so, Miss Scarlett? Do y'all sit on the veranda and sip mint juleps?"

Fiona ignored me. "Seriously," she said. "We should turn around, get the hell out of here, and forget this whole damn thing."

"Nobody's leaving. Noone's getting electrocuted. No dogs will be involved. No man with a gun will shoot us." My nerves were getting the better of me. "We're simply sneaking in there, taking the slippers, sneaking out, then going our separate ways."

"If we die, I'm going to kill you," she spouted.

I ran out of patience and said, "Put on your gloves, strap on your toolbelt, and find some cowardly lion courage. It's time to walk the yellow brick road."

Before slamming the trunk shut, I took out my gym bag, which was full of burglarizing tools. We slogged down the steep planted slope that led to Bowman's tennis court. I carried a crowbar. Fiona carried Ruben's Super Soaker. A rumble of thunder made us scurry down the slippery hill as fast as we could. In our full length, foil-hooded ponchos we were a couple of human lightning rods ready to fry.

I jumped a low retaining wall bordering Bowman's tennis court, then turned to give Fiona a hand. She didn't need my help. All her yoga was paying off. We crept across the mushy grounds and hid behind a large palm tree. The downpour was intensifying.

"See the red box on that pole?" I said, pointing it out. "It houses the security system. Step one of our mission, Operation Molasses." I pulled out a large bottle of maple syrup from my gym bag. "You stay here, out of sight. I'm going to slather me some hotcakes." I started to slink toward the pole.

Fiona grabbed hold of my poncho and hauled me back behind the trunk of the tree. Out of nowhere, two hulking moving men came around the corner carrying an antique armoire covered with a waterproof tarp. We huddled low, our metal bodies scraping against each other.

When the men passed, Fiona said in a shaky voice, "What if they saw us?"

"We're safe. Not exactly camouflaged, but safe."

"What are we doing here? This is insane." She shifted her weight from one foot to the other. "I gotta go."

"No. I can't do this alone."

"I mean, I need to use the little girl's room."

"What?"

"It happens when I get nervous," she whispered.

"It'll have to wait."

"It can't."

"I don't believe this. I fucking don't believe this."

"It's not my fault. I drank vats of coffee at lunch with Eddie. And the sound of this rain isn't helping. Besides, my bladder is the size of a Tic Tac."

"Okay, I get it. And I've had enough of Eddie."

"So have I," she said, hiding on the other side of the palm tree. "No peeking."

"Just do it. And do it quietly." I ran to the pole, then pried the lock off the security box with the crowbar and popped open the cover. I poured the entire bottle of syrup over the wires and the circuitry in the box, licked my fingers, and returned to the palm tree.

Fiona looked relieved to see me. At least her bladder was relieved.

Chapter 56

FIONA

We ran through a torrent of rain along the side of the decaying mansion, squishing through muck.

Jack craned his neck to peer through the leaded glass window for a better view of Bowman's study. "The display case is still there. I can see our slippers."

"Do you see anything else?" I asked.

"Laser beams crisscrossing the room. But the syrup will soon take care of them."

We skulked along the edge of the house until we came to a crawl space leading underneath the manor. Jack removed the protective vent cover and gestured for me to enter inside. The opening looked like a little mineshaft, just wide enough for a person's hips to fit through.

"Okay," Jack whispered. "This is it. Stick to the script. Trust the research."

"Okay. You go. I'll wait here," I whispered.

"Get in there and stop jabbering."

"I can't."

"Yes, you can. Just close your lips."

"I mean, I can't crawl in there."

"You're wasting time."

I just shrugged my foil shoulders, lips closed.

"Do we have to make wee-wee again?" he asked impatiently.

"No."

"Caca?"

"Jack."

"Then, get in there," he commanded.

"I can't."

"Why?"

"I'm too embarrassed to say."

"It *is* caca."

"It's claustrophobia."

"Are you kidding me?" Jack said, walking off.

"I should've told you earlier."

He turned to me. "Claustro-fuckin'-phobia? Really?"

"Closed spaces freak me out. Elevators, closets, caves, MRI machines, some relationships—"

"This is crazy."

"I could possibly stick my head in, but that's as far as I go."

Jack looked up at the dark clouds, looked down at the marshy mud. "Fiona. We have to do this together. I can't do it by myself. You can't back out now."

"I'm scared. I'm cold. I'm wet. And come to think of it, I do have to go potty again."

"We'll be in and out of that study within two minutes, three at the most. Can you give me three more minutes of your life? That's all I'm asking."

We had come this far. I didn't want to let him down. I had to face one of my many fears. I also had to face the fact that I was falling harder and harder for Jack Reynolds, and that felt riskier than wriggling under a five-hundred-ton house. Nothing is better than being in love. But nothing hurts more than heartache. I was deathly afraid of going through that kind of pain again.

"I'll do it under one condition," I whispered.

"Do I have to take my shirt off again?"

"If we live through this—"

"That's a big 'if.'"

"We'll go our separate ways," I said.

"Yeah. Sure. I told you we would."

"I mean it, Jack. We need to get on with our lives. Our separate lives."

"Separate ways. Separate lives. Agreed."

"Promise me."

"I promise you. Now, can we get on with committing our crime here?"

I knew he hadn't really heard me, and that we would have to revisit the conversation when we weren't in the act of breaking and entering, so I took a deep breath, switched on my headlamp, squatted down, crawled in, and slithered on my stomach under the house through the mire. Rusty and leaky galvanized pipes dripped above me. Thin colored cables were strung overhead.

Jack followed me in. With the limited headspace, he had to army crawl on his belly, pushing his gym bag ahead of him.

I froze.

"What now?" Jack asked, my butt in his face.

"I have a problem."

"Are we talking number one or number two?"

"It's not that," I said over my shoulder. "I feel another phobia coming on."

"Fear of dirt?"

"Arachnophobia. There better not be any spiders down here," I said.

"I can assure you, there aren't."

"Well, that's a relief."

"They're eaten by the rats."

"Rats?"

Jack took out our script from his gym bag. "Give me some light," he requested.

I directed my headlamp beam Jack's way. The light was shaking as I continued to contemplate the probability of rats.

He found a dog-eared page in our script and read aloud, "'The communications cable is red. Backup generators, white. Power, yellow.'"

"I can't breathe," I said. "This is a dungeon."

"We're almost there."

"A tomb, far worse than an MRI," I whimpered. "There's no air down here."

"Hang on."

"I think I saw a snake."

"Stop it," he barked.

"What if there's an earthquake?"

"Then, we're stuck down here with the snakes and rats."

"That's really not funny. I'm going to be in therapy for years."

"In two minutes, you'll be able to afford it. Now, just clip the cables."

"Did someone say 'please?'"

"Oh, my god. *Pah-leez.* Okay?" He quickly referred to the script. "'The lights stay on for now.'"

I took a pair of cable cutters from Jack's bag and snipped the red, then the white cable above our heads.

"Good," Jack said. "Now, point your light toward the floorboards."

I glared at him.

"Pleeease," he said.

I aimed my light upward.

Jack started to pry through the floor above our heads with his crowbar. Clacks of thunder masked the sound of termite-ridden wood splitting. He began to sweat and puff heavily, but he was dogged. And strong. The floorboards cracked, and a couple planks rose into Bowman's study.

In no time, Jack had made an opening in the floor large enough for us to squeeze into Bowman's study. He peered through the jagged hole and assessed the room. "Molasses did its thing. The laser beams are gone. That sticky stuff killed 'em."

"Wahoo. Now, get me out of here," I pleaded.

"Take your best shot, Elsa. Then, we can make our move."

I raised the barrel of young Ruben's Super Soaker, poked it through the hole in the floor, and took aim, just like my daddy taught me, at the security camera mounted in the corner of the ceiling. "She shoots," I said, squeezing the trigger repeatedly, squirting an inky stream of motor oil, which splattered on the camera, blackening the lens.

"She scores." Jack was having the time of his life.

"Yay."

"How's the bladder?"

"It's a super soaker," I said.

"Sorry I asked. Let's go to work." He climbed into the room, then reached down to pull me up. And just like that, we were both standing inside the mansion, inside the study, inside seconds of snatching the ruby slippers. We stepped daintily to the tall cabinet containing the cherished relics and gazed at our prize. They rested on the top shelf in a protective glass box.

Outside the open double doors, in the foyer, we heard movers approaching. We darted behind the doors, hiding beside the doorframe, our backs pressed to the wall. After the men passed by, we gently pushed the double doors closed.

As Jack locked them, he whispered, "Which brings us to page eighty-seven." He quietly read the lines. "'Ethan lifts Elsa up and holds her legs, while she stretches to reach the object of their desire, displayed upon a tall pedestal, the treasured gold dragon.'" In a pathetic impersonation of John Wayne, Jack added, "Up ya go, littl' Elsa."

I took the crowbar.

Jack lifted me, supporting my lower body.

Once again, my tin foil ass was inches from his nose. His grip felt so good. I prayed that I wouldn't pee in his face.

"'She reaches for the precious dragon,'" Jack quoted from the script.

I reached toward the precious pair of ruby red slippers. With Jack still holding my hips high in the air, I used the crowbar to break the glass case protecting our treasure and deftly slipped the tip of the crowbar inside the first shoe, all the way to the toe. It was as if I were fishing for a red slipper instead of a red snapper.

There was thumping on the stairs. And a voice shouting. "Steve. Steve."

I looked down at Jack, who whispered, "It's Bowman. Hurry."

I carefully transported and deposited the first slipper into my fishing basket.

Bowman shouted again, "Steve. Am I the only fuckin' one watchin' the security monitors?"

I stretched to reach the second slipper, poked the crowbar inside, carted it toward me, and gracefully grasped it with my free hand. I placed the second iconic slipper inside my basket, where the world-famous artefact joined its mate.

"Let's get the hell outta Kansas," I said.

Jack was eyeing Charlie Chaplin's cane.

"Don't get greedy," I said.

Bowman was right outside the door, screaming, "Steve. I'm being robbed."

Jack and I aimed for the opening in the floor, hopped down that rabbit hole and, on all fours, rapidly wiggled through the grungy tunnel. I was Charles Bronson in *The Great Escape*. Jack was Tim Robbins in *The Shawshank Redemption*. I couldn't wait to get into open air. Jack wormed out of the crawl space first, dragging the crowbar, his gym bag, and the Super Soaker with him.

Just before I clambered out, I clutched my cable cutters and reached up. "Lights out, campers."

And I clipped the yellow power cable.

Chapter 57

JACK

THE EXTERIOR FLOODLIGHTS arced and burned out, staging a blazing firework display before plunging Bowman's outdoor property into total darkness.

Fiona climbed out from under the foundation into the rain. "Oh, damn." she said.

"What?"

"I broke a nail."

"Can we obsess over that later?"

"How did Bowman figure out he was being robbed?" she asked.

"He probably saw a blacked-out lens on one of the security monitors."

The two of us, looking like commandos with our muddy faces, bolted through Bowman's backyard. The slimy terrain made it difficult to keep our footing. We stumbled in the dark, crossed the tennis court, and ended up at the retaining wall on the hillside.

Fiona was laughing wildly. She was having the time of her life. "We made it," she exclaimed. "We made it."

We stealthily scaled the stone wall, then struggled to climb the grassy slope, which led up to the cul-de-sac where we had parked the Mercedes. I gave Fiona the Super Soaker to use as a walking stick, to help her mount the muddy hill.

I turned around to see several dark figures charging through the tennis court. Things weren't going exactly according to my plan.

"Uh, Fiona. We need to pick up the pace a little. We haven't quite made it yet."

The relentless rains had caused our path to become more slippery and sloppier than earlier. For every stride upward, we slid two back.

The goons gained ground, as we clawed our way up the grubby hill. We were close to the top when one of the thugs caught up, gripped Fiona's ankle, yanked her to the ground, and pulled her silver-wrapped body part way down the slope.

She screamed and pounded her assailant over the head with the Super Soaker, but he was thick skulled.

I slid down the hill on my rump, ripped the attacker's meaty hands off of Fiona, and slugged him senseless.

By that time, big Steve had reached us.

I whacked his kneecaps with the crowbar, causing him to somersault downhill and over the wall onto the tennis court.

Other bruisers, however, were still giving chase, straining to climb the slippery slope.

I took them on, one by one. It was the Alamo. I was Davy Crockett. Fiona had waited for me. "Get your ass up that hill," I hollered. And I pushed her tin-foiled buttocks forward, inch by inch.

Chapter 58
FIONA

WE CRESTED THE hill and got to the Mercedes before any of Bowman's men saw which direction we had gone. "We did it." I whispered to Jack. "Let's get out of here."

We jumped into the car, I put the key in the ignition and turned it hard. But my disobedient engine refused to catch. I desperately turned the key again. Nothing. Tried a third time. Nada. Once more. Zilch. We could hear grunts from the thugs as they hiked the hill.

I threw open my door and yelled to Jack, "Eject."

"What?"

"Out."

"Keep trying," he shouted.

"No. Get out," I insisted.

"They'll kill us."

"I'm your mentor. Do what I say."

There was a blinding flash of lightening and a ferocious crash of thunder. We jumped out of the moody Mercedes, slammed the doors, and ran madly down the street, two highly reflective scarecrows fleeing for their lives.

"Wheels. We need wheels," I said.

The gasping goons summited the hill and spotted us escaping through sheets of rain. One of them got on his walkie-talkie, and we heard him yell, "They're headed back to the house."

I could see men with walkie-talkies and flashlights in Bowman's driveway fanning out, searching the grounds.

"Run," Jack yelled over a cloudburst.

"I *am* running," I yelled back, trying to keep up with him.

"You run like a turtle."

The road circled down to the front of Bowman's estate. Loading trucks and vans were parked in his muddy courtyard. We ran up the driveway toward the mansion in search of a car that we could "borrow." We frantically bound from vehicle to vehicle, taking cover behind each.

I looked through the window of one of the unoccupied moving vans. Its rear doors were open, revealing a half-packed cabin. I spotted a key in the ignition. "We're saved," I bellowed.

Jack slinked into the driver's seat. I sneaked into the passenger seat. Jack turned the key.

Unlike the old Mercedes, the motor started immediately. Success.

Jack floored it. We were on our way.

Almost. The wheels spun in the mud, seeking traction. We were stuck. When it rains, it pours.

On his front portico, Bowman, with a walkie-talkie to his ear, scanned the driveway with a powerful Mag-Lite.

Jack sprang out of the van, calling back to me, "Take the wheel."

I climbed behind the steering wheel as Jack streaked to the rear of the minivan.

"Gun it," Jack demanded.

I stepped on the accelerator.

He pushed the vehicle with all his might, managing to force the van an inch forward, creating just enough improved surface for the tires.

"We're free," he called out. "We did it."

Jack had rescued us. His once shimmering foil poncho was now thoroughly mud-splattered, as was his face. He was my knight in almost shining armor.

"Jump in," I yelled.

Jack dove inside the van through the back doors, imploring me to, "Go, go, go."

Bowman must have witnessed our van fishtailing away because I saw him in my side-view mirror hightailing it for his Hummer.

My eyes were focused straight ahead as I raced the van through the rain, around other parked vehicles, out of the driveway, and into the street. The windshield wipers were wigwagging at full speed.

Jack locked the rear doors of the van and climbed over priceless cargo, working his way to the front cabin. "Oh, yeah. That's what I'm talking about," he said, spitting mud. "We made it."

Our relief was cut short when a barrage of bullets—BOOM, BOOM, BOOM—blew out the back windows of the van and unhinged the rear doors.

I shrieked.

"It's Bowman. Keep driving," Jack shouted, scrambling toward me as the vehicle veered from side to side, slamming my partner against the walls of the van and thrashing him about like a bat in a bag.

I noticed that I had been slightly grazed in the forearm. "Uh, oh," I said. "Don't get upset, Jack."

"Did someone make poopoo in her panty-pants?"

"It's not that."

"Bullet phobia? Don't worry. I have the same fear."

"I've taken one for the team," I said bluntly.

"What are you talking about?"

"A bullet. I've been winged." A tiny trickle of blood had begun to drip down my arm. A pin prick at best. I was one lucky ladybug. "Could've been a piece of glass, or I may have picked a scab, but—"

We were whizzing through the calm and quiet streets of the fashionable Pacific Palisades neighborhood. Because of the late hour and the storm, the residents were tucked safely in their beds.

"Faster. And what does 'winged' mean?" Jack asked.

"You need to watch more TV. It means wounded," I said. "It's probably nothing. Just take the wheel for a moment."

Jack's eyes fixed on a single droplet of blood dribbling toward my right elbow. He panicked. "Oh, no. You've been killed."

"It's a scratch," I said. "Just drive."

"I hate blood. My father hated blood. His father hated blood. It's in our blood to hate blood."

"Hold the wheel, Jack."

"No problem. I'll drive. Here I come. Help has arrived. Just don't die on me."

Bowman was on our tail. We had to get away from him.

Jack had become delirious, lightheaded, useless. And he was now clumsily trading places with me. "Don't pass out," he blubbered. "Fifi. Please. Stay with me."

"It's only a nick," I said, hoisting a leg over his head at fifty miles an hour. "Don't *you* pass out on me."

Our van slid around curves, the rear doors banging open and shut, jettisoning valuable cargo onto the winding road in our wake.

Bowman swerved behind us to avoid running over several costly keepsakes as his Hummer bore down on our van.

Jack managed to make it into the driver's seat, steering the van stiff-armed like a student driver. He sneaked a fleeting peek at my grazed arm. It was still oozing a small amount of blood. "Okay. This is getting way, way, way out of hand," he said as the van drifted across the street toward oncoming traffic.

"Everything's fine, Jack. Dandy, in fact. Just watch where you're going."

"There's red blood here."

"Think of it as a nosebleed."

"I'm not gonna lie to you. I'm feeling a little faint." Jack's eyes were rolling up in his head.

I reached over and took control of the wheel, my bleeding arm stretched across his body.

A close look at my forearm caused Jack's head to swivel. "I'm going down. I'm going down fast. Mayday, Mayday." He was swooning, ready to keel over.

"Can you do the pedals?" I yelled.

"The pedals?"

"The things under your feet."

"The pedals? My feet? Who's Eddie?"

He was in bad shape.

Suddenly, our van was hit hard from behind. We pitched forward, our necks snapping.

The jolt shocked Jack back to life. "Hold on," he screamed to me. He tightened his grip on the steering wheel and slammed on the brakes, giving Bowman no time to react, resulting in the Hummer smashing us solidly in the backend again. The front grill of the Hummer crumpled, metal fragments and shards of glass spilled into the street.

Jack sped the van away.

Bowman recovered and continued his pursuit.

"I hate myself," Jack yelled.

"Just steer. You can hate yourself in the morning."

"I forced you into this. Now, you're all shot up, and there's blood gushing everywhere. It's all my fault."

"Is my face as muddy as yours?"

"You're worried about how you look at a time like this?"

"Indulge me."

"Your face is muddy, and your arm is bloody. But you're still beautiful. And we're still in big doo-doo here."

Beautiful. Had I heard that right? "We're going to be totally fine," I said. "Make a left at the next corner."

"This is so messed up," he said, checking the rearview mirror.

Bowman's car was pulling around to the passenger side of the van. He drew even with my window, sneered, and aimed his gun at us.

"Here it comes," Jack screamed. "I knew it. We're gonna be shot in the face."

"Okay. But first, let's make that left."

Jack spun the steering wheel hard to the left. The van took a two-tire turn onto a narrow road.

The Hummer missed the turn and kept going straight.

Jack checked the side mirror. "We lost him."

"See? No problem. Just like Ethan and… the other guy." I checked my side mirror.

Bowman's Hummer skidded to a stop. He threw his car in reverse. His tires screeched and burned, returning him to the mouth of the street we'd turned onto. Through the open rear doors of the van came the blinding headlights of the Hummer.

"Oh, shit," Jack said. "I'm going for broke." He stomped down on the gas.

"Oh, shit. Oh, shit," I yodeled.

The van engineered the tight turns much better than the Hummer. In its attempt to clip our rear fender and affect a pit maneuver, the Hummer lost control and spun out, crashing into a fire hydrant, sending a geyser of water sky high.

Bowman staggered out of the smoking Hummer, stunned and livid, but uninjured.

"Best day ever," Jack squealed. "Except for that blood thing."

"Ding, dong, the witch is dead," I sang, checking that Dorothy's red slippers in my fishing basket had survived. They had.

The road merged into the Pacific Coast Highway. Our van with back doors flapping open and closed, bumper hanging off and sending out a spray of sparks, ran a traffic light and rashly sailed across four lanes of traffic onto the highway, facing south. Several cars managed to avoid colliding with us, but some came very close.

I was ecstatic. "It's over. We made it."

Jack was euphoric. "We're safe. We did it."

It was our eureka moment. I was sure Jack was going to slam on the brakes, bringing the van to a stop, and we would kiss.

He didn't. We didn't. But everything became quiet and peaceful. We were traveling smoothly at the speed limit. It was just the two of us, our mud-blackened faces reveling in victory. I felt liberated, enjoying a leisurely, rainy drive along the oceanfront. It was like Jack and I were on a romantic road trip. Until, behold. We were treated to a holy experience.

The interior of the van became bathed in an intense white light, as if from Heaven. Did I hear angels sing? The moment felt sacred. It felt special. It felt surreal. It felt like the universe was giving us its blessing, its permission.

Unfortunately, I had grossly misjudged the holiness. I was blinded by the light, as Bruce Springsteen might say.

Jack looked skyward out the front windshield, up at the universe. "Holy shit," he announced.

I followed his gaze. "The plot thickens," I said, upon seeing that the van was under the hot spotlight of a police helicopter's sun gun. I looked behind us. Numerous cop cars followed in single file with lightbars flashing, headlights blinking, and sirens blaring.

"Oh—" Jack said.

"Just a minor rewrite."

"My—"

"One more twist."

"GOD." Terror was in Jack's eyes. "We've got to stop."

"We can't stop now. It's just getting interesting."

"A police chase isn't interesting. Stealing a car with stolen goods inside isn't interesting. Spurting blood isn't interesting."

"It's my blood. And I'm not giving up."

"I'll just tell them we're doing research for a movie," Jack said, trying to calm down.

"Oh, sure. They'll buy that."

"Everyone else has. This is L.A., remember? Where everybody wants to be in show business."

Over the lead cruiser's loudspeaker came, "This is the California Highway Patrol. Pull over."

"We're going to be arrested, charged, and imprisoned," Jack said. "Maybe Benny will bake me a cake with a file inside."

"Look at it this way," I said. "In a hundred years, none of this will matter."

"The police are after us. That's what matters in the here and now."

"Yeah. Somebody wants us," I said. "Cherish the moment."

"We're not Thelma and what's-her-name—"

"Ethan."

"We're law-abiding—"

"Relax, Jack. We've got two million dollars' worth of slippers and a script that shows us how to make a perfect get-away. The movie's not over yet."

"What's-his-name and what's-her-name are fiction. We're not. We bleed," he said. "Well, one of us bleeds."

"We wrote an airtight ending," I said. "If we continue to do what our characters did, we'll be home free."

The police car behind us had moved to within feet of our rear bumper. The sirens had become louder, the lights brighter, and the loud speaker more insistent. "Pull the van over and stop now."

"What if our script doesn't work?" Jack asked.

"It has so far."

"But what if it *doesn't*?"

"We're already in a world of trouble. Why not go out in style?"

He thought. He winced. He grinned. "Okay, I'm in. But I forgot what to do."

"We do what writers do. We make stuff up. We're creative artists. I'm revising the script a bit." I placed the Super Soaker on Jack's lap. "Take Elsa hostage, Ethan."

With his left hand, Jack steered the van. With his right hand, he raised the Super Soaker and gave the cops in the cars behind us a great view of a carjacker with a weapon to his prisoner's head. "This rewrite better work," he mumbled.

"Or what?" I said.

"Or we'll never see Rathbone again."

That touched me deeply. I decided to cry later.

The chase continued over the rain-slick highway. Due to the heightened hijacking situation, the police cars had dropped back. But we remained under the severe scrutiny of the helicopter's relentless searchlight.

Chapter 59

JACK

I WAS RACKING up a long list of moving violations as I led the chase through the flooded streets of Culver City. A long line of police SUVs continued to follow us, as did the police helicopter from above.

Fiona flicked on the radio.

"...but the rain is expected to clear out by tomorrow," a newscaster said. *"This just in. We have breaking news about a police pursuit taking place in the west L.A. area. It all began about thirty minutes ago in Santa Monica."*

"We're newsworthy, Jack," Fiona boasted.

"We're famous."

The newscaster continued. *"We are now being told that the driver is a suspected carjacker. And that he or she has taken a hostage, and he's holding a rifle to his victim's head."*

"It's working. Our script is working." I rejoiced.

"Once again, for those just joining us," the broadcaster announced. *"The Highway Patrol is in low-speed chase of a minivan carrying two occupants. Both appear to be African American, and one is being held captive."* The announcer cleared his voice. *"We see this so often in Los Angeles. Each time, we speculate what in the world is going through the suspect's mind. He's risking the lives of innocent citizens as well as those in law enforcement. Our prayers go out to that poor hostage."*

"Thank you," Fiona said. "We can use all the help we can get."

My neighborhood was coming into view.

"We need to shake the cops," Fiona said more urgently.

The newscaster prattled on. *"Nearly all these pursuits end up in an arrest and conviction, or worse,"* he informed us. *"Whoever this knucklehead is, whatever he or she may be wanted for, they simply have no chance of escaping. He may outsmart the ground units for a second or two, but the police airship with its Night Sun spotlight can never be outrun."*

"Wanna bet?" this knucklehead said. I made a quick turn into the ARCO gas station on Overland Avenue, but I was forced to stop the van at a row of rubber traffic cones blocking the entrance to the alley. It was shut down for repaving. "Ah, shit. My shortcut is closed."

"Go through the cones, Jack."

"That's illegal."

"Oh, honey. We passed illegal ten miles ago."

Hearing the endearment "honey" shocked and sort of delighted me. Had we crossed a line? I guess we had crossed all kinds of lines many miles ago.

I rolled the van's tires over the orange cones and proceeded down the alley. So far, so good. No traffic. Only potholes. I accelerated, sending a rooster tail of dirty rainwater into the air. The police cars followed but kept their distance, knowing that I had a hostage with a rifle muzzle stuck in her pretty, half-shell ear.

"The cops are still on our tail," I said. "They're way back there now. But that damn helicopter—"

"Jack. Look out."

Coming straight at us was a dump truck. I had to turn sharply to evade a head-on collision.

Fiona covered her face with her hands. "Did we make it? Are we alive?" she said, peeking through her fingers. "Am I dreaming this?"

"This nightmare is about to get very real," I said. "Now might be a good time to buckle your seatbelt." I drew a deep breath and sat up tall in the driver's seat as we approached Palm Gardens. I turned into my driveway, leading to the underground parking garage, and headed down the ramp toward the closed wrought iron gate. "If I enter my security code on the keypad, the cops will assume I live here. That could be a bad thing."

"Well, here's a good thing," Fiona said, gesturing toward the front entrance. "Check this out."

Luckily, a purple Jeep—driven by dear Violette—was exiting the garage, having opened the automatic security gate from inside.

Fortunately, she was oblivious to the pandemonium. Fortunately, she didn't recognize a blackened me. *Unfortunately*, the heavy iron gate was now slowly sliding shut behind her.

"We can't make it in," I said. "We don't have time."

"We have to. Once we're underground," Fiona said, "the cops will be locked out, and that pesky helicopter will be neutralized."

"Can't do it."

"Hold on and don't watch." Fiona extended her left foot, stamped it on top of my right foot, forcing our feet down with great power and pushing the gas pedal flat to the floor. She and I squeezed the steering wheel as strongly as we could. We zoomed forward.

Her eyes widened.

I shut mine.

Our van veered around Violette's exiting Jeep as we barely fit through the small opening formed by the closing gate. By the time the police cars reached the entrance, the gate had fully and securely closed, preventing the cops from proceeding.

The radio newscaster seemed thrilled by the sudden turn of events. *"Oh, my. What's this? The carjacker has led authorities to an underground garage, trapping himself inside. What a buffoon. This chase is over, folks. This van is boxed in. This gunman has been caught. Proof that you can run, but you can't hide."*

I PULLED INTO a distant parking spot, out of sight from the gate entrance. We could hear vicious barking from the just released K9 units, which were restrained at and by the gate. We also heard the whirling rotor blade from the police helicopter hovering outside overhead.

Still wearing our filthy foil ponchos, Fiona and I hopped out of the van, taking with us our belongings. I broke away to prop open the tenants' exit door at the opposite end of the garage leading to the street level, giving the impression that we had fled on foot via that route. I rejoined Fiona, grabbed her hand, and ran toward the door leading to the indoor stairwell.

We bounded up the stairs, two at a time, to the fifth floor. I slammed open the hall door and burst into the exterior corridor. Sirens were screaming, and the xenon light from the helicopter prowled the building. We lowered our heads and sprinted down the narrow landing along the railing to my unit. Not once did Fiona let go of my hand. Not once did I let go of hers.

Just as alarmed tenants cracked their doors open to investigate the hubbub, Fiona and I slipped into my apartment.

I turned on the lights. I double bolted the door.

We were sweaty, soaked, and shaking. Our faces were mud-caked. We waited there, still wearing our latex gloves, trying to catch our breath, tying to believe we were really safe this time.

The harsh light from the police chopper swept across my windows. I lowered the blinds.

"Nice place," Fiona said nonchalantly.

"Thanks. The utilities are included," I quipped idiotically. I stood there, probing her eyes, looking for some sign that she hadn't bled out.

"Do you think they'll find us?" she asked.

"The cops won't, and Bowman won't."

"Did his goons see who we were?"

"Our faces were too muddy. There's no way."

"Reassure me," she purred.

"They never made it to your Mercedes," I said. "Never saw where we parked."

"Go back to the cops. Won't they—"

"We wore gloves. We left no prints," I said.

"How about here, now?"

"We wore foil. We foiled the dogs."

"Go back to the mansion."

"We blacked out the security camera. No evidence there."

"Tell me more," she begged.

"The van is a rental. It'll trace back to Bowman."

"Anything else?"

"Bowman didn't know it was you and me tonight. And even if he did, he couldn't squeal on us. He'd incriminate himself. Don't forget, that's the beauty of robbing a robber. Besides, I think when the police retrieve the stuff that was falling out of the van, Bowman will be facing some heavy-duty jail time." I laughed, tasting the victory. "We just executed the perfect crime, Miss Logan."

We still hadn't moved a millimeter.

"Now what?" she asked. "What now?"

"We keep following the script. We lie low for a while. Sell the slippers through Carlo on the black market. Take the money and go our merry million-dollar way."

"Million-dollar *separate* way." Fiona let her shoulders fall. She was spent.

"This again?"

"We wrote a script," she said. "We've now been paid. The job's over. The partnership is dissolved." She straightened her muddied glasses. "You promised we would separate. I have to return to LBJ."

"Lyndon Baines Johnson?"

"Life Before Jack."

Those words took my breath away. "Well, we can't separate now. We're surrounded by cops. So, sit down, relax, and don't enjoy the view." I discreetly moved to the balcony's sliding glass door and pulled the drapes in front closed, eliminating a view, in or out. "How's your arm?" I asked.

"It's numb."

"Really?"

"I'm kidding," she said, taking off her poncho. "Does this place have a shower?"

"No. But there's a kitchen sink."

"Really?"

"I'm kidding," I said, slipping off my poncho.

As we were disrobing in front of each other, we started to chuckle. It was the release we had long needed. The giggle grew into knee-slapping, nose-snorting, eye-watering, belly-aching hilarity. Just like Steve McQueen's fit of laughter after completing his heist in *The Thomas Crown Affair*.

Gradually, our merriment subsided. Little by little, we regained a small degree of decorum. Slowly, we returned to reality.

"May I borrow a towel?" Fiona asked.

"You can keep the towel. I'm rich now."

"And perhaps something to wear. Preferably new or recently dry-cleaned."

"I suppose you want a mint on your pillow as well."

"Pillow?" she asked.

We mulled the implications.

"In case the police lockdown the apartment complex overnight," I said.

She half-smiled. Such a muddy face. Such a stunning black woman.

I PARTED MY kitchen curtains just a bit to observe the police activity outside. They had created a perimeter around the entire apartment building with yellow tape. Cops were interviewing various residents and witnesses. Police dogs were trying to pick up a scent, sniffing every square foot. And the whirlybird was still circling above, flying low, its searchlight slicing through the rain, still on the hunt. TV news crews covered it all.

Chapter 60
FIONA

JACK'S TELEVISION WAS tuned to the eleven o'clock news, but I muted the sound after the anchorwoman, wearing a deep cleavage top, characterized the subject of tonight's police chase as *"reckless, with a total disregard for human life."*

I stood in Jack's startlingly spotless kitchen wearing a loose-fitting Ohio State sweatsuit, my hair wrapped in a towel. I sipped hot tea and listened to the rain quiet down to sprinkles.

"I found band aids and an antibiotic cream," Jack said, joining me in the kitchen. "And some tongue depressors." He wore a royal blue, terrycloth bathrobe. And he had shaved and put on cologne. "If I have to remove a bullet, you can't scream. They'll find us."

"I'll swallow some whiskey and bite on your tongue depressor," I said, rolling up my sleeve and presenting my badge-of-courage injury.

"Where is it?" Jack asked.

"There." I pointed to my little souvenir scrape.

"That? I nearly fainted over that?"

"Nearly?"

Jack attended to my scratch with a tender touch. "You're lucky. An inch closer, and you could've lost a freckle."

"Okay, no more of that," I said.

When he had finished dressing my "wound," I sat on his comfy couch and declared that, "We achieved something wonderful tonight. We wrote a script about the perfect crime, and we executed it flawlessly. And now, the reviews are in. It's the feel good, unproduced movie of the year, created by two fugitives from justice."

"The police are out there, going door to door," he said, joining me on the couch. "What do we tell them?"

I removed the two ruby slippers from my mud-stained wicker basket. "Tell them there's no business like shoe business." I handed him a slipper. "A million for you." I put the other slipper in my lap. "A million for me." We honored the moment. "We got away with it, Jack." My heart was pumping hard. Our eyes were making love.

A loud knock on the door startled us and decimated the magic of the moment.

Jack looked to me, seeking support.

"You're a writer," I said quietly. "You'll think of something."

He stuffed his ruby slipper into his bathrobe pocket and crossed to the door. "Who is it?"

A gruff voice replied, "Los Angeles Police Department."

"The entire department?"

"Open the door."

"How do I know you are who you say you are and not the one they're looking for, and you're trying to break into my apartment to hide and maybe kill me?" Jack stammered.

His nerves had gotten the best of him. This could easily lead to our undoing.

"How do you know I'm looking for someone?" said the voice on the other side of the door.

Jack froze.

I pointed to the television.

"It's all over the news," he said.

"Then, you know we may have a hostage situation going on somewhere in this building," the voice said through the door.

"Yeah, my big sister and I are scared to death," Jack responded.

I would have thrown my hot tea in Jack's eyes, if the timing had been better.

"Open the peephole, and I'll show you my identification," the voice said, losing patience.

Jack looked through the eyehole, then opened the door. A mustached officer in a yellow rainslicker stood there looking ten feet tall. "Sorry to disturb you folks. But we're making sure the suspect hasn't forced his way into one of these apartments. He's not afraid of taking captives."

"I appreciate that, sir," Jack said. "Thank you for checking up on us. And while I'm at it, thank you for protecting and serving us, day after day, night after night, week after—"

"Do you mind if I take a look around?" the cop asked.

Jack was stuck in his neurotic, compulsive mode. "Mind? I insist. Please, come in. Make yourself at home. *Mi apartamento es su apartamento.*"

I surreptitiously buried my slipper under a couch pillow.

Jack followed the big cop as he wandered through the apartment, inspecting the bedrooms, the bathroom, opening closets and cabinets, before returning to the living room. Jack kept up a skittish, running dialogue. "Hell of a storm last night," he said. "It was raining, so hard the animals were pairing up."

"Funny," the cop muttered, checking behind the curtains.

Jack couldn't stop blathering. "Here's one you might not have heard. What is the Mexican weather forecast?"

"What?"

"Chili today and hot tamale."

The cop was all business. He stopped his search. "Everything checks out."

"You would know," Jack said gleefully. "Your department is the best in the world. As a citizen of Los Angeles, I'm grateful for the job you and your troops do, month after month, year after—"

"Thanks." The cop cut him off. "Did you hear anything odd tonight?"

"No, sir. Nothing odd or out of the ordinary. Or unusual. Or abnormal. Or peculiar." He turned to me. "It's been a silent night. Right, sis?"

"All is calm, all is bright, bro," I sneered.

"Have you seen anything or anybody strange?" the cop inquired of me, his eyes darting about.

"I'm just visiting from Ohio. *Everything* in L.A. seems strange." Then, I muttered to myself, "Mostly my brother."

"Well, stay alert and keep your doors locked. Call 9-1-1 if you need us."

"Hope you catch them, officer," I said as I rose, eager to have him leave.

He paused. "Them? One's an innocent victim."

A chill shot down my spine. Had *I* messed up?

"Poor lady," Jack said, attempting to help.

"How do you know the hostage is a woman?" the cop asked.

Jack was noticeably shaken. Had *he* messed up?

"I don't," Jack said in a jittery voice. "I'm a writer. I'm in the movie business. We make things up. Always creating. Lady. Guy. I could've said 'kid.'" He did a little soft shoe and sang a couple bars of "Hooray for Hollywood."

I jumped in with a life preserver. "We got a call about all this from our Uncle Manuel. Manuel Lopez, who—"

"*Lieutenant* Lopez," Jack said. "Top dog on the Force. I can put in a good word for you."

"Yeah. Everybody knows Manny," the cop said, studying our faces.

"He knows my brother lives in this building," I said. "So, he gave us a little heads-up."

We all stood there, caught in the tension.

"Welllll…." Jack said. "I'm sure you'll nab your man. Or woman. Or kid."

"Oh, we will," the cop said. "I can promise you that."

Jack started in again. "Once more, on behalf of all Angelinos—"

The cop immediately left.

Jack immediately closed and re-locked the door. After taking a big sigh, he leaned against the door and said, "I think that went quite well."

"Really? We almost freakin' blew it," I said.

"But we didn't. We're all good."

After a moment, I said, "Big sister?"

"I was a nervous wreck. I didn't know what to say."

"Is that how you think of me?"

"No, of course not," he said.

"Because, for the record, I don't think of you as my little brother."

"I would hope not. I'm taller than you."

I decided to scamper to the end of the proverbial limb and ask the question that had been burning within my heart. How *do* you think of me? But, true to form, I simply sat back down on the couch and asked, "Do you have anything around here to drink?"

"The night we sold the script, I bought a bottle of cheap champagne. Beth and I never opened it."

"How cheap?"

"Bubbles would've cost extra."

"If it doesn't come in a can, bring it on."

"How about a carton?"

I just looked at him, this endearing young man.

"I don't have much else," he said. "You know, being a bachelor and all."

"I understand."

"I might have some leftover sardines."

"Yum," I mocked.

"We'll eat old sardines, sip flat champagne, and watch them try to find us on TV."

We were safe and alone in his apartment. We were flush with success. Two-million dollars' worth. We would never feel more triumphant or sexier. Where was all this leading? To the bedroom? I couldn't let that happen. But I wondered if Jack would.

"I'll get a candle, just for atmosphere," he said, popping the cork from a bottle of champagne.

"We're just toasting to our success," I said. "Just two ex-partners celebrating."

He joined me on the couch and poured the champagne in a debonair fashion. "Just two millionaires celebrating."

"That's all."

"Nothing more."

"I mean it, Jack," I said out of self-preservation.

He raised his glass and pledged, "To dying with no regrets."

I examined his face, searching for signs that he would abide by my call for abstinence. "To winners who never quit," I said.

We clinked, we sipped, and we turned up the sound on the TV just in time to see our "borrowed" minivan being towed from Jack's underground garage. According to the newscaster, *"The carjacker managed to elude authorities. The police have completed their search of the neighborhood and have concluded that the suspect is still on the loose and still has his hostage."*

We got away with it. We were winners. Take that, Hollywood. The news reporter was right, though. Jack did have me hostage. But if one of us had enough willpower to resist temptation, I would make it out of this night emotionally unscathed. We would go our separate ways. And my heart would remain intact and at large.

I WAS AWAKENED by the harsh bawl of a blue jay. The best I could do was open one eye. Night was becoming day. And the rain had stopped.

There were two empty flutes on the coffee table, as well as one drained bottle of ten-dollar champagne. One empty bottle of wine. One crushed can of beer. And three unopened cans of sardines. I noticed that the couch where I was last seated was also empty, that I was now on the floor, on a soft sheepskin rug, and that my head was resting on Jack's solid chest. He was fast asleep, still wearing his blue bathrobe. I still had on the gray fleece sweatsuit. Although the preceding few hours were all a blur, I distinctly remembered that we both conked out from a combination of fatigue, alcohol, and a common syndrome known as "Post Conquest Letdown." Evidently, no lovey-dovey business had been part of the festivities. Just as well. It's what I had asked for. Why complicate my life? Why set myself up for failure? For the pain? I would endure. I had Rathbone and Jane Austen. And one ruby red million-dollar slipper. I could take a cruise around the world. Fourteen times.

I lay there thinking. And listening to Jack's heartbeat. His arm was around me. A down comforter was around both of us. I didn't want to move. I never wanted to leave.

After a few marvelous minutes that I hoped would last me a lifetime, I silently got up off the floor.

Jack continued to sleep.

I studied him. I felt so connected to him. I had spent the night. We had slept together. It would become my last image of him. And one of my fondest memories.

I looked out the window. The police were gone. The neighborhood was quiet. The sun was shining over Sony Pictures Studios.

I took the number 217 morning bus from Culver City to West Hollywood. I had to stand because the seats were taken by nannies, nurses, maids, and caretakers, all going to work with wrinkled faces in starched uniforms.

With a precious shoe in my pocket, I walked down a seedy alley from the bus stop to the 24-hour Veterinary Clinic. The on-duty surgeon, Dr. Ralph Butler, met me at the front desk.

"Go Buckeyes," he said, starring at my chest.

"Excuse me?"

"Your sweatshirt. Ohio State."

I was in no mood to chat. "I called earlier about visiting my dog, Rathbone."

"Right. He's progressing well, but he's still sort of spaced out."

"I just need to see him."

"Okay. I understand. Follow me." Dr. Butler led me to the rear of the hospital, into a small recovery room.

Rathbone lay in a large cage, on absorbent pads, on a heated tile floor. His hindlegs were heavily bandaged, and various tubes ran in and out of his body. A plastic cone encircled his head. His eyes were open but milky. I felt sick.

The doctor started to leave. "Stay as long as you want."

"Can he see me?" I asked.

"He's pretty doped up, but I'm sure he'd like to hear your voice." Dr. Butler closed the door.

I crawled into the cage and sat cross-legged next to my faithful friend. "Hey, baby."

Rathbone remained motionless.

I delicately stroked his coat. "We're going to be all right. We're going to lick our wounds and get back on our feet." A heart monitor chirped at equal intervals. "I couldn't stay there. I couldn't stay with him. I couldn't fool myself any longer. Do you know what I'm saying?" I swear his left ear perked up a little. "Other than calling me beautiful once, he never said or implied that he was interested in a relationship. I saw what I wanted to see, whereas he saw me as what? Too old. A mentor. A professor. A, Lord help us, sister?" I stuck my head inside Rathbone's lampshade and kissed him on his wet nose.

His tongue flopped out of his mouth. Had he had the energy, he would have licked me a kiss.

"We're going to be all right. Did I already say that?" I crawled out of the cage like a dog and stood up.

Rathbone's monitor beeped more rapidly.

"I love you, baby. But, next time, we both have to remember this. Look before you leap."

Chapter 61

JACK

It was noon when I awoke disoriented in my own living room. First of all, why was I on the floor? Oh, right. That's where Fiona and I had lost consciousness. Where was Fiona? Taking a shower? Taking a walk? Taking a tinkle?

I struggled to my feet and saw a handwritten note on the kitchen counter.

Nice writing with you.
Nice robbing with you.
I'll mail your sweatsuit back.
Gone her separate way,
Fifi

My heart raced. I hastily reached into my bathrobe pocket. For a moment, my stomach sank, until I found that my red slipper was still there. I felt horrible for doubting Fiona's veracity. I had never known anyone more honest. Maybe Hollywood had corrupted me. I felt worse, however, that Fiona had left without even saying goodbye.

There was an earsplitting bang on the door. I jumped. And called out, "Who's there?"

A deep, muffled voice responded, "Police. Open up."

I almost vacated my bowels. I looked through the peephole. I was not pleased.

Violette was standing there in a Brazilian bikini, smirking.

I opened the door. "That was hilarious," I said, trying to recover.

"What about that hostage business last night. Nothing hilarious about that, right?"

"Yeah, not much," I said, still in need of a defibrillator.

"That murderer's van almost hit me. I could've been *killed*. It was awesome."

"He didn't murder anyone. He just—"

"What happened with your aunt?" she asked. "Or was it your uncle?"

"Aunt. She's still dying."

"Poor thing. Hey, guess what. I got a job in a movie."

"That's great."

"I'm just an extra in a crowd scene. We're filming across the street at Sony."

"How convenient."

"They don't need me until after lunch. So, I thought we could drive to the beach and take a run together," she said, sticking her violet head inside my apartment. "Or just hang around here. Hinty-hint-hint."

"I'm sorry, but I'm busy."

"Got company?"

"No."

"Then, what? Is someone else 'dying?'" She used air quotes.

"No. Just my aunt. I'm going there now."

"How convenient." Violette stamped her foot, the start of a tantrum. "Don't you find me attractive, Buck?"

"Yes, of course I do. Who wouldn't? But seriously, why me?"

"Cuz you're hot. And you seem smart."

"Seem?"

"This is L.A., Buck, where we can just have some naughty time together. You don't have to marry me."

"I have a girlfriend," I said impulsively.

"I thought you dumped her."

"This is a new one." Did I just say that?

"Ask her to join us." Did she just say that?

I didn't react to her chipper ménage à trois offer. Violette stood in my doorway with her bottom lip jutted out.

"I've got to go. I'm really sorry," I said. "She's my favorite aunt. She let Kevin and me stay with her when we first moved to L.A."

"You owe me. Next time, we're going to do something that rhymes with Buck."

Such a clever and classy woman.
Violette swiveled on her bare feet and clomped away.

I NEEDED SOME sort of closure. After all, Fiona and I had grown very close in a very brief period of time. She had changed my life. And turned my heart upside down. We couldn't just exit each other's lives without a proper farewell. But she didn't return any of my text or voicemail messages. So, I took an Uber across town to Casa del Sol, where I had left Kevin's motorcycle the night before.

I LOPED THROUGH the garden, down the walkway, to Fiona's front door. There was a written note taped to the doorknocker.
Gone Fishin'.
P.S. If it's an emergency, dial 911.
P.P.S. If it's not, I'll get to it when I get to it.
I retrieved Kevin's motorcycle from Fiona's garage and raced downtown.

THE UNIFORMED OFFICER at the Information Desk called Lieutenant Lopez, who granted me permission to come upstairs. I took long strides down the hall of the police department, hoping there weren't any wanted posters of me lining the walls. I entered Lopez's office and approached his desk.
He stood up, shook my hand, and offered me a chair.
We both sat.
"My lucky day," he said. "First Fiona, now you."
"Fiona was here?"
"Came and went just minutes ago."
"What did she want?" I asked slowly.
"I guess she thought I'm the Lost and Found department. Gave me this." From his bottom desk drawer, he withdrew Fiona's ruby red slipper.

"Judy Garland wore it in *The Wizard of Oz*. It's half the pair, but worth twice my house."

"Why would she turn it in?"

"Good Samaritan? I don't know." He sighed. "She said she found only one slipper." The lieutenant looked at me, head tilted, eyebrows raised. I had the right to remain silent. "She also named names," Lieutenant Lopez said.

I almost choked on my tongue. "Really? Anyone I know?"

"Do you know Roger Bowman?"

"Sounds familiar."

"Full-time club owner. Part-time producer. Small-time tax evader. Big time crook."

"All-time schmuck," I couldn't help from saying.

"Thanks to Fiona's tip, we caught him at the Tijuana border with his caravan of goodies. Things missing from Tinseltown for years."

"Does she get a reward or anything?"

"Absolutely. We towed that classic car of hers from the Palisades to our auto shop. The mechanics are fighting over who gets to fix it."

"Did she say where she was going?"

"Yeah," said the lieutenant. "First, to rent a car."

"And then?"

"'Somewhere over the rainbow.' That's a direct quote."

"Did she say anything else?"

"Let me think," he said. "Oh, yeah. 'See ya at the movies.'" The lieutenant looked me square in the eyes, already knowing the answer to his question. "So, what brings you here, Jack?"

"My conscience." I took the matching ruby red slipper out of my jacket pocket and placed it on the lieutenant's desk next to Fiona's slipper. "I think they belong together."

"So do I," he said with a tinge of irony. "I guess you and Fiona think alike. That's why you're partners."

I stood up, leaned in, and whispered, "Are the partners in any kind of trouble?"

"Fortunately, last night's storm kept a lot of people off the roads because I heard there was some sort of nutty car chase," he said. "Trouble? Hell, no. You're Hollywood heroes."

"Thanks, Lieutenant."

"Be careful out there. Writing scripts can get you killed."

"Yes, it's a dangerous business," I said as I turned to leave. "But you meet the greatest people."

Chapter 62

FIONA

I NEEDED TO air out. Get away during Rathbone's recuperation, away from Jack's magnetism, away from another Eddie encounter. I needed a change of venue. Solitary confinement. In the words of the great Greta Garbo from the movie *Grand Hotel*, "'I vant to be alone.'" And luckily, autophobia, the fear of being alone, wasn't one of my many irrational fears.

Rivers, more so than oceans or lakes, made me feel calm, content, contemplative. And so, I let nature soothe me in the most peaceful place on earth, the sacred surroundings of Crystal Cove, Colorado. My special place. There was no more exquisite spot than the middle of Lone River at twilight with not a human around for miles. That's where I stood casting my fly rod, with my vintage fishing basket hanging over my shoulder and my bird watching binoculars draped around my neck. I was just twenty yards away from the river's bank, where my little dome tent was pitched beside a magnificent Ponderosa Pine. Soon, a canopy of stars would illuminate the heavens, and a silver moon would send long shadows throughout the forest.

It took me years to realize why I enjoyed fishing so thoroughly. Sure, it was always good to break away from the familiar, from one's comfort zone, from the glare and blare of the city, the pressures and stresses of daily living, the rut of an indoor routine, away from the ball and chain, otherwise known as my desk and chair. Fishing cleansed the soul and nourished the spirit.

But more importantly, there were lessons to be learned in, on, by, and from the river. I just had to be receptive to its knowledge. It required that I open all my senses in order to soak up its meaning. For example, witness the moving water. Nothing in life remains static. Like a river, our lives are constantly changing, winding, widening, narrowing, being joined by and joining other tributaries during our twisting journey. I learned from rivers that a boulder in my path is merely a challenge to seek a different, less resistant, and perhaps better course, that according to the laws of nature, although there would be rough rapids ahead, smooth water would always follow.

Standing there in the leaf-dappled water for hours, with pole in hand, with the clear liquid swirling between my legs, engaged in an age-old hunt to outsmart and snag a scaly opponent, the river inspired me to think about where I stood in the larger picture. The *much* larger picture.

There are two trillion galaxies in the universe. Our Milky Way, with its two hundred billion stars, was just a single one. I was just one of nearly eight billion people on just one of eight planets in our solar system, absorbed, at that sublime moment, in the primitive survival practice of catching dinner at the end of a hook. I was connected to the continuum of basic human necessities, food and water. It was daunting. And humbling. And life-affirming.

Oh, and love. Did I list love as a basic human necessity? I could live without a full belly. But not without a full heart.

I didn't have to be religious or even spiritual to recognize and marvel at the life cycle of my river. Somewhere upstream in the Rockies, a snowcap was melting, filling Mother Earth's arteries and veins with fresh ice water and supporting the fish, flora, and fauna that call the river home. From miles away, with miles to go, around my rubber hip waders, flowed a life-sustaining fluid headed toward its destination, its own oceanic galaxy.

How fortunate I was to be amidst the wilderness, nuzzled by river water, tasting its mist, smelling its vapors, hearing its ripples, watching its current, as wisdom sprung from its very depths, placing my infinitesimal existence in perspective, and providing me the profound metaphor that Life is but a Stream.

I felt strong and confident being by myself on the river, in the woods. I felt strong and confident being alone in the world. I felt good about myself. I felt Marvin would be proud that I had finally moved on and was able to feel again. Laugh again. Write again. Love again. I had an improbable acquaintance to thank for that.

I closed my eyes. The evening wind caressed my cheeks, and the brook babbled sweetly below my knees. My fingertips would know if a rainbow trout had been lured to my hand-tied fly. Several placid seconds went by. But then, the deafening roar of a rude and raucous engine echoed off the ravine and inside the cove, shattering nature's tranquility and ruining my meditation.

All thanks to an improbably acquaintance of mine.

Chapter 63
JACK

I ARRIVED ON a promontory above Fiona's encampment at golden hour and stopped next to her rental car. I had entered paradise, a green refuge, Fiona's secret sanctuary. I set the kickstand, dismounted the pearl-white Harley, took off my gloves, and removed my helmet.

"Fiona," I yelled out, hiking down the ridge to the riverbank.

Her expression held little surprise and, I'm sorry to say, no joy.

"Not speaking," Fiona yelled back.

"You make waders look fashionable," I said.

"You should have called," she snapped.

"I did. You didn't answer. It's becoming a pattern."

"One doesn't bring a phone to a place like this. Much less a motorcycle."

She was as feisty as ever.

"Aren't you going to ask how my butt is? I've been riding for thirteen straight hours."

"It's going to be a lot sorer riding thirteen hours back. Goodbye, Jack."

"You can hide," I said, arriving at the water's edge. "But you can't run."

"How'd you find me?"

"I clicked my heels three times."

"No, really."

"I followed my heart. And some directions from the locals." I pointed to a giant Ponderosa Pine. "And I recognized that tree from the painting."

"You shouldn't have come."

"I needed to talk."

Fiona reeled in her line. "I needed to run."

"From what?" I asked.

"You."

"Why?"

"It's for the best," she said.

"It's best when we're together."

"Haven't you noticed how people look at us?"

"Yeah. With envy." I kneeled at the river's bank and let my hands be washed by the rushing water. "Why did you return the slipper?" I asked.

"It didn't fit," she said. "And how do you know I did?"

"Found out when I returned mine."

Fiona stiffened. "What? Why?"

"*You* were the one that fit. The slippers were, well, just an excuse to be with you."

"Get back on your white horse. And get the Harley outta here."

I had a choice to make. But isn't that what life is? A series of choices? I could turn around, head back to L.A., and pack for Ohio. Or stay and endure further rejection from this nature woman.

Defying all logic, I tossed my wallet and phone on the shore and forged, fully clothed, into the river, heading toward Fiona, stepping carefully over cragged, silt-covered rocks. The frigid water took my balance and breath away.

"Jack, 'go' means go," Fiona pleaded.

"This water is so wet." My teeth chattered.

"We're wrong for each other, for so many reasons."

"Name one," I said, moving unsteadily in her direction.

"I'll name many. You're just starting out, and I'm just finishing up."

"I want to start out with you. And you want to finish up with me. Next?"

"I'm too old, and you're too young."

"You have a youthful spirit, and I have an old soul," I said. "Go on."

"And together, we have no money."

"And this water's too freakin' cold." I pressed forward, struggling for footing, trying not to fall. "And you talk too much." I was making progress, step by slippery step, closing the distance. "And we don't need money. We have each other. That's worth way more than a pair of old slippers."

"This isn't a movie," she said. "It's real life. We can't write the ending."

"I already have. Boy meets girl."

"Older woman."

"Boy loses girl."

"Older woman."

"Boy finds ageless woman. In a freezing river."

"Don't do this," Fiona insisted.

"And they live happily ever laughter. Just like Evan—"

"Ethan."

"And Ethel."

"Elsa."

I had reached her. The slate cobalt water reflected the azure sky against which pink cumulous clouds floated like giant cotton candy. A red-tailed hawk carved a circle overhead. My green eyes looked into her blue eyes. My feet were ice cold. My legs were shaking. My knees were knocking. Everything about that colorful moment, except for my numb body, was ideal.

"Don't say it, Jack."

The world stopped spinning long enough for me to say what I honestly felt. "I want you."

Her eyes glistened. "Say it again."

"I want you, Fifi."

"Really?" she whispered.

"Write it down," I whispered.

We faced each other. This time as lovers-to-be. This time, no one was dreaming.

She removed her eyeglasses and let them dangle from their strap around her neck. "Are you going to kiss me?" she asked.

"I'll get to it when I get to it," I said, prolonging the inevitable.

"You're *not* going to kiss me?"

I smiled. "I've come too far not to. Just ask my butt." With that, I held her impossibly beautiful face in my hands.

She closed her sapphire eyes, surrendering, at long last, to our fate. Her eyelids were quivering.

I kissed each one softly.

"Jack, you realize this can't go anywhere." She sighed, keeping her eyes shut. "There's no way we can—"

I kissed her lips. Again and again. Until we were making out in the middle of a river. It was amazing. Glorious. Oscar worthy.

I picked her up, like in the film *An Officer and a Gentleman*, and carried her across Lone River to terra firma. I could hear envious ladybirds flapping their wings, applauding my gallantry.

Chapter 64
FIONA

Jack set my feet down on the grass near my tent. I was breathless. The sun was slowly fading. So was my confidence. If I didn't like him so damn much, none of this would matter. But was I ready for where we were headed? What would Deana say? What would my daughter think? What would Marvin want? How would Rathbone react? What would I do? My heart was pounding. I wanted him.

"Seriously, Jack. This can't be a whim, a quickie on an air mattress."

"It's not. Not for me."

"I mean it. I'm not having any slam, bam, thank you, ma'ams."

"The altitude is affecting you."

"I'm not twenty-something. I'm no longer thirty-anything. I'm—"

"Gorgeous. Smart. Funny. Sexy-something." He kissed me, then stood back. "I want a relationship with you. An all-out, in public, full throttle relationship with you. That's the truth."

My truth? I was scared.

He cranked his head toward the tent. "Are you going to invite me in?"

"Are you asking whether you can spend the night?"

"I suppose I could sleep out here with the rhinos."

"You're a city boy, right?"

"Hippos. I meant hippos."

I was done talking. The moon was rising. The crickets and frogs had come to play their evening serenade. Our time had arrived. I took Jack's hands and led him inside my tent. To be in my life. In my body.

Undressing in front of a man after a certain age was terrifying under the best of circumstances. But trying to be seductive while pulling off sticky, squeaky, stinky, wet chest waders inside a small tent? Well, we couldn't keep from laughing. It was the emotional relief we needed.

I lowered the light in the kerosene lantern.

Jack turned it back up.

"Must you?" I said.

"Yes."

"The first time?"

"Yes."

"You may not like what you see."

"I liked what I saw the first day you walked into class."

"I've had a baby. Some of my body parts have drifted."

He held up a condom. "No babies tonight."

And then his mouth was all over mine. He wasn't listening to any more of my excuses or falling for any more of my stall tactics. He cradled my back and laid me down softly on my sleeping bag. He took off his shirt. And in the flickering light, sober this time, I saw that he was built like a Michelangelo statue. His skin was tight, his muscles were toned. Foreplay with a new partner. Nothing was more exhilarating while, at the same time, more intimidating.

The next thing I knew, my panties were off. We were naked. And sharing body heat. I halted to catch my breath, holding Jack at arm's length. I needed a moment to accept the moment. A moment to take in the moment. A moment to live in the moment. I hoped Marvin would understand, approve, and cheer me on.

"What is it?" he asked.

"I've made a decision."

"What?"

"You can spend the night."

"I'd like to, but damn. Tonight's my bowling league."

That was our last laugh. From then on, it was all nibbling and touching and kissing. His fingers, reading me like my skin was braille, were gentle, patient, and experienced. And then, he rolled on top of me, pinning my hands against the canvas floor. He was selfless, savoring the act, giving more than receiving. He was fulfilling me in every way.

I hooked my ankles around his neck—thank you, yoga—drawing him closer, deeper.

Jack never saw the single tear that trickled down my face. A tear in memory of Marvin. A tear celebrating a page turned.

Finally, at long last, I was ready.

We greeted the dawn enveloped in each other's arms, my head resting on his muscular shoulder. This time, no wine, no sweatpants, no bathrobe separating our bodies. Just skin on skin. This time, I wouldn't have to get up and escape.

Jack smiled at me. "How are we doing?"

"Somehow, the tent is still standing."

"And a fun time was had by all."

"Fun? Like bowling?"

"Fun like balling." He kissed me softly. "Fun like making love to someone you love."

Did he just say he loved me? "It wasn't just sex with an older woman?" I asked softly. "Something to check off your bucket list?"

"It's like that pool guy and that nanny. Love came first." He kissed my neck. "Sex came second."

And indeed, a second serving was upon us. We went at it again. Another long, slow, sweet, sweaty round.

Passion ruled our new world. The basic necessity of love had been met. Along the banks of Lone River.

Chapter 65
JACK

WE RESTED, CATCHING our breath. Side by side. Facing each other as the morning sun brightened the tent. We shared some trail mix. Eventually, two dreamers would take a dip in the river, then return to the city, return to their regular lives, return to managing rental units and frosting fruitcakes. Tossing reality aside, I basked in the afterglow of an all-consuming romantic night.

"Fiona?"

"Speaking."

"Do we ever have to leave this place?"

"Not as long as the fish keep biting. Winters can be brutal, though."

I smiled. "Did you ever think we would get together?"

"No. But I hoped for a miracle."

"I don't believe in miracles."

The strains of *As Time Goes By*, my ringtone, broke the stillness of the morning. "Huh? Do I really have cell service way out here?" I reached for my phone.

Fiona cringed. The intrusion of urban technology into that sanctum of serenity irked her.

I read the caller ID, and my face fell. "It's Benny. I've been ducking him," I said. "Wanna hear me get canned?"

"No. I don't want anything to spoil our—"

I turned on the speaker. "This is Jack," I said into the phone.

"This was your boss," Benny blasted back.

"I was going to call, but—"

"You're a little late. Where the hell've you been? Can't get a hold of Fiona either. We've been trying to reach you forever."

"I'm sorry, Benny. We're in Colorado. We smoked a trout. But I didn't inhale," I said, winking at Fiona. "And what did you mean by 'we've' been calling?'"

"*I'm with—*"

An urgent voice came on the phone. "*Kim Fleishman, Fiona's agent. We're in a bar at the Beverly Hills Hotel.*"

"*The Polo Lounge,*" Benny said in the background. "*Very fancy schmancy. But a glass of Pepsi, mostly ice? Twelve dollars.*"

Fiona talked into my phone. "Hi, Kim. What's up?"

"*Benny and I are having a drink,*" Kim said. "*Well, I am. He's eating the peanuts.*"

Benny came on. "*Jack? You still there?*"

"Yeah," I said. "Am I fired?"

"*You're not going to need your job anymore,*" Benny said. "*You're going to be doing what you should be doing. You're going to be writing movies. No more scribbling on wedding cakes.*"

"I'd like to believe that," I said.

Kim came on the line. "*That script you two wrote? Benny gave it to Gordy Schaffner.*"

"What's a Gordy Schaffner?" Fiona asked.

Benny spoke up. "*He's a long-time customer and some big mucky-muck at some hoity-toity studio. He read the script because he owed me a favor for hiring his bagel-brain nephew.*"

"Duncan?" I asked.

"*Duncan-the-Dunce,*" Benny said.

Kim continued. "*Anyway, Schaffner called me and offered some serious money for your screenplay.*"

I looked at Fiona. She looked at me. Our mouths were agape.

"*Of course, I negotiated a higher number,*" Kim said. "*How does two-hundred and fifty thousand dollars sound?*"

At the same time, Fiona and I said, "WHAT THE—"

Kim wasn't finished. "*For each of you.*"

Benny quickly added, "*Minus, of course, my ten percent.*"

Fiona had sprung into my arms.

"*So, get your tokheses back here. You've got a half-million-dollar contract to sign,*" Benny said before hanging up.

Fiona and I celebrated the miracle by hitting the air mattress one more time.

Chapter 66
FIONA

THE NEXT MORNING, we broke camp, returned my rental car, and rode Kevin's Harley back to California. My arms were wrapped around Jack's waist for four states and two spectacular days.

This trip, those weeks, that partnership revived me. Saved me. I had given up on love. I had resolved to live a single existence, enjoying my daughter, waiting for grandchildren. I would have been satisfied to feed off fond memories for emotional sustenance and embrace the status quo, considering the future as merely a countdown to wearing jodhpurs in my coffin.

But a student named Jack, an enticing young man from Dayton, signed up to learn a little something about screenwriting. He reminded me that life is like writing a movie. It should have compelling characters, a great story to tell, and a happy ending.

My happy ending was just…

THE BEGINNING

ACKNOWLEDGMENTS

My thanks to the supportive publishing staff at Roan & Weatherford, especially George "Clay" Mitchell. Also, a round of applause for the keen eye of line editor Lisa Lindsey. And, as always, my deepest gratitude to my family and friends—past and present—for their encouragement and love.

Printed in the USA
CPSIA information can be obtained
at www.ICGtesting.com
CBHW020932271124
18025CB00022B/286/J